BARLEYBRIDGE

Books by Richard Muir

The English Village
Riddles in the British Landscape
The Shell Guide to Reading the Landscape
The Lost Villages of Britain
History from the Air
Visions of the Past *(with Christopher Taylor)*
The National Trust Guide to Prehistoric and Roman Britain
(with Humphrey Welfare)
A Traveller's History of Britain and Ireland
The Shell Countryside Book *(with Eric Duffey)*
The Shell Guide to Reading the Celtic Landscapes
The National Trust Guide to Dark Age and Medieval Britain
The National Trust Guide to Rivers of Britain *(with Nina Muir)*
Landscape and Nature Photography
Hedgerows *(with Nina Muir)*
Old Yorkshire
The Countryside Encyclopaedia
Fields *(with Nina Muir)*

BARLEYBRIDGE

*the chronicles of
Herbert Postlethwaite*

Richard Muir

M
MACMILLAN
LONDON

First published in Great Britain in 1989 by
MACMILLAN LONDON LIMITED
4 Little Essex Street London WC2R 3LF
and Basingstoke

Associated companies in Auckland, Delhi, Dublin, Gaborone, Hamburg, Harare, Hong Kong, Johannesburg, Kuala Lumpur, Lagos, Manzini, Melbourne, Mexico City, Nairobi, New York, Singapore and Tokyo

ISBN 0-333-483472

A CIP catalogue record for this book is available from the British Library

Typeset by Matrix, 21 Russell Street, London WC2

Printed in Hong Kong

Any resemblance to places, organisations or people, living, dead or in limbo, is purely coincidental.

For Philippa Harrison

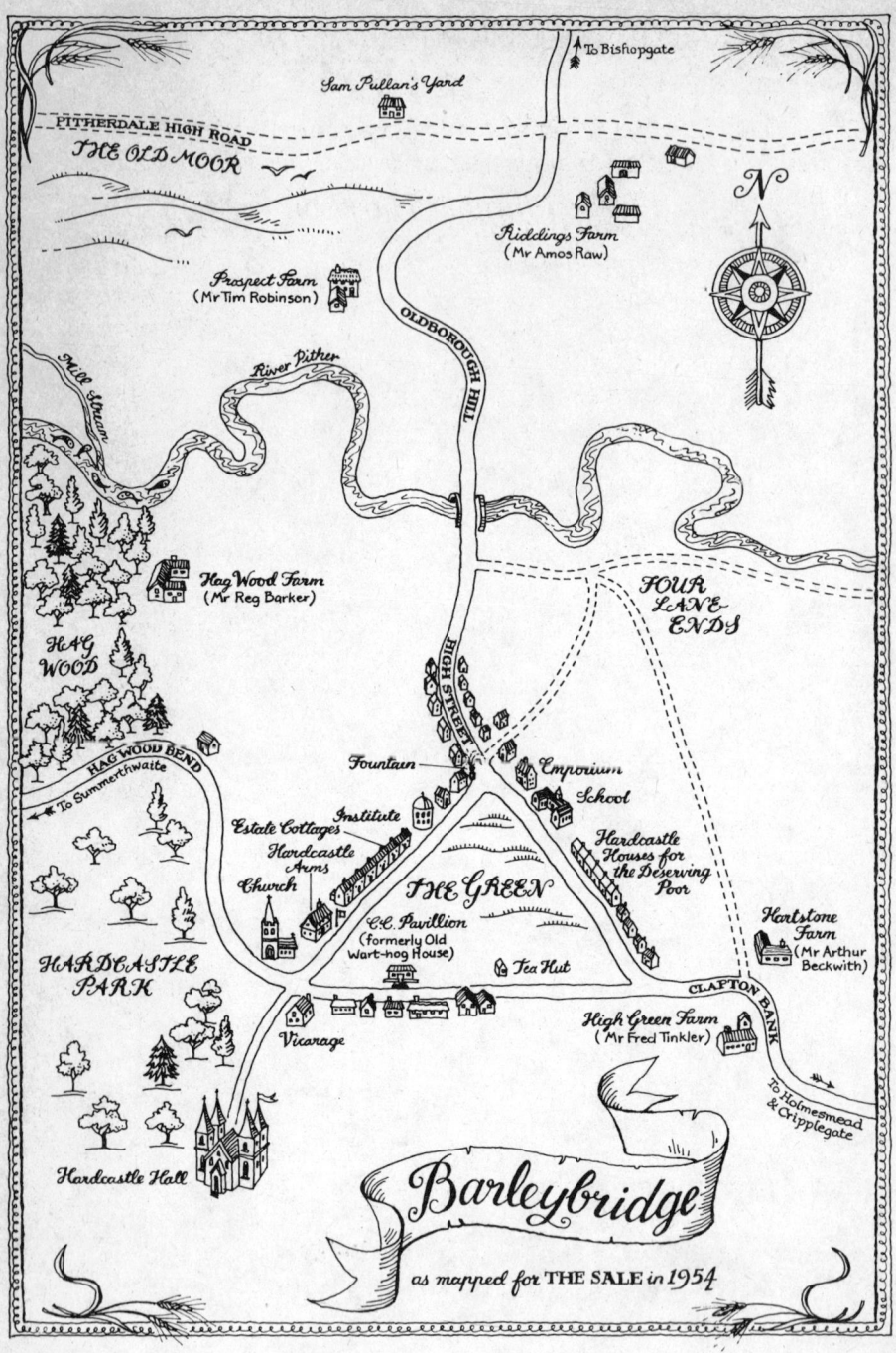

To Bishopgate

Sam Pullan's Yard

PITHERDALE HIGH ROAD
THE OLD MOOR

Riddings Farm
(Mr Amos Raw)

N

Prospect Farm
(Mr Tim Robinson)

OLDBOROUGH HILL

River Pither

Mill Stream

Hag Wood Farm
(Mr Reg Barker)

FOUR
LANE
ENDS

HAG
WOOD

HAG WOOD BEND

To Summerthwaite

Fountain

Emporium
School

Estate Cottages   Institute
Hardcastle
Arms
Church

HIGH STREET

Hardcastle
Houses for
the Deserving
Poor

THE GREEN

C.C. Pavillion
(formerly Old
Wart-nog House)

Tea Hut

Hartstone
Farm
(Mr Arthur
Beckwith)

HARDCASTLE
PARK

Vicarage

High Green Farm
(Mr Fred Tinkler)

CLAPTON BANK

To Holmesmead
& Cripplegate

Hardcastle Hall

Barleybridge

as mapped for THE SALE in 1954

A Note from the Author

Though never one to brag, I can fairly assert that there is nobody better fitted than myself to record the social history of Barleybridge, my native village in Pitherdale. My readers will appreciate the validity of this claim when I reveal that for thirty-nine years I was 'Dalesbred Tup', author of the weekly 'Pitherdale Gleanings' column for the *Yorkshire Gazette*. By kind permission of the proprietors, certain relevant examples of these Gleanings are reproduced in this book; I fancy they add a certain distinction to the narrative. (I must add, however, that unpardonable interference by editors and sub-editors all too frequently devalued my copy and I would not wish to be judged by everything published under the renowned 'Dalesbred Tup' by-line.)

Not everyone will realise that in addition to my literary career I was also employed as organist and choirmaster at the church of St Tracy and St Karen in Cripplegate. Moreover, as circumstances allowed, I would often and most generously offer my services entirely free of charge to the congregation of Barleybridge, specialising in the more energetic pieces of church music which Mrs Fawcett could not manage on account of her wooden leg. Now I wish that my generosity could have been yet greater, for I hold her oaken appendage entirely responsible for spreading woodworm throughout the organ loft.

Time changes, and seldom for the better. Even men of distinction are now denied the respect that is their due. Only the other day I could swear that I overheard young Danny Kendal refer to me as a 'boring old cart'. As to the first adjective, I fancy that my record speaks for itself. For twelve years I served on the committee of the Cripplegate Round Table; I am an Hon. Vice-Chairman of the Pitherdale Chrysanthemum Society, and served King and country as a full corporal in the Green Howards from 1940 until invalided out of service in 1942 with sinusitis. Hardly the profile of a boring life! As to being old, let me merely remark that seventy-eight is considered a relatively youthful age by Pitherdale standards. The cart allusion I cannot understand, so I will simply state that I have no vehicular ambitions or inclinations.

Here I have attempted to present a sober account of a typical village society. I might add that my neighbours regard me as a sociologist of some standing. I have watched a good many of the programmes in the Open University D100 social sciences foundation course on BBC 2, desisting only when they brought on a bearded Marxist with a pink tie.

In compiling what I modestly expect will prove to be a major landmark in rural sociology, I have avoided all temptations to sensationalise, preferring to compose a factual chronicle of day-to-day events in village life. Never one to interfere in village affairs – my status as 'Daleshead Tup' precluded that – I have recorded what I have observed as a privileged onlooker from the sidelines of Barleybridge life. If it seems prosaic then I can only reply that that is the way things are in Barleybridge. And long may they remain so!

Herbert Postlethwaite
The Old Mastiff Kennel
Barleybridge

1

In which we encounter Barleybridge, find the village in mourning and learn the secret of the phantom mourners

From the Yorkshire Gazette, *12 April 1969*
Pitherdale Gleanings by 'Dalesbred Tup'

Today I write about Barleybridge where I have lived since 1923 in a delightful gritstone cottage converted from the former mastiff kennels built by Captain Julius Hardcastle JP in 1854. Still remembered fondly as the 'Justice with the iron nose', Captain Julius dispensed with his mastiffs after the loss of his nasal equipment when one of the dogs tripped him as he was inspecting the man-traps in Hardcastle Park. Yet despite his grievous loss and the heavy hand-forged replacement, he still claimed to be able to scent a poacher at two hundred yards – and woe betide any of that calling who faced him across the bench!

I write about Barleybridge to dispel rumours circulating in the correspondence columns of this and other newspapers which suggest that there is something odd about the village. As a resident of long standing I can assure my readers that Barleybridge is not 'rum', as our correspondent from Holmesmead asserts. If anything we are a rather sedate and reticent little community, as a closer familiarity with the facts would have revealed.

'The lady with the live chicken under her headscarf' is, in fact, Mrs Batty, a stalwart supporter of the Wesleyan cause. Mrs Batty suffers from lugwark, or 'earache' as they call it in the south. A lifelong breeder of tablefowl, Mrs Batty finds that by strapping a Rhode Island red to her ear she can keep out the March chills most effectively. I have personally tested the remedy and can recommend it to one and all.

Turning now to 'the funny red-faced man asleep on top of the hedge', this was in fact one of our most distinguished parish councillors and a leading organiser of the Barleybridge Show, Mr Amos Raw. He tells me that he went to check his sheep following the loss of two of his neighbour's ewes. He scrambled atop the hedge to obtain a better view but fell asleep when counting the flock. Since counting sheep is a well-known cure for insomnia there is nothing odd whatsoever about Mr Raw's conduct. There is always the possibility that the gentleman referred to was not Mr Raw, but another parish councillor of note, Mr Frederick Tinkler. Mr Tinkler often loses his young partridges to sparrow-hawks and may sometimes be seen lying face upwards upon a hedge with a tempting morsel of meat on his green waistcoat and a coal hammer in each hand. However, following the complaint to the RSPB and the incident when he missed the hawk and struck his kneecaps, I thought he had resorted to other forms of pest control. 'Concerned of Cripplegate' should have been more specific.

All this goes to show that there are perfectly normal explanations for these and the other phenomena reported. We in Barleybridge welcome visitors. All we ask is that you take us as you find us – and if you find us just as conservative and conventional as the folk of a hundred other northern villages then I for one will not be surprised.

Mrs Hetherington-Cohen of Barleybridge WI requests me to mention that the prize for the most woodlice found under a backyard doormat was won by Mrs Carperby with a total of fifty-eight. Mrs Carperby goes through to the national championships quarter-finals.

Somewhere to the north of Worksop and to the south of Wallsend lies Barleybridge. Here, in the dappled green valley of the river Pither, it nestles, lingers, slumbers or lurks, depending on your point of view. Barleybridge is a typical English village – in other words it is quite unique. With characteristic conviction Samuel Harbottle's *Guide to the Antiquities, Topography and Singular Monuments of Enchanting Pitherdale* (published by Harbottle and Smythe of Buxton in 1871) informs us that: 'The name of Barleybridge recalls those distant times when creaking tumbrils laden with the bounteous produce of far-flung granges crossed the torrents of the Pither here bound for the copious granaries of Delacroix Abbey. In those black times when the realms of Popery spanned all Pitherdale and serpents in monkish garb cavorted and gorged in the taverns which besmirched the fair face of the village . . . ' Further research reveals that Samuel Harbottle, isolated by his fellow Fundamental True Baptists for what they felt was an excessive antipathy to the Church of Rome, was not the most objective of historians. And so, in the absence of an alternative history, let us simply accept that Barleybridge appears in Domesday Book as *Berebrig* and was granted a Thursday market and a fair on St Eric's Day by King John in 1204.

The bridge which now spans the Pither at Barleybridge, a fine stone structure of three arches, was built by a special levy imposed upon this and neighbouring parishes in 1792. Local people are still known to grumble about this iniquitous tax, the exaction of which is made far worse by lingering suspicions that the folk of Holmesmead, just two miles downstream, contributed less than their proper due. As one crosses the stone bridge the lane from Bishopgate becomes Barleybridge High Street (and only street) as it ascends the southern slopes of the valley. Then it forks to border the triangular green which was created to accommodate the Fair of St Eric, one branch soon bearing eastwards towards Holmesmead and the other westwards to link up the hamlets of the upper dale. At the head of the green stands the church of St Eric and St Brian, while far above and pinnacled like a row of pines looms Hardcastle Hall, a spiky intrusion on the skyline.

Built in 1832 in what one commentator unkindly called the Count Dracula school of Gothick architecture, this is the seat of the Hardcastle dynasty. The Hardcastles, descended from a long line of pedlars and packhorse drivers, finally gained their fortunes in the mills of Oldham. Through a steadfast pursuit of the time-honoured virtues of hard work, thrift and the unbridled exploitation of their fellow men, women and children they won great wealth and all the respectability that this entails. Having left half the millworkers of Lancashire broken and exhausted, Josiah Hardcastle (soon to become Sir Josiah) chose to cross the hills to enjoy the life of a rural squire and to vent his newly acquired taste for uncompromising benevolence upon the unsuspecting population of Barleybridge. Hardly had the walls of Hardcastle Hall begun to rise than Sir Josiah had bought up every farm and house in the parish. With the ink on the deeds scarcely dry he began the demolition of all the stone cottages necessary to make way for the new church, the school, the inn, the Hardcastle Institute and the Hardcastle fountain. Each edifice bore the Hardcastle arms and motto: 'The Lord abominates an idle shuttle'; plus tasteful individual epigrams: 'Time watched is time wasted' round the face of the school clock, 'The pure water of the Lord surpasseth the Devil's wine' on the fountain, and so on. So grand was the scale of these endowments that when the time came to begin work on the Hardcastle Houses for the Deserving Poor there was space left to accommodate only one quarter of the families inherited from the cottage demolitions. The remaining homeless were provided with their coach fares and guaranteed employment at the Hardcastle mills in Oldham.

Once secure in their lofty hall the Hardcastles devoted their energies to rural pursuits, public service and Empire. Captain Frederick Hardcastle was devoured by a crocodile when surveying the route of East Africa's first railway, the Rev. Hannibal Hardcastle was consumed by cannibals at a bible reading in Borneo, and Col. Ernest Hardcastle surrendered his leg to a tiger whilst on leave from the North-West Frontier. Indeed, it is fair to say that Hardcastles were eaten whenever and wherever the cause of Empire so required. However, when Brigadier Sir Humphrey Hardcastle survived the Second World War without being eaten – not even nibbled – by anything, percipient students of the family's history realised that its fortunes were faltering. On the Brigadier's death Sir Cecil Hardcastle inherited the hall, its estates and such a heavy burden of taxation that an auction (known for ever more in Barleybridge as 'The Sale') was inevitable.

At The Sale, held in the Hardcastle Arms, Barleybridge, on 1 June 1954, the entire estate, excepting only the Hall, its park and gardens and Barleybridge green, was sold. The green has an unusual history for as soon as Josiah Hardcastle had completed his purchase of the properties in Barleybridge he applied for, and obtained, the Parliamentary Enclosure of the common lands in his parish: Barleybridge Moor and the village green. Under the terms of Enclosure the commons were to be shared amongst all the landowners of the parish – namely Josiah Hardcastle. Only one smallholder, Jacob Pullan, had resisted all pressures to sell to Josiah, and at Enclosure he was awarded a tiny parcel of the Moor high on the northern flanks of Pitherdale. Josiah's plans for the green included zoological gardens, an arboretum and a Hardcastle family museum. However, a shortage at this stage of heirlooms suitable for exhibition (two dozen sets of packhorse harnesses and grandfather Hardcastle's copper-beating tools being deemed of insufficient merit), the stubborn refusal of date palms to endure the Pitherdale winter, and the escape of the first zoological exhibit (a wart-hog which devoured three toes from the left foot of the infant Victoria Hardcastle before being shot by gamekeepers at a picnic in Hardcastle Park) were all factors which conspired against the courageous venture. Thereafter the green was again made available to the village. It provided a venue for home matches of the Barleybridge Cricket Club, founded by Sir Marmaduke Hardcastle in 1893 to encourage different standards of manly virtue and sportsmanship, while the Fair of St Eric was revived in the previous year in the form of the annual fête of the Barleybridge Society of Horticulturalists, another of Sir Marmaduke's innovations.

As Josiah's passion for benevolence and great works had mellowed, so the hand of the Hardcastles had settled more lightly on Barleybridge. Rents were modest, patronage bearable, and only the poacher, conscientious objector or suffragette had cause to quiver. The conditions of The Sale were such that virtually all the properties in Barleybridge were purchased by their tenants. The farmers became men of substance, even though their gates, hedges, walls and buildings seemed rather less sprucely maintained than before.

Last in the line of Josiah's descendants, Sir Cecil Hardcastle was a gentle soul, lacking the ardour for public service and the affairs of Empire which had sustained his forebears. He was a childless widower, and the profits from The Sale allowed him to pass his days at Hardcastle Hall in modest dignity, supporting a housekeeper-cum-cook and a chauffeur/gardener. Though lacking the vim and vigour of his ancestors he had inherited two of their qualities: an abiding interest in the estate and parish and a morbid fear of being eaten.

His days followed a similar pattern, a late breakfast taken in bed, a progress by wheelchair round his gardens, followed by an afternoon of contemplation spent in the trophy room. This room commanded a splendid panoramic view across the parish, and via his magnificent tripod-mounted four-inch refractor telescope Sir Cecil could keep abreast of the most intimate affairs of Barleybridge without suffering the stresses and inconvenience of consulting the villagers. The Sale had imposed such a shock on his delicate sensibilities that he chose to disregard it. Hardcastles had boasted that they owned everything that they could see from Hardcastle Hall, and Sir Cecil preserved a proprietorial interest in events both within and beyond his shrunken domain.

The lofty walls of the trophy room were studded with the remains of animals which had fallen foul of the muskets and Mausers of Hardcastles now as dead as themselves. Oryx, eland, kudu, sambur deer, buffalo, Amos Pullan's lurcher and other beasts unknown to science or too eroded by dust and maggots to be identified jostled for places in this mural mausoleum. However, several shield-shaped ochre patches on the smoke-cured walls revealed the former locations of trophies removed and burned on the express instructions of Sir Cecil. Any animal with exposed fangs, ranging in size from the roaring lion to the gaping weasel, had been consigned to the flames, a victim of Sir Cecil's unsympathetic attitude to all things that bite.

On one particular clear July day Sir Cecil could have

6

been found just where one would expect to find him, seated at his telescope. Scanning the northern marshes of the parish he could see but one small cloud in the sky. This cloud is present from May to October. It is not composed of wafts or vapours but of the bluebottles which swarm above Sam Pullan's knacker's yard. How Sir Cecil loathed that cloud! A man of restrained emotions, his capacity for hatred was entirely concentrated on Sam Pullan, his yard, his plot and the flies that hovered above it. Ever since the Enclosure of Barleybridge Moor each succeeding Hardcastle had sought to dislodge, evict, imprison or otherwise inconvenience the Pullans, whose tiny freehold endured as a blemish on the Hardcastle empire. Steadfast to the last, the Pullans replied by devising ever more elaborate yet inscrutable methods of poaching and provocation. Long before the days of the hunt saboteurs, when foxhunting was generally regarded as no more than a convenient way of simultaneously reducing the numbers of vermin and of landed gentry, old Jack Pullan established England's first fox sanctuary on Barleybridge Moor. He even used the by-products of his knacker's yard to lay a trail of delicacies from each earth, via devious routes, to the haven of his holding. Every time the hunt met at Hardcastle Hall the hunt servants and gamekeepers arrived spent and frustrated from their attempts to disentangle offal from thicket. After the forty-third unsuccessful hunt (by which time Brigadier Hardcastle had been obliged to have his entire staff of gardeners and estate workers provided with mounts to swell the attendance at the increasingly unpopular meets), the Barleybridge hunt was disbanded. Three foxes on leads then accompanied old Jack at his celebrations in the Hardcastle Arms.

Since the Pullans had no apparent means of support, each succeeding Hardcastle prayed that one day they would sell up their plot and go. Quite how they managed to fare is not a matter of public record, though they were not unknown to local dealers in game. After The Sale, when the farmers of Barleybridge no longer faced eviction if caught consorting with those of Pullan blood, old Jack saw his knacker's yard begin to prosper and Sam inherited it in 1969. It lies encircled by pines on the edge of the moors overlooking Pitherdale and

7

is reached via a rocky track which is part of the ancient bridleway known as Pitherdale High Road. Sam Pullan is a hefty, ruddy fellow given to yellow waistcoats, bold checks and elderly American convertibles, his example of which can be found outside one or other of the Pitherdale pubs on any night of the week. Though jovial and talkative when encountered at the bar he does not encourage casual visitors to home or yard. Ramblers using Pitherdale High Road tend to bypass the yard, the approaches to which are richly festooned with the heads of a variety of Sam's animal clients, some less fresh than others.

On the day in question Sir Cecil was rather tense and unsettled. Desiccation and moth damage were affecting the surviving exhibits in the trophy room and several sets of teeth were gradually being revealed. Gazing through his telescope Sir Cecil detected a diamond-shaped speck surging upwards through the customary cloud of bluebottles, above the Pullan yard. A kite? How odd! The first kite ascended, towing up a second kite which was twice as large. Very odd! Third, fourth and fifth kites followed, the last the size of a blanket. Below this fifth kite there fluttered a length of cloth bearing letters. A banner. As the stiff breeze held the banner taut Sir Cecil was able to read the legend: 'The Lord abominates . . .' It was nothing less than a gross and unprintable parody of the Hardcastle motto. His heart pounding and fingers twitching, Sir Cecil wiped the perspiration from the eyepiece of his telescope in time to see the kites now raising a sail-sized sheet of white canvas, which was doubtless a sight screen purloined from the cricket pavilion. Depicted on the ascending sheet in deft black strokes was the image of an elderly man being eaten by a fox.

When Mrs Atkinson entered the trophy room with tea and scones at four o'clock she found Sir Cecil hunched stiffly over his telescope, a look of terror in his frozen, staring eyes. Thus ended the noblest era in the history of Barleybridge. Before the Hardcastles there had been the Fitzherberts of Delacroix Hall; before them the Abbots of Delacroix; before them Count Alan of Brittany; and before him, Earl Edwin. How will the folk of Barleybridge manage without someone important to tell them what to do?

At least Sir Cecil had left the most meticulous instructions for his funeral arrangements. In the normal course of things he would have been buried in the Hardcastle vaults beneath the great family monument in Barleybridge churchyard. However, two years after his father's funeral, while dozing aloft in the family pew he had heard one villager say to another 'T'owd Brigadier thowt he'd got off wi'owt gettin et. But he were wrong, for t'worms are munchin' him reet now.' After this chastening experience Sir Cecil resolved to be cremated. He would have liked to have had his ashes scattered on the Pither at his favourite fishing spot, fanned by alders and washed away to eternity on the peat-red waters. However, the thought that some fire blackened fragment of knuckle or splinter of pelvis might be taken by a myopic trout urged a different course of action.

On 12 July 1982 the ashes of Sir Cecil, the last of the Hardcastles of Hardcastle Hall, were buried in a bronze urn amongst the roots of an ancient bourbon rose in the Hall gardens.

Two nights later Sam Pullan dug them up and threw them in the river at Otter Cliff, followed by a handful of wasp grubs which set the waters swirling as Sir Cecil disappeared in a frenzy of fins, gills and blindly snapping jaws.

Prior to his engagement at Cripplegate crematorium, Sir Cecil was the subject of a funeral service at Barleybridge church. This was a notable occasion for several reasons but the only one we have time to consider is that this was the last funeral ever reported by Barry Harding of the *Pitherdale Messenger*. Barry's initial career in local journalism culminated brightly in the offer of a post as columnist for the *Yorkshire Standard*. Thereafter it regressed, via a series of popular hostelries and lesser newspapers, to his appointment as chief, and only, reporter on the *Pitherdale Messenger*. There he assembled the reports of the local Women's Institutes, established a network amongst the less unreliable local gossips and supplemented his modest salary by selling the best of the local stories as news tips to rival and superior publications. The *Messenger* was really the *Cripplegate Announcer* but with different front and second pages.

Readers unfamiliar with the procedures of local journalism may not realise that the reporting of funerals is accomplished in the following manner. The undertaker provides the attendant reporter with a list of family and chief mourners; the 'other mourners included . . .' section which follows is then compiled by the reporter as these other mourners progress glumly through the lychgate. Never one to tarry at scenes of grief, Barry had swiftly realised that lists of other mourners could be invented in any convenient and convivial bar without further risk of contracting colds, boredom or sobriety. Since the reports of funerals were tucked away in the recesses of page two, between the perpetual advertisements for the Cripplegate Eventide Home and Stanley Moreton, undertaker ('A discreet and caring service'), there was little chance that they would ever be read.

However, Barry Harding's funeral system contained a fatal flaw: having invented a mourner he developed an affection for this fictitious personage and became increasingly reluctant to exclude him or her from his reports. At the very moment when Stanley Moreton was handing over the list of family and chief mourners outside Barleybridge church the editor of the *Cripplegate Announcer* was rifling Harding's desk in the hope of finding the odd cigarette. Instead of cigarettes he found an envelope stuffed with payslips from the *Yorkshire Standard* and a curious list headed 'Other mourners: Grades I, II and III'. While Harding was downing his second pint of Stoat's Old Particular with an unusually jovial Sam Pullan in the Hardcastle Arms, his editor was checking 'other mourners' in the back issues of the *Pitherdale Messenger* and scouring for names in local directories.

At a hastily convened meeting between the editor and the chairman of Grimsdale Newspapers it was decided *either* that Pitherdale was the haunt of a morbid band of homeless and itinerant mourners whose Grade I members had been present at every funeral held in or about the dale for the last six years *or* that the following people and page 2 stalwarts did not exist: Alderman and Mrs Percy Cake; Lt-Col. Monty Featherstonhaugh (retd); Ms J. M. Flowers and her daughter Petal; the Arkwright family of Spofforth; Mr Sidney Heptonstall representing the Airedale Society of Ironfounders; Mme Sabatini; the Abbot of Delacroix; W. H. Ipping; Professor D'Eath, DD; and Mrs I. Shoppatesco. Though reluctant to dismiss a promising story ('Bishop Offers Shelter to Homeless Mourners') the establishment at Grimsdale Newspapers accepted that only the second option could be correct.

Barry Harding was fired, but lived quite comfortably after enrolling his phantom mourners as claimants at the Cripplegate Social Security office.

From the Yorkshire Gazette, *22 July 1982*
Pitherdale Gleanings by 'Dalesbred Tup'

Normally at this time of the year I report on the prospects for the second crop of hay. Today, however, my thoughts are dominated by the recent tragic death of Sir Cecil Hardcastle, the last of his line to occupy Hardcastle Hall in Barleybridge. Sir Cecil remained a bachelor and misfortune has dogged his dynasty. The estates would have passed to his great-nephew, Julian Hardcastle, of Cootamundra, New South Wales, but for the unfortunate incident involving the crocodile when he attempted to paddle across the Murrumbidgee on what he took to be an old dead log. Sadly, he was the third member of the dynasty to have made this fatal misconception. Our thoughts turn to the fates of Captain Frederick Hardcastle in 1887 and Esmeralda Hardcastle in 1908. Had young Julian paid more attention to his family history there might yet be a Hardcastle enshrined in our noble Hall.

For the last one and a half centuries the Hardcastles have cast a caring eye over our little community. I have good reason to remember the kindness of Lady Ophelia Hardcastle. As a child in 1916 her servants caught me gathering chestnuts in the Hall park. Her ladyship had me taken directly to Richmond, but

11

on discovering that the Green Howards could no longer enlist six-year-old drummer boys she graciously returned me to my parents just as soon as I had polished all the hooves in the Hardcastle stables. Legends of similar acts of benevolence are still rife in Barleybridge.

During the latter years of his life Sir Cecil engaged in regular communications with our parish council. Without his eagle-eyed observations we might not have discovered the illicit use of the Horticultural Society's tea hut by the infant pipe-smokers guild, or have known that Mrs Shutt was cultivating mushrooms in the crypt, to the detriment of the fabric and wholesomeness of our beloved church. Sir Cecil's incarceration of the gas board officials in 1968 was sensationalised by the 'popular' media. They might well have been Russian agents – and I am assured that at least two of them *are* Labour voters. Seen in the context of the Soviet invasion of Czechoslovakia then in progress and the similarities with Russian naval uniforms, Sir Cecil's prompt action should have been roundly praised. Better safe than sorry, say I!

A stern task now confronts our parish councillors, deprived as they are of Sir Cecil's perspicacity and guidance. Yet they are all men of stalwart yeomen stock and will doubtless rise to the challenges which confront them. Prominent amongst these challenges will loom the boundary dispute with Holmesmead parish. Let us pray that no more blood will be shed over this already bloodstained half-acre of contested ground. But if the need should arise, our leaders will not be found wanting – and the prowess displayed at the recent clay pigeon shoot should be heeded by all concerned.

Preparations are well in hand for the Barleybridge Show, scheduled for St Eric's Day. The organisers request me to advise readers that in the under-nines section the prize in Class 9b will be awarded for the best hand-painted *balloon,* not baboon as printed in the catalogue. Any youngsters misled by the misprint should contact the RSPCA and also obtain an anti-tetanus injection forthwith. If the behaviour of its close relative, the barbary ape, is anything to go by, the baboon is an animal to avoid. It was one of these apes which severely incapacitated the Hon. Septimus Hardcastle when he paused for relief during an inspection of the defences of Gibraltar in 1892. Had this vile ape not been lurking behind the porcelain fittings there might now be Hardcastles alive to inherit the ancestral home.

2

In which we meet the pillars of local democracy and discover how Barleybridge educates its young

The old grey cottages of Barleybridge huddle in a setting noted for its ancient oaks and for the ribbons of alder which fringe the gushing waters of the Pither. Were we dilettantes, we might consider the many dippers, admire the lady's smock bobbing in the meadows or quest for the kingfisher. But as serious students of the social life of this village we prefer to discover more about the local power structure, the processes of decision-making and the operation of democracy. These interests lead us directly to Barleybridge Parish Council.

The members of Barleybridge Parish Council are as follows: Arthur Beckwith (Chairman), farmer; Fred Tinkler, farmer; Reg Barker, farmer; Amos Raw, farmer; and Tim Robinson, farmer. Astute readers will have recognised that the agricultural vocation is well represented on the Parish Council. In fact, it is totally represented, for not only are all the parish councillors farmers, but also all the farmers in Barleybridge are parish councillors. This helps to ensure that farming interests are not neglected. For example, when thirty-nine local residents complained about the nuisances and danger resulting from a recent clay pigeon shoot (three of the complainants bearing small wounds and another brandishing a dead cat) the Parish Council had the corporate expertise needed to set the matter in its proper perspective. Councillor Beckwith (shoot organiser) and councillors Tinkler, Barker, Raw and Robinson (his guests) assured the delegation that, not only had they always shot clay pigeons in the company of their chosen friends, but so too had their fathers before them and *their* fathers before *them*. Parishioners were advised that people who could not enjoy good old country sports and were afraid of a few bangs and bits of lead could always 'beggar-off to Holmesmead for t'day'.

The pronouncements of Barleybridge Parish Council were not always so forthright. In former days, when chairmanship of the council was handed down from Hardcastle to Hardcastle and other members did not exercise their speaking rights, the deliberations had taken the form of a monologue delivered from the chair. This covered matters such as the painting of gates, trimming of hedges, availability of foxes, absences from church and the needs of the village needy. In his later years Sir Cecil had relinquished his chairmanship, though his observations (local, telescopic) were delivered to Chairman Beckwith on the eve of each meeting.

Following the sad demise of Sir Cecil, the council, now bereft of his recommendations, was obliged to formulate its own policy. The one which emerged had all the virtues of brevity and lucidity. Whenever Cripplegate District Council invited the Barleybridge Parish Council to present its views on issues of local import the reply returned came in the form: 'The Barleybridge Parish Council has no observations to make on this matter'. However, lest we should unfairly assume that the judgements of the Council are perhaps a little stereotyped, indecisive or lacking in that lustre endowed by vigorous debate it must be remarked that the Council had two other policies.

Firstly, there was the Holmesmead policy. This was a policy of outright antipathy towards the neighbouring parish in general and its council in particular. Holmesmead Parish Council was articulate, democratic, popular and effective, and as such a prime target for the elected representatives of Barleybridge.

Secondly, there was the policy towards barn conversions and holiday chalets. This was also a policy of vehement opposition, although its eventual adoption demonstrates the flexibility of attitudes held by the parochial councillors

15

of Barleybridge. During the period 1983–4 unused barns belonging to the Beckwith, Raw, Robinson, Tinkler and Barker families had been successfully and profitably converted into new dwellings, while both the Beckwiths and Raws introduced clusters of holiday chalets beside secluded reaches of Pitherdale. The descendants of several former smallholders and commoners also owned barns quite suitable for conversion, but suddenly, Messrs Beckwith and Tinkler having just secured planning permission to convert their two remaining barns, the members of the Councillor realised that further applications of this nature would not be beneficial to the amenities of the parish. As Councillor Beckwith explained the situation to the meeting held at Barleybridge C. of E. School on 12 February 1985: 'Enough is as good as a feast. Tha can go too far, tha knaws. I reckon that we've got t'barn situation abaht reet.' Thereafter all subsequent applications for the conversion of barns, pigsties, or stables were vigorously opposed. Even Mrs Wharton's application to erect a hen-house in her front yard was rejected on the grounds that one thing might lead to another. 'If'n t'fowls should dee then who's to say but she might let t'ouse out to campers? Think on.' In this way the Council strove to achieve a proper balance between native, newcomer and visitor and preserve the remaining architectural legacy of farm buildings.

Sadly to report, the abilities of the Parish Council were not always highly regarded in Barleybridge. On more occasions than one Jim Wharton had confided that the Council would be incapable of organising a dance in a disco – or words to that effect. Some of the doubts were rooted in a lack of confidence based on experience concerning the annual erection and illumination of the Barleybridge Christmas tree. But the councillors are grieviously traduced by such idle chatter, especially when one considers that a stalwart devotion to husbandry combined with an overriding desire to feed the nation had deprived all members of the Council and all their relations of the benefits of military service. Though deprived of organisational training the councillors nevertheless sought to apply a martial efficiency to 'Operation

16

Spruce'. Councillor Beckwith drew up the schedule along the following lines:

a) Cut down tree donated from the small plantation in Hardcastle Park.
b) Load it on Tinkler's trailer and lead it down to the green.
c) Look for empty barrel at back of Hardcastle Arms.
d) Put tree in barrel and fill with earth.
e) Stand tree in barrel on edge of green outside Pitherdale Emporium.
f) Add fairy lights.
g) Run electric cable from plug in Pitherdale Emporium, out via letter box, to tree and wire-up to fairy lights.
h) Wind insulating tape round the join in the wires.

'They messed it up last year, t'year afore, t'year afore that – and they'll mess it up this,' observed Jim Wharton.

In the event the capabilities of the Council proved to be wickedly traduced, for by midday on 4 January the tree was installed and illuminated. Grass-roots democracy had accomplished every stage of Operation Spruce from *a* to *g*. The weather was crisp and dry and the lights blinked-out a multicoloured message of joy until 6 January when one of Sam Pullan's lurchers cocked a leg over the naked wires. Poor Snapper was electrocuted, though the fire in the Pitherdale Emporium was insufficiently severe to prevent a return to trading by March.

Members of the Parish Council regarded Operation Spruce as a reasonable, if not unqualified, success. In fact, it was just as well that the tree did burn down, as Arthur Beckwith had not devised a schedule for its removal.

The infrequent meetings of Barleybridge Council are held in the infants' room at Barleybridge C. of E. School, a fitting setting. Naturally the affairs of school and council overlap quite considerably. For some time Councillor Barker had nursed hopes to build a small housing estate in his local

17

meadow, Dole Plash. The trouble was that observations far more persuasive than the Council's standard response would be needed to steer the transfiguration of the orchid-rich wetland safely past the planners and councillors of Cripplegate. It might even fall foul of the Barleybridge barns policy, the scope of which was ever-widening. A muted mention of the plan produced grunts, growls and much head-scratching until Chairman Beckwith called for the parish map. 'Now sither, if a few 'owses 'ad to be built, Fower Lane Ends would be the only spot wi' proper access. Access is important in planning, tha' knaws.'

Coincidentally, the farms of Tinkler, Beckwith, Barker and Raw converge at Four Lane Ends and the spirits of enthusiasm and public service blossomed as each land-owner expressed a reluctant readiness to sell an acre or two to the right developer. Only Councillor Robinson remained unmoved until it was demonstrated that his second-ary occupation as a haulage contractor would allow him too to serve the community during the building operations. All were agreed that there was a definite local need for such development and the next few hours were devoted to attempts to identify it. An enrolment board on the class-room wall provided the clue: 35 pupils in attendance. Since the school had been built by Josiah Hardcastle in 1833, the enrolment had oscillated between the extremes of 29 and 36 pupils in attendance. Of course, what the school needed was a new influx of pupils and these new pupils could only come from the new estate at Four Lane Ends.

Fred Tinkler bore a heavy countenance as he dropped in at the Hardcastle Arms to inform customers of his fear that the school might have to close on account of its 'falling numbers'. The following night Amos Raw was to learn of the school's difficulties but cheerfully reassured all present that he had heard rumours of a new housing scheme which would bring in all the new pupils that one could wish for. 'Just trust in t'owd Parish Council,' he said, as he had said so many times before. Planning approval was duly secured at a meeting between Arthur Beckwith and Kit Jackson, Chairman of Cripplegate Area No. 2 Planning Committee, held at Arthur's cost in a private dining suite at the Leeds

Hilton. Few meetings between leading servants of the electorate can have been so cordial and productive. Not only was Councillor Jackson persuaded of the manifold merits of the Barleybridge housing scheme but he was also able (in his quite different capacity as a butcher) to negotiate a ten-year lease of grazings on Barleybridge Old Moor at rates which were amazingly generous. The entire episode was an object lesson in local democracy harmoniously at work.

The estate that arose at Four Lane Ends was named Pitherdale Garth. The plans depicting the spacious four and five bedroom houses were submitted in various architectural competitions but only secured an award from RNIB. Dwellings were arranged round and within a circular road located at the junction of the four old lanes, now renamed Beckwith Drive, Raw Drive, Tinkler Drive and Barker Drive, both in recognition of the estate's founders and in the hope that each drive might become an avenue for further expansion into the property of the named patron. Each dwelling faced another across their open-plan gardens and a tall cypress screen excluded the rural sights, sounds and, to some extent, smells. 'All the pleasures of suburban living without the inconveniences of country life,' proclaimed the estate agent's hoarding.

Forty-eight householders took up residence in Pitherdale Garth. They included thirty-one retired couples, ten families with teenage children, two couples devoted to the cause of celibacy, a widower and his housekeeper, and four families with children of junior school age. These children all attended distant public schools. Councillors Beckwith, Raw, Tinkler and Barker sold their lands for £80,000 per acre; dwellings in Pitherdale Garth were bought at prices ranging from £120,000 to £180,000 by purchasers no less public-spirited than the Barleybridge councillors in their determination to do the very best for their offspring.

Whilst cynics might argue that in the final analysis the Pitherdale Garth enterprise did a great deal for the councillors and nothing to swell the enrolment at Barleybridge School, more open-minded observers appreciate that it resulted in the paving of roadside verges leading towards the village school. The improvements to road safety were

19

installed by the County Highways department after several Barleybridge pupils were narrowly missed by Volvos and other vehicles of expensive and alien manufacture bound at great speed from the Garth and conveying infants to the select nurseries and colleges of Cripplegate. When the paving scheme was mooted, Barleybridge Parish Council advised that it had '. . . no observations to make on this matter'.

The Barleybridge Church of England School superseded a dame school held in the cellar of the village cobbler. It has two classrooms: a little classroom for little children and a big classroom for big ones. The little classroom is the domain of Miss Bliss. Activities here consist largely of colouring bits of paper; cutting them out; sticking them together; removing the glue and paint from the infants, and first aid, with a specialisation in scissor wounds; little else of interest occurs.

Peter Gavestone, BA, is headmaster and conducts affairs in the big classroom. Although the attainments of Barleybridge scholars in prosaic areas of learning such as reading, mathematics or environmental studies are rather modest, the school can boast that it leads the world in the education of the 8–11-year age group in so far as the subject of Edward II (1307–1327) is concerned. Mr Gavestone has devoted his life to the historical rehabilitation of what he believes to have been a grossly maligned monarch. He is the founding member of the Edward II Society with a nationwide membership of thirteen. Previously the seven members who were not confined in institutions of various kinds would meet each year on 25 April to dine at a hotel near Edward's resting place in Gloucester Cathedral, dressed in early fourteenth-century attire and conversing only in the archaic French of Edward's court. Sadly, this event was cancelled after mistakes in the booking arrangements led to the arrest of the entire unconfined membership in the lobby of the Black Swan Hotel, Gloucester, where they were mistaken for foreign transvestites.

Barleybridge parents do not generally complain about what some educational purists might regard as a somewhat imbalanced curriculum. It can after all be demonstrated that there are no set classes pertaining to Edward II on Thursdays *or* on alternate Mondays. There were a few muted murmurings of dissent when the entire Christmas concert was acted in Chaucerian (actually slightly pre-Chaucerian) English. However, the majority of parents attending assumed that the nativity play was being performed in Norwegian, revealing an impressively precocious command of European languages, while the Edward II character was variously mistaken for Our Lord, one or other of the three kings or, in the case of Mrs Tinkler, the Archangel Gabriel. Some weeks later a few eyebrows were raised when the Robinson twins were seen re-enacting the assassination of Edward as ordered by the evil Bishop of Hereford, which was, as historians will appreciate, a somewhat unwholesome form of execution. But such minor quibbles apart, it is true to say that Barleybridge people would fight tooth and nail to preserve their village school – even if none can explain why.

In all his spare time Mr Gavestone concentrates his scholarly talents on constructing a genealogical tree which, he believes, will eventually demonstrate that Josiah Hardcastle was a direct descendant of John, the second son of Edward II. Had he been able to prove that the late Sir Cecil was the rightful King of England he had hoped to be rewarded with the Earldom of Cornwall; now his ambitions are more limited. Having traced Prince John's descendants forwards and Josiah's ancestors backwards, only one link remains to be forged. If only Mr Gavestone can establish that Ephraim Hardcastle (1712–52), tinker and poultry-dealer of Rawtenstall, Lancashire, was the first-born son of the Marquis de Camenbert (1702–63), plantation owner of Louisiana, then his life's work will be complete.

3

In which we meet the village stalwarts at leisure and find that all is not what it appears to be

From the Yorkshire Gazette, *7 August 1973*
Pitherdale Gleanings by 'Dalesbred Tup'

As summer draws to its close, thoughts in Pitherdale turn to the village show season, which begins at Barleybridge on the day of St Eric and continues until the Summerthwaite Feast on the last Saturday in September. Assuredly there is nothing to compare with the heady atmosphere of the grand marquee which basks in the warmth of the August sun! Never one to shirk a challenge, at last week's Barleybridge Show I accepted a wager with Mr S. Pullan, our local livestock terminator, maintaining, in the face of his protestations, that I could navigate blindfold around the main show tent. With utter certainty I correctly identified each of the floral classes; the bread, wholemeal and plain; the confectionery; and, no great achievements these, the onions and shallots. Having successfully negotiated the beetroot and currant classes I proclaimed with unsullied confidence that I had now reached Mrs Armitage's entry in the turnip wine class. At this point Mr Pullan unceremoniously removed my blindfold, revealing that he had introduced a donkey to the marquee. Although she would not accept my explanation at the time, let me now say to Mrs Armitage, with all the authority of the *Yorkshire Gazette* behind me, that I consider the donkey to be the most wholesome and fragrant among beasts, qualities which it undoubtedly shares with Mrs Armitage's country wines.

This Show was unfortunately marred by one of those little

disputes which so frequently erupt at such fiercely competitive gatherings. Mrs Batty's prizewinning entry in Class 104: 'six brown eggs', was challenged by Mrs Shutt, who indicated to the Show Executive Committee members that each victorious egg bore the stamp of a little lion and had therefore been purchased at an unspecified egg emporium, contrary to Rule 54b. In defence of her produce Mrs Batty maintained that the lion brands were, in fact, birthmarks present on all eggs laid by her buff Orpington, Gertrude.

To resolve the controversy Messrs Raw and Bell, of the Executive Committee of the Barleybridge Society of Horticulturalists (BASH), spent the following night stationed beneath Gertrude's nest box in Mrs Batty's hen-house. Unfortunately both observers fell asleep in the course of the night, although when they awoke in the morning the nest box was found to contain three eggs, all bearing the lion birthmark. Therefore under Rule 293b of the BASH handbook, covering the official surveillance of laying, the prize is retained by Mrs Batty.

However, the BASH Executive Committee has disqualified the entry by Mr Reath in Class 91: four slices of homecured bacon. When the slices were stacked together letters spelling 'DAN' formed on the rind, and the judges suspect that the bacon may have been entered on behalf of Mr Dan Arncliffe, who is currently suspended from competition on account of the Tesco label found in association with his entry in last year's cabbage class. Readers who follow the results should amend their catalogues substituting Mr A. Beckwith as winner of Class 91. His bacon carried the letters 'ISH', but the judges decreed that this had no special significance.

It can be claimed with some confidence that members of the Hardcastle family brought civilisation to Barleybridge. Nowhere is this more true than in the recreational arena. Until the tradition was quashed by Captain Julius Hardcastle in 1849 a particularly violent form of camp ball was played between the menfolk of Barleybridge and Holmesmead parishes on the eve of the feast of St Eric. The contestants assembled on the disputed half-acre which forms the marchland between the two parishes and a pig's head was lobbed into the midst of the throng. The men of Holmesmead would seek to win by impaling their trophy on the weather vane of Holmesmead church tower, while Barleybridge stalwarts sought to achieve victory by suspending it from their wooden bridge. A draw was declared if, within the heaving mêlée, the contested item was nibbled right away by the poor of the parishes.

Since the game had objectives but no rules neither side could be accused of cheating, though Barleybridge, having fewer residents, was always prepared to regard fair play as a luxury. This was certainly true of the outcome in 1497, when a small but élite force of Swiss mercenaries contributed mightily to the Barleybridge victory. Fatalities were not uncommon and many an old score was settled in the anonymity of the shoving mass of competitors. Captain Julius, the 'Justice with an iron nose', ended the tradition when it was found that the head impaled on the weather vane of Holmesmead church was probably not that of a pig and more likely to belong to Belling, his head gardener and Chief Steward of Barleybridge Show (the differences being less distinct than one might imagine); it remained for his grandson to provide substitute entertainments.

The Barleybridge Society of Horticulturalists was created at the instigation of Sir Marmaduke Hardcastle in 1892. Sir Marmaduke was disturbed by the eruption of an unbridled enthusiasm for ferreting amongst his tenants. After the amputation of his hand, which turned septic after being bitten by an escaped ferret seeking refuge in his cigar box, he decided to direct the attentions of the community away from livestock and into horticulture. The Barleybridge Fair of St Eric had lapsed in 1531, and its revival in the new guise of the Barleybridge Show occasioned much excitement. Each village in Pitherdale stages its own show, and each is different. In the case of Barleybridge the emphasis lies on the exhibition of fruit, flowers and vegetables, a specialisation which can be traced back to the opposition of the show's founder to livestock classes. Indeed, a clause banning the exhibition or attendance of ferrets and empowering stewards to deny admission to any person suspected of harbouring same was written into the original BASH constitution.

Following the death of Sir Cecil a relaxation of attitudes resulted in the introduction of a number of classes for ponies and their young riders. Thereafter the BASH committee became divided between the Traditionalists or 'Big Tent Folk' and 'T'oss Crowd': members of the former persuasion seek to preserve the pre-eminence of the produce display in the main marquee; T'oss Crowd and their supporters are rather more monetaristic in their outlook. Whilst conceding that the juvenile equestrians are an utterly obnoxious collection of brats, the latter wish to increase the number of pony classes from nine to forty-four, since the participants are prepared to pay extravagant entry fees for the right to compete for lollipops, sherbet dips and bunches of carrots.

BASH has a General Committee and an Executive. Almost every resident of Barleybridge is a member of the General Committee, while the seven members of the Executive are attracted into service by the prospect that once a year they can don a red and gold badge, order hordes of bustling minions around, escape any arduous work and jump the queue in the beer tent. Meetings of the Executive resemble those of the Parish Council, being, if anything, more decorous and uneventful since the Show takes care of itself rather well and is only mildly disrupted by the efforts of the Executive. On one memorable occasion, the Executive *was* obliged to take strong and decisive action. Major Hetherington-Cohen, chief steward of the equestrian events, reported that Sam Pullan had been observed approaching the losing competitors in the 7–9-year-old show-jumping class, handing chastened riders his business card and slapping stickers bearing the legend 'Sold to Pullan's Barleybridge Slaughter House' on the rumps of their mounts. In consequence he incurred a five-year ban from the pony ring and its immediate precincts. T'oss crowd would accept nothing less.

Barleybridge Show is prosperous and attended by a high proportion of the Pitherdale population and some visitors from yet further afield. Sam Pullan apart, the only problem facing the Committee has been a failure to attract famous personalities to open the show. As a result the opening ceremony has been performed by various local figures, some of whom are not even well known within the limited confines of Barleybridge parish. For four consecutive years the show was opened by Amos Raw whose address unerringly runs as follows:

'Na'then, I'm pleased you've all came. I reckon we've got t'barn situation abaht reet. Just trust in t'owd Parish Council. I want to thank Mrs Wharton and t'Women's Institute for providing cakes for t'Executive and if anybody wants a load o' muck deliverin' come November I've got some good stuff that's rotting down nicely. It's not all watter and straw like they'll sell you at 'Olmesmead 'Ollins Farm.'

The summer of Sir Cecil's death, the BASH celebrity crisis was terminated in a most singular manner. Amanda Cheshire combines an ego of intergalactic proportions with a total absence of talent. She cannot sing, paint, write, or sit quietly and is quite incapable of intelligent conversation on any subject. Plainly she was predestined to become a very famous television personality. Her stardom rests heavily on two attributes, an ear-to-ear grin which reveals teeth like ranks of ivory tombstones and a quite disproportionately large posterior. The former attribute speaks for itself, as it were, and the second is emphasised by her celebrated black leather slacks.

As all but the most discerning readers will know, Amanda is the star of the top-rated programme 'Mandy Drops In!' in which our celebrity descends upon some apparently unsuspecting locality in a hot-air balloon, dashes across to the nearest member of the public, invariably a 'local character', and invites this 'guest' to relate recollections of their most embarrassing moment, honeymoon, and parents-in-law and to give their views on capital punishment and left-wing politicians, the observations being interspersed by old television clips selected by the guest (usually featuring James Last, Benny Hill or Red

26

Rum). The scene which features both Amanda's attributes prominently as she alights from the wicker basket of the balloon is generally regarded as one of the great moments of television.

'Mandy Drops In!' is not so easy a programme to stage as one might imagine. Spontaneity and *ad lib* comments must be carefully rehearsed; a special lighting crew is needed to illuminate Amanda's outstanding features properly; while the destination of hot-air balloons, once launched, is not easy to control. The problem is solved by launching the balloon within a mile of the selected random place of descent. Thus, if Mandy is to drop in by chance at Cromer, film is taken in advance of the balloon ascending from the car park of the television centre, old footage of Mandy and her balloon sailing above the Cairngorms, Bristol Channel and Snowdonia follows, the lighting crew and local character assemble at the purely-by-chance landing place and the balloon is launched nearby and upwind.

Although invariably the subject of glowing reviews in the popular press, the programme has been less generously received by the television critic of the *Sunday Examiner*, who asked his readers whether Mandy's previously purely-by-chance arrivals at Stonehenge during the winter solstice celebration, Cowes at the start of the Fastnet race or the parade ring at Aintree on Grand National day could be entirely coincidental. This unhelpful critique caused discussions amongst the production team, which culminated in the decision that the forthcoming series of 'Mandy Drops In!' would begin with their star's arrival at some quite unheard-of location in what the director describes as 'the utterly tedious and boringly butch North of England'.

Being roughly as far from London as it is from Edinburgh, Glyndebourne and Stratford, Barleybridge emerged as the ideal venue to be honoured by Mandy. Filming was scheduled for Show Day, which would provide the star with the facility spontaneously to judge the baby show (opportunities for good bending-over-pram shots) and to make impromptu marrow jokes coyly in the grand marquee.

Auditions in Barleybridge School failed to produce a

local character of sufficient intellect, eccentricity and spontaneity of wit and repartee to merit selection as Mandy's unsuspecting guest. (Moreover, a snap survey revealed a staggering 87 per cent of the village population have not heard of Benny Hill while 15 of the 26 who have believe that he runs a chain of turf accountants). The difficulty was therefore to be resolved by the importation of a little-known Lancashire comedian, Percy Preston, whom Mandy would recognise by his ruddy countenance, loud check suit and yellow waistcoat.

Show Day dawned bright and warm. Half the village horticulturalists headed for the grand marquee to secure the foremost display positions for their produce. The other half headed more furtively to Cripplegate open market in their vain annual attempts to purchase marrows to beat the monsters reared by Herbert Farrar in deep beds of Amos Raw's top-grade muck and to seek for other produce of monumental dimensions and prize-winning symmetry. For the past seven years Appleyard's stall at the Cripplegate market has produced the top three exhibits in the cabbage class – and cynical growers have muttered that the Bill Holroyd trophy should be removed from Reg Barker's mantelpiece and displayed on the Appleyard stall.

Soon the trestle tables in the grand marquee were sagging under the weight of exhibits. The warm air was heavy with the scent of rose, sweet pea, viola, beetroot and onion. Jars of honey and jam, fruit cakes, country wines and floral displays testified to the diligence and competitive instincts of the WI members, while silver sparkled in the Committee tent. With the Bishopgate Silver Band tuning up beneath an elm, kegs of Stoat's Old Particular exploding in the beer tent, exhibitors being harried by members of the Executive and appeals for owners of a box of beetroot marked 'Appleyard's of Cripplegate' to *please immediately* report to the Committee tent!' booming forth from loudspeakers, the stage was set for another perfect day.

After Amos Raw's traditional opening speech the show began, as ever, with the fancy dress parade, judged, as ever, by headmaster Gavestone. The first prize was awarded to the

Robinson twins dressed as Edward II and Queen Isabella, the second to Martin Swales as the evil Bishop of Hereford, and the third to David Wharton as Edward II. The anguish of eight unsuccessful Edward II look-alikes and a brace of Queen Isabellas was exceeded only by the wrath of Mrs Sherman of Pitherdale Garth who had invested heavily to attire her youngest daughter, Faith, as the old woman who lived in a shoe, in an outfit rushed from London by special courier.

In the beer tent a nervous Percy Preston was discovering the qualities of Old Particular and becoming less nervous but more emotional by the minute. Outside the great moment arrived. The famous pink balloon bearing Amanda dropped like thistledown to a perfect landing right beside the waiting lighting crew. 'Good heavens, where can this be' she exclaimed as she alighted from the basket, repeating the episode five times for the benefit of the camera team. Then, with cameramen running close behind to capture every angle (and curve) she bounced towards the distinctive figure in the check suit and yellow waistcoat.

'*Hello!* I'm Amanda Cheshire,' she gushed, embracing her unsuspecting guest. 'And who are *you?*'

'I'm Sam Pullan,' replied the guest.

'No you're not, you're Percy Preston,' stuttered our star, having rehearsed no *ad lib* to cover such an occasion.

As Amanda wobbled away in search of the real Percy Preston the rearward camera captured in close-up a large sticker attached to her black leather rump: 'Sold to Pullan's Barleybridge Slaughter House'.

'Cut!' squeeled the director as Amanda, distraught, rampaged through the baby show, kicking aside prams and filling the air with flying bairns and pampers. And when the star had been tranquillised with gin in the back room of the Hardcastle Arms the crew decided to retreat to Holmesmead. There Amanda completed a successful encounter with 'Nutty' Ramsbottom, who was released from family custody for the afternoon to vent his colourful views on corporal punishment, modern art, immigration and the Irish problem and to request highlights of the royal weddings, Torvill and Dean, Red Rum and the Benny Hill Show.

Deprived for ever of television exposure, Percy Preston retired to the Hardcastle Arms with Sam Pullan, where they celebrated their joint life-long bans from Barleybridge Show, imposed at the hastily convened emergency meeting of the BASH Executive. Amos Raw carefully folded the text of his speech and placed it in the breast pocket of his lovat suit; neither suit nor speech would emerge until the next Barleybridge Show.

When not accommodating Barleybridge Show, the green provides the venue for home matches of the Barleybridge Cricket Club. The Club was established by Sir Marmaduke as the second prong in his ferreting elimination strategy; it enjoys the use of an unusually splendid pavilion, modified from the ruins of the Old Wart-hog House.

The most singular match in the history of Barleybridge CC was held to commemorate the tenth anniversary of the Club. It was inspired by Sir Marmaduke following his realisation that, with sundry offspring on leave or down from Sandhurst, Oxford, Cambridge, Marlborough and Harrow, he and his brother-in-law, Rev. Mortimer Drury, possessed the nucleus of a crack Barleybridge Public Schools side capable of thrashing any eleven that the village could muster. The scorecard of this match reads as follows:

Barleybridge Public Schools XI versus
Barleybridge village and tenants
Played on Barleybridge Green, 13 August 1903

Village and Tenants
S. Beckwith	run out		3
H. Raw (capt.)	bowled Drury (A.V.)		7
Z. Wharton	caught Hardcastle (H.V. St J.)		
	bowled Drury (A.V.)		0

M. Raw	bowled Hardcastle (C.M.J.)	2
J. Pullan	run out	32
I. Swales	lbw bowled Swaffham-Bulbeck	9
J. Smith	stumped Drury (W.J.) bowled Drury (A.V.)	29
Z.I. Robinson	lbw bowled Swaffham-Bulbeck	0
L. Tinkler	bowled Drury (A.V.)	2
R. Barker	bowled Swaffham-Bulbeck	3
P. Beckwith	not out	2
	Extras	5
	Total	94

Public Schools XI

Lt E.M.J. Hardcastle	retired hurt	3
Mr A.V. Drury	bowled Smith	0
Rt Hon. I.A.M. Hardcastle	retired hurt	2
Rev. G.O.D. Drury, DD	retired hurt	0
Capt. J.C. Drury	bowled Smith	1
Rev. L.O.V. Hardcastle	retired hurt	3
Mr. H.V. St J. Hardcastle	retired hurt	0
Lt J.X.C. Swaffham-Bulbeck	refused to bat	–
Mr W. J. Drury	did not bat	–
Mr C.M.J. Hardcastle	did not bat	–
Mr L.S.D. Drury	did not bat	–

Result: Match abandoned

Sir Marmaduke's decision to abandon the match was immediately followed by his instructions for the summary eviction of his homicidal tenant, John Smith. Had he been more familiar with his tenantry, better versed in the county cricketing scene and able to recognise the significance of sweaters trimmed in light blue, yellow and dark blue the disaster need never have happened. As the carriage bearing the five injured members of the Public Schools XI marked its progress up Clapton Bank towards Dr Earl's surgery by a trail of blood, teeth and finger nails, Harold Spittlehouse, the county's leading pace bowler (aka John Smith), was in Jeremiah Pullan's cottage sharing the keg of Stoat's Stone Trough Brew which his host had promised.

This brief chapter from the annals of Barleybridge CC reminds us that two quite different forms of cricket are played in England. We refer not to the trivial distinction between the county game and the provincial leagues but to the northern and southern departments of the game. In the south, perceptions of the game are broad and include images of sociable picnics round the boundary; brightly striped caps and blazers; teams undivided by class distinctions in which any stockbroker, merchant banker or insider trader can feel at home; drinks shared with opponents in village inns; and girlfriends clad for the occasion by Laura Ashley. The northern perceptions of the game of cricket are narrower. They concern only winning.

When the Pitherdale Cricket League became the Stoat's Old Particular Pitherdale League (SOPP) in 1979 the sponsors demanded the removal of certain image-denting irregularities. A tightening-up of registration procedures virtually eliminated the incorporation of visiting professional players and the use of pseudonyms. Eighty-five per cent of the serving umpires were debarred from future participation in the game. A new rule, unique to the SOPP League, was introduced which required that wicket-keepers should not stand within two feet of the stumps. This attempted to eradicate the traditional local form of dismissal, whereby stumpers would toe-tap the base of the stumps sufficiently firmly to dislodge the bails whenever a slow bowler almost hit the wicket.

Each club responded to the awesome new restrictions in its own way. At Holmesmead, blessed by opening bowlers of rare speed and penetration, the leading wicket-taker was octogenarian groundsman, Oliver Rawden. Messrs Hadlee and Rice may have thought that the pitches prepared for them at Trent Bridge were perfect, but the greenness of the Nottingham strip has the pallor of dead straw when compared to the lushly verdant Holmesmead tracks. From October to early February the Holmesmead square is cosseted in a blanket of the much-maligned though highly nutritious muck from Hollins Farm. Before the February frost can gain a hold the entire pitch is periodically flooded when Oliver dams the flanking brooks. This flooding stimulates the grass into a vigorous early growth, so that in March the field glows like a square-cut emerald amongst the grey-green of the Pitherdale pastures. What happens to the pitch between April and September is a secret known only to Oliver, though when he dies and his testament is taken from the vaults of Scarsdale and Scarsdale (solicitors) of Cripplegate the hallowed secrets will be passed on to his successor. Meanwhile, the precincts of the ground are patrolled at dawn and dusk according to a rota of players and supporters compiled by club captain Arthur Bramley. It is widely believed that members of this vigilante group were responsible for the multiple injuries inflicted upon poor Hector Ewbank, who was encountered approaching the pitch at dusk with a sack full of scrabbling moles on the eve of the Barleybridge match.

Though lacking a groundsman of the mystical sagacity of Oliver Rawden, members of Barleybridge CC are fully aware of the strategic value of pitch preparation. They place their trust not in the pace of Albert Swales nor the guile of spinner Hector Ewbank, but in a roller of truly heroic dimensions. A vast cylinder of millstone grit some five feet in girth is entrapped in a cast-iron frame which terminates at either end in bars against which four generations of Barleybridge cricketers have pushed and hauled. This match-winning roller can break up a dry pitch to create a dust-bowl the equal of anything seen in Oklahoma, squeeze up lingering dew, or impart a seam-gripping encrustation on a damp pitch, and the plateaus and indentations on its gritty surface endow a wet pitch with the texture of crazy paving.

Readers of a discerning nature may be quick to point out that the advantages of roller technology enjoyed by the Barleybridge team could equally be exploited by visiting players. There is, however, a fatal flaw in this analysis. Though many attempts have been made, at the time of writing no visiting team comprising eleven players and a twelfth man has yet succeeded in moving the Barleybridge roller from its concrete launching pad beside the pavilion. The Barleybridge roller squad comprises twelve first team members, five former players and two umpires. Roller training begins on the net pitches in mid-March and the club takes out special insurance to cover any slipped discs, hernias or broken toes which may be incurred.

In the most recently completed season the record of the Barleybridge team was as follows:

	Won	Lost	Drawn	Rained off
Home Games	35	4	1	6
Away Games	4	13	0	3

When evaluating these statistics one should bear in mind that Barleybridge plays its most serious home and away matches in the SOPP League on Saturdays, while on Sundays the Club plays host in 'friendly' games to visiting sides which lack their own grounds. The Sunday games are used to blood promising youngsters who take the places of certain religious Nonconformists or absentee farmworkers.

A careful analysis of the Barleybridge statistics accomplished by the scorer, Mr Gavestone, reveals that in twenty-seven of the home matches won, victory was the direct result of judiciously applied roller technology. Moreover, three of the four home defeats occurred on Sundays in June or August, when the resources of the team were so depleted by the calls of hay-making that excessive numbers of youngsters were inducted and the team members were unable to move their match-winner from its concrete pad. To insure against such defeats in years to come Mr Gavestone decided to cancel two classes in mathematics and replace them with instructions in elementary roller technology and body-building for the under-elevens.

In recent years Puddle's, the vast London-based brewing conglomerate, has been advancing into Stoat's territory, gaining control of one public house after another in order to market their Puddle's Instant Sunshine Ales and Lagers. Sponsorship has played a major role in the strategy for expansion, and in Barleybridge the year when Mandy dropped in is also remembered as the one when the Puddle's Instant Sunshine Ales and Lagers League (PISALL) was created. In principle this provided a welcome addition to the competitive cricket scene, although some of the rules revealed a woeful ignorance of northern cricketing conditions. The relevant rules are outlined below, accompanied by comments in parenthesis kindly supplied by Hector Ewbank, spinner and sage of Barleybridge.

Rules of PISALL Knockout Competition (Pitherdale Division)

1) Clubs shall compete for the PISALL Cup. (Fair enough)
2) Games shall be played on Wednesday evenings in May, June and July, commencing 6.45 p.m. (Good idea)
3) Games shall consist of 20 overs per innings. (Sounds right)
4) A new ball will be provided at the commencement of each innings. (Sheer folly!)
5) The final will be played on a neutral ground. (Ayup!)
6) PISALL officials will appoint neutral umpires. (Barmy lot!)
7) The wicket-keeper shall not stand within two feet of the stumps. (They're learning summat)
8) The final shall be played between the two teams scoring most points in the preceding league matches. (OK)

Mr Ewbank points out – though it is scarcely necessary – that every man, woman and child in the county remotely familiar with village cricket is fully conversant with the traditional new-ball strategy. The following brief explanation is provided for foreigners.

During the opening overs of the game non-batting members and supporters of the batting side are spaced out round and beyond the boundary. Opening batsmen take every opportunity to hit the new ball to the boundary or, preferably, out of the field. In the scramble to retrieve it the new ball becomes lost, stamped into the turf or otherwise concealed, if possible, in a hedge or burrow from which it can later be retrieved for future use. The game then resumes with an old ball.

The ruling requiring neutral umpires posed a new challenge. Having each won all six of their home games and two away matches, Barleybridge and Holmesmead qualified to meet in the final, which was to be played at the Bishopgate ground on the lofty plateau overlooking Pitherdale. The neutral-umpire ruling was regarded as a problem of such magnitude that an unprecedented meeting between the two captains, Albert Swales of Barleybridge and Arthur Bramley of Holmesmead, was convened on neutral territory in the Carpenter's Arms at Hartley.

The deliberation between the two captains went as follows:

A.S. Na'then, Arthur, I see they've appointed Jack Richmond and Bert Stockdale as t'umpires.

A.B. Aye, and if tha goes to bribe owd Stockdale 'ow's tha to ken that I 'aven't been and bribed 'im fust? And after I've bribed 'im 'ow's I to ken that tha 'asn't bin back and bribed 'im some more?

A.S. Aye. And 'ere's summat else. If I go to Jack and tell 'im as 'ow I saw 'im in t'back o' t'churchyard with Mrs Tinkler, tha can allus go and tell 'im who tha thinks Polly Ramsden's dad really were. Think on.

This tantalising issue was eventually resolved by a careful scrutiny of the PISALL rule book, which revealed a clause allowing captains to object to any appointed umpire. A sustained barrage of objections mounted by the opposing captains eliminated all the registered umpires in the league, excepting only Ron Chadwick of Holmesmead and Jim Wharton of Barleybridge. In this way a unique instance of cooperation between Barleybridge and Holmesmead achieved a favourable outcome.

All the village cricket fields in Pitherdale are prettily situated and the Bishopgate field is one of the loveliest, commanding views of pasture and woodland with glimpses of the crumbling tower of distant Delacroix Abbey to the east and with the verdant cleft of the Pitherdale Gorge and Clapham Rocks visible to the west. Did the mellow richness of the scene inspire the men of Barleybridge as they tumbled from the back of Sam Pullan's horse wagon? We may never know. They certainly did not pause to admire the pastures gilded by the evening sun but gathered in a sullen group round the Bishopgate roller. Albert Swales encapsulated their collective sentiments when he announced that he had rolled cigarettes with bigger rollers than this. Meanwhile, Holmesmead's finest were disconsolately pacing the immaculate Bishopgate wicket. 'Call this a pitch!' said Arthur Bramley. 'I've seen more grass growing on a saddleback sow!' Plainly the PISALL committee's concern for fair play had introduced an unfamiliar and traumatic dimension of even-handedness into the cricketing affairs of Pitherdale.

Barleybridge won the toss and elected to bat. 'Slogger' Bellamy was promoted up the order to handle the new ball situation and in the second over it was seen sailing over the bordering hedgerow, hotly pursued by the players and supporters of Barleybridge. 'Ayup!' shouted Fred Tinkler, holding aloft a tangled bundle of string, leather and cork. 'He must 'a thumped that one 'ard—'e's 'it beggar right out of its case.' ('Ho'd on to t'new ball' whispered Albert Swales, 'I want to use 'er in t'Summerthwaite match.')

As the game proceeded umpire Ron Chadwick was emerging as a potential match-winner, the first seven Barleybridge men being dismissed leg before wicket, most of them while attempting to pull the leg-breaks which young Wayne Chadwick pitched just outside the off stump. This immediate crisis was forestalled in captainly fashion by Albert Swales, who called a quick single and, on reaching the opposite crease, tripped with such violence that his flying bat hit the unfortunate umpire full in the teeth. By special dispensation from his attendant relatives, 'Nutty' Ramsbottom was allowed to deputise, whilst Chadwick senior was rushed to the casualty department of Cripplegate Hospital. When the last Barleybridge player headed towards the crease (the time-honoured instructions to dig in his heels on or about a length as he ran up and down the pitch still ringing in his ears) the Barleybridge score was a modest 84. His opportunities to accomplish the traditional pitch-mangling duties of number 11 batsmen in Pitherdale were limited by the dismissal of his partner with the score on 89 although he still was able to impart a few heel-sized dents where Hector Ewbank could be expected to land his 'wrong-uns'.

The Holmesmead opening batsmen and their supporters quickly solved the new ball problem ('I reckon we'll see t' new ball again when we play Holmesmead in t'Saturday League' mused Albert Swales). Had there been a fair-minded observer in Pitherdale cricketing circles, this divine being would have acknowledged that, other things being equal (as they never were), Holmesmead had the better players. The premature departure of umpire Chadwick certainly helped redress the imbalance and umpire Wharton did all he could to uphold the honour of his fellow parishioners. Even so, the game seemed to be swinging inexorably in Holmesmead's favour with 'Nutty' Ramsbottom achieving a string of unexpected decisions. With Holmesmead needing only to score one run without loss from the remaining 3.4 overs Wayne Chadwick cut the ball firmly to Albert Swales at point.

Before the batsmen could cross, Albert launched his 52-year-old frame in the direction of young Chadwick, hurling the batsman across the pitch. 'OWZAT?' yelled Albert to Wharton. The umpire was rather perplexed, the ball having run crisply along the ground from bat to fielder which restricted the potential for caught and lbw decisions to an embarrassing degree.

'OWZAT?', repeated Albert.

'Quite possibly, but what for?' queried the umpire.

'Obstructin' t'fielding side,' said Albert.

'Out,' said Wharton, hastily gathering the bails and scurrying for the pavilion.

Thus the first PISALL final ended in a draw. Neither side wishing to undergo the tensions of a replay it was agreed that the PISALL trophy would be retained by Holmesmead for six months and then handed from Bramley to Swales across the parish boundary at midnight on 31 January. While neither side was entirely content with the result and a fiery contest was promised at their next encounter, members of both teams felt satisfied that they had taught the PISALL committee something about the intricacies of the game of cricket as it is played in Pitherdale.

4

In which we encounter the arcane traditions of the WI and meet the compleat unofficial anglers

From the Yorkshire Gazette, *10 November 1981*
Pitherdale Gleanings by 'Dalesbred Tup'

During my long association with the 'Pitherdale Gleanings' column the reporting of the activities of our redoubtable branches of the Women's Institute has been one of my most pleasurable duties. This week I am pleased to report that a truce has been declared between Bishopgate WI and the Bishopgate Countrywomen's Guild. Followers of recent events will be aware that the competition for members between these two admirable organisations has been intense, and we must all hope that during the fortnight's 'cooling-off period' following the release of hostages by Bishopgate WI, the friendly rivalries can be placed on a more stable footing. All seven hostages are in good health and all have been reclaimed by their husbands, with the exception of Mrs Openshaw. Under the terms of the truce the WI ladies have agreed to provide Miss Harper with a new hat to replace the one damaged during the hijacking of the Countrywomen's charabanc.

On Wednesday last I fulfilled my invitation to talk to the ladies of Barleybridge WI on the subject of 'The Chrysanthemum Through the Ages' (I am Hon. Vice Chairman of the Pitherdale Chrysanthemum Society and not unknown in the most elevated circles of the chrysanthemum world). To enthuse and edify the ladies I took along a selection of my favourite specimens, including a bronze bloom of majestic proportions which was Highly Commended at my Society's exhibition at Summerthwaite on 3 November – the winning exhibits were, I maintain, quite inferior in both hue and formation.

Much time was devoted to the formal business of the organisation, while during the discussion of the branch minutes the ladies became seized of a fascinating issue: are there whist drives in heaven? Mrs Batty maintained that playing cards would not be allowed within the pearly gates and that there were probably security machines, like the ones at airports, to check for cards amongst the luggage. But Mrs Reynard asserted that Miss Fossdyke, who died in 1939, would not have even considered going to heaven if there were no whist drives – and she was far too saintly a lady to have been destined for the other place. So since Miss Fossdyke is no longer with us there must be whist drives in heaven, Q.E.D. Then the ladies calculated that Miss Fossdyke would be 152 years old if still alive. Finally Mrs Batty suggested that she thought she glimpsed her in Woolworths last week, so perhaps she *had* decided not to go to heaven – or had been thrown out for trying to sneak in playing cards.

Only eight minutes remained for my talk, but I fancy that I did full justice to my topic in the time available before the departure of the last bus to Summerthwaite. One thing does puzzle me: Mrs Holroyd and I have been neighbours for more than five decades and I cannot imagine why she introduced me as 'Mr Pitherwhite'. And one small point: at my numerous other speaking engagements I have afterwards been rewarded with tea and sweet biscuits, and I can wholly recommend this hospitable practice to the good ladies of Barleybridge.

The resourcefulness and capability of our Women's Institutes is truly remarkable. At the time of writing, members of the Grassingham branch are launching their assault on the north face of K2, while ladies of the Folliholm branch rode five of the six winners on Lady's Day at Wetherby Races, including the winner of the prestigious Stoat's Old Particular Gold Cup. On the other hand, Barleybridge Women's Institute has a rather more conservative reputation. Its members care not for mountaineering or National Hunt racing; the source of the Nile would still be a mystery if its discovery depended on the exertions of the Barleybridge branch. No, the enthusiasm of the Barleybridge members is for minutes. Ladies who would jabber like magpies during a recital by Mozart himself or happily walk blindfold through the Louvre become absorbed and attentive whenever minutes are being read. The greatest reverence is reserved for the WI London minutes, every word, syllable and comma of which is eagerly devoured. When each crumb which falls from the London table has been savoured and digested the members then immerse themselves in the minutes of the local Barleybridge branch. Anything that follows is merely regarded as light relief and of little consequence, which partly explains why this branch encounters such difficulties in attracting visiting speakers.

Elsewhere in Pitherdale explorers of the Amazon, experts in patchwork, noted naturalists and renowned raconteurs jostle for invitations to entertain the Bishopgate, Holmesmead or Summerthwaite WI members, but when confronted by invitations to speak at Barleybridge, diaries fill, relatives die and the symptoms of flu materialise in an instant.

As hardened public speakers know, there are two types of venue. There are those where the organisers are perfectly competent in providing slide projectors that work; magazines that fit the projectors; extension leads that run all the way from power point to projector; electric plugs that are compatible with the apparatus concerned and with the sockets of the hall; projector tables of a suitable height, and screens which are large yet do not collapse. Equally, there are venues where most or all of these essential aids are deficient in one or any respect. Strangely, venues of the second type seldom achieve translation into venues of the first type. Barleybridge WI operate a venue of the second type.

Having had thirty-seven invitations to guest speakers apologetically declined, the lecture secretary of Barleybridge WI, Mrs Thelma Wharton, was recently reduced to inviting Mr Gavestone to present a talk on 'Edward II, A Much Maligned Monarch'. As always, the meeting was held in the school, and after the scholars had departed Mr Gavestone set up the projector and screen; when he returned in the evening his arrangements had only been mildly disrupted by the WI organisers, so that one of the greatest obstacles facing guest speakers was largely removed.

The meeting began almost promptly at 7.45 p.m. with the reading of the London minutes. At 8.30 Mr Gavestone tip-toed into the little classroom to mark some homework. By 9.20 p.m. both London and Barleybridge minutes had been negotiated and the attention of the members turned to the annual branch competition for 'The Greatest Number of Objects Contained in a Matchbox'. (Currently the record stands at 5, Mrs Ewbank's record-breaking entry containing half a nutmeg, a drawing-pin, a used return bus ticket to Cripplegate, a button from Mr Ewbank's cricket shirt, and a small piece of silver paper.)

Mr Gavestone began his talk at 9.52 p.m., and we are grateful to Miss Clarkson for providing the shorthand notes upon which the following transcript of his talk is based:

Mrs Holroyd (Chairwoman Barleybridge WI): 'Now, ladies, we can't go home yet because we've got to listen to Mr . . . er . . . Gravestone who wants to talk to us about Henry VIII.'

Mr Gavestone: 'Thank you, Madam Chairman. Edward II was the eldest surviving son and the fourteenth child of his predecessor, Edward I . . . '

Mrs Ewbank: 'I don't like his tie very much.'

Miss Bliss: 'He needs a wife to take him in hand.'

Mr Gavestone: ' . . . sometimes known as Edward of Caernarvon, he was born at Caernarvon on 25 April, 1284.' (Shows slide of Caernarvon Castle.)

Mrs Reynard: 'We went there on t'WI trip in 1953.'

Mrs Hetherington-Cohen: 'No, we did not, we went to Richmond. That was when poor Mrs Fawcett fell down all those horrid steps.'

Mrs Farrar: 'No, that was at Whitby!'

Mrs Hetherington-Cohen: 'It was at Richmond. I remember because it was the year before The Sale. It was when the Brigadier was taken badly and he waved us all off from his wheelchair.'

Mrs Farrar: 'Well, they do have steps at Whitby.'

Mrs Ewbank: 'She fractured her femur. She was never the same again. They used to keep a pig in a pen at the bottom of the garden. I can still smell it now.'

Mr Gavestone: 'At the age of twenty-three Edward succeeded as King of England, titular Overlord of Ireland and Scotland . . . '

Mrs Ewbank: 'And after she broke her femur it was *Mr* Fawcett that had to muck it out. She used to give me some for t'rhubarb.'

Mr Gavestone: ' . . . and Duke of Aquitaine. In January 1308 Edward married Isabella, known as the She Wolf of France'

Mrs Armitage: 'That's what they used to call Mrs Poireau who used to run t'village stores at Holmesmead!' (laughter)

Mr Gavestone: 'This union produced four children, Edward, John, Eleanor and Joanna . . . '

Mrs Farrar: 'It was that Mrs Poireau that ran off with Sam Pullan's cousin from Bishopgate.'

Mr Gavestone: 'Now, Edward II's second son, John, is of very special significance to Barleybridge and I am sure that you ladies will be very interested to learn about my latest discoveries . . . '

Mrs Holroyd: 'We will have to stop here because two of our ladies want to catch the last bus to Summerthwaite. So I'll thank Mr Graveyard for telling us all about Richard the Lionheart and we can all get along.'

The difficulty in obtaining guest speakers continues, and for the following meeting Mr Amos Raw was invited to deliver his 'opening Barleybridge Show' speech. Sadly he was unable to attend.

While the ladies of Barleybridge are immersing themselves in the heady affairs of the WI, many of their menfolk may be found in solitary contemplation on the shady banks of the Pither. The Barleybridge Unofficial Angling Club (BUAC) was founded by Jacob Pullan in 1835, and its existence was discovered and proscribed by Josiah Hardcastle in 1838. Until The Sale, membership of BUAC consisted only of members of the Pullan family. At The Sale fishing rights on the Pither between the parish boundaries of Summerthwaite and Holmesmead were purchased by a consortium of Cripplegate surgeons, dentists, estate agents and account-ants, who formed the Barleybridge Private Angling Club (BPAC). Meanwhile the membership of BUAC was swelled by former Hardcastle tenants who no longer faced eviction or transportation if caught drowning worms in the peaty waters of the Pither. BUAC is a commercial and sporting association. Its founding member could have sold the plump brown trout to any landlord in Pitherdale (with the possible exception of the landlord of the Hardcastle Arms). However, he chose to sell to Harburton's of Cripplegate, 'Purveyors of Superior Fish and Crustaceans to the Quality'. He drew great satisfaction from the thought that Hardcastles were paying top prices to eat their own fish.

After The Sale, Herbert Farrar was retained as water bailiff. His task was not an easy one. Should members of BPAC see BUAC members fishing unimpeded in the hallowed waters, his livelihood would be at risk. On the other hand, should he deal heavy-handedly with any anglers of the BUAC persuasion, the chance that any of his marrows would arrive at Barleybridge Show in competitive condition was less than remote. These weighty conflicts of loyalty were resolved at a secret meeting held in the back snug of the Hardcastle Arms between Mr Farrar, representing himself, and Sam Pullan, representing BUAC. The result was an unwritten concordat, which can be summarised as follows:

1) Should any BUAC member actually be caught in the act of fishing by Mr Farrar it was their own silly fault.

2) The aforementioned Mr Farrar would undertake to patrol the Barleybridge to Holmesmead section of the Pither on Mondays, Wednesdays and Fridays and the Barleybridge to Summerthwaite section of the Pither on Tuesdays, Thursdays and Saturdays.

3) In the course of his patrols Mr Farrar will sing or

whistle. During the trout season he will vocalise selections from *Oklahoma* and during the coarse fishing season (grayling and chub) he will enliven the riverine setting with traditional carols, preferably 'The Holly and the Ivy'.

4) Any BUAC member caught in the act of fishing shall, on the first occasion, render to the aforementioned Mr Farrar one barrow load of Amos Raw's best pig muck; on the second occasion he shall render one trailer load of the aforementioned fertiliser, but on the third occasion he shall suffer a confiscation of tackle.

5) So long as this agreement remains in force then all marrows and other vegetable produce grown by the aforementioned Mr Farrar shall be regarded as sacrosanct by BUAC members. Moreover, the reputation of Mrs Farrar will be held in similar esteem and shall not be introduced into any conversations in which BUAC members participate.

With this understanding in place a competitive but harmonious relationship was established, with Herbert Farrar tempering his undoubted skills as a water bailiff with a judicious restraint, the aim being to maintain an equilibrium which permitted his marrows to receive the optimum amount of fertiliser without risking defacement. Thus far only one case has had to go to a special arbitration panel composed of Messrs Pullan, Beckwith and Gavestone. This concerned old Tom Stott's third conviction. Mr Farrar testified that he was patrolling the Barleybridge–Holmesmead stretch on Wednesday 17 June and singing 'Oh! What a beautiful morning' as loudly as was compatible with his duties when he caught Tom Stott fishing for the third time that week and confiscated his tackle. That evening he heard noises outside and found that Mr Stott was throwing empty Stoat's Masham Ewe Ale bottles at his cold frame.

'What's the use of him singing?' appealed Old Tom. 'Everybody knows I'm as deaf as a post! Why can't he bang a dinner gong or something?'

The panel rejected the appeal and decided that it would be unseemly for a water bailiff of Mr Farrar's standing to proceed about his duties banging a dinner gong. Mr Stott was instructed to repair the cold frame and provide three barrow-loads of organic fertiliser by way of compensation, his tackle to be retained by Mr Farrar until the start of the coarse fishing season.

Let us hope that it is not presumptuous for the author to anticipate that many readers will be wondering how, should they take a stroll beside the Pither in Barleybridge, a member of BUAC can be recognised and differentiated from a member of BPAC. One is pleased to provide the following identification notes.

Members of BPAC wear loosely cut suits of tweed, soft tweed hats festooned with flies, and thigh-length waders. Their presence in or about the river is largely confined to the trout fishing season. They are restricted to the dry fly method of angling, although they may occasionally fish for grayling using the wet fly method during the coarse fishing season. They use rods of split cane and greenheart and catch very little.

In contrast, members of BUAC wear a variety of garments, camouflaged jackets being currently much in vogue, and Wellington boots (only in black) are standard issue, not only for BUAC members, but for the entire population above the age of two (apart from Mrs Hetherington-Cohen). The unofficials find the float method of fishing best suited to Pither waters. A variety of baits are used. Three-year-old accumulations of Amos Raw's grade A pig-and-cattle mixture produces a crop of particularly appetising small red worms. Wasp grubs are used in season and are said to be surpassed only by a species of maggot cultivated in a unique blend of offal and marketed to BUAC members by Sam Pullan at a discount rate of 75p per pint. Unofficial anglers use a type of rod manufactured from Second World War tank radio aerials. The particular advantage of this form of equipment is that when tossed into the river it sinks and can then be retrieved after Mr Farrar has passed. BUAC members catch a great many fish, some for private consumption and some for sale to local innkeepers at the standard rate of £1 per pound. Conservational policies introduced by Sam Pullan in 1967 limit the number of fish taken to five trout or three pounds weight of fish per member per day. The restrictions were introduced after heavy catches threatened to destabilise the price of trout in Pitherdale. Fortunately the Pither is such a paradise for brown trout that the river stocks itself and the fish population is undiminished by the activities of the BUAC fraternity.

BUAC is, emphatically, an *unofficial* angling club and its existence is denied by all the good people of Barleybridge, particularly the membership and Mr Farrar. Its policy towards BPAC members is hostile but intricate. The premier plank in the policy is a desire not to compromise the position of Mr Farrar and its second objective is to prevent BPAC members from occupying the best fishing stances or otherwise disrupting the pleasures of unofficial anglers. The best fishing places are Old Ford Bend, Otter Cliff, where the old millstream rejoins the river, and Ramsbottom Deep. These spots are so superb and so inviting that no trout in its right mind would be seen in the stretches near Four Lane Ends or Beckwith's Meadow. Consequently all BUAC members seek to concentrate the gentleman anglers in the two last-named locations. When Sam Pullan caught a monstrous trout, worth £3.75 at current rates, on the sloping shelf of shale below Otter Cliff he sacrificed all thoughts of financial gain. Instead he had the fish stuffed, mounted and displayed in the saloon bar of the Hardcastle Arms which is so favoured by BPAC members. The commemorative plaque on the case reads: 'Brown Trout weighing 3 lb 12 oz, caught by Sir Cecil Hardcastle 14.7.1978. This fish took a March Brown and was caught in the R. Pither at Beckwith's Meadow.' Ever since the trout arrived in the Hardcastle Arms, lines terminating at one end in a March Brown and at the other in a private angler have been lashing the Pither into a foam at Beckwith's Meadow. Thus far, however, nobody has taken a fish of more than 3 lb, the closest approach being an eel of 5 oz.

Some of the other tactics used by BUAC members are club secrets, but some information was recovered in the form of a tape recording made at Ramsbottom Deep by Arnold Pickersgill, who was attempting to capture the mating call of the yellow wagtail:

(piercing note of kingfisher rapidly receding)
    'You're doin' fine Oklahoma!' (approach of Mr Farrar)

'Plop!'(Hector Ewbank's tank aerial rod drops in the river)
'Ow do, 'Erbert?'
'Ow do, 'Ector, 'ow is t'?'
'Fair to middling, tha' knaws.'
'Oklahoma's OK.' (Mr Farrar departs)
'Schlop.' (sound of rod being retrieved)
'Plop.' (rod returns to river)
'Plod, squelch, plod, squelch.' (approach of BPAC member).
'Good day to you, fine weather we are having!'
'It's a bit nowt to summat an' too mitherly for lakin' wi' t' 'ay.' (special incomprehensible BUAC dialect used only in conversation with BPAC members)
'Quite so. I say, have you been here long? Have you seen any trout rising?'
'Nae, lad, tha'll not catch owt 'ere. T'last trout catched 'ere were catched by owd Sir Marmaduke 'Ardcastle back in 1883. It were that contaminated wi' muck from Robinson's sewer that 'e were rushed t't'ospital straight after 'e et it. T'sewer comes in over there tha knaws, just past t'place were Mother Ramsbottom drowned 'ersen. She were that green and bloated by t'time they found 'er they thowt she were a gurt big frog. Aye. But I saw some right big 'uns rising down by Fower Lane Ends.'
'Is that so! Well then, I'll bid you good day.'
'An' t'best o' t'wether tuppin' season t'thee.' (more BUAC dialect).
'Schlop.'
'The corn is as 'igh as an elephant's eye.'
'Plop.'
'Na'then, 'Erbert.'
'Na'then 'Ector. 'As t'daft beggar gone?'
'Aye.'
'And it looks like it's climbing right up to the sky.'
'Schlop.'

5

In which we explore the public buildings and services of Barleybridge and Mrs Addyman stuffs a cat

Samuel Harbottle's observations concerning the patronage of Barleybridge taverns by members of the Delacroix Abbey community were not unfounded. After the Dissolution the village supported a variety of inns and ale-houses. However when Josiah Hardcastle purchased the village the *laissez-faire* processes of free competition, typhoid and arson had reduced the village hostelries to one: the Black Swan, known to its patrons as 'The Mucky Duck'. This, the only surviving timber-framed building in Pitherdale, was gutted by Josiah's agents and furnished with an imposing mock-Elizabethan façade the better to harmonise with the new Vicarage which was rising nearby, its original Elizabethan frontage being considered undistinguished. A new landlord was installed and each St Brian's Day (31 January) tenants assembled in the first-floor dining-room of what was now the Hardcastle Arms to pay their rents. A few years later generous investments in the political system actually secured a family coat of arms (a weaver, rampant, supported by overseers), and the arms and family motto were emblazoned above the entrance to the inn.

Barleybridge is renowned for the longevity of its inhabitants. Some observers attribute this to the beneficial effects of imbibing large quantities of Stoat's Old Particular. Others blame it on the air, the water or even a wholesome lifestyle. In fact it may solely be due to the stubborn nature of the typical Barleybridgian. The mere thought of funeral expenses is sufficient to prolong the life of the average

50

villager by a good five years, no matter how coaxing the advertisements placed in the *Pitherdale Messenger* by Stanley Moreton, undertaker, may be.

It has been calculated that the average lifespan of the Barleybridge male would be 103 were it not for the statistical distortions wrought by the Great War of 1914–18. Many men bade their farewell to the village at the Hardcastle Arms in 1914. On the outbreak of hostilities, Lady Hardcastle summoned a meeting of the entire tenantry in the rent collection room above the saloon bar. To her right stood the vicar, to her left a recruiting sergeant of the Green Howards, while in a corner the church organist played patriotic tunes on an upright piano.

'In times of grave national emergency such as these,' she announced, 'it behoves us all to make the deepest personal sacrifices. I myself have decided to soldier on as best I can without the services of my coachmen, grooms, gardeners, gamekeepers, water bailiff and tenants. Their duties will be shouldered by retired members of our staff and wives of our tenants, who will report to my agent at Hardcastle Hall at 6.30 tomorrow morning to receive their instructions. My existing employees are therefore relieved of their obligations and will enlist immediately and then depart promptly for Richmond. Let me only add that Colonel Hardcastle and I love you all dearly and know that it is in your own best interests that you should cross the sea to defend the honour of your King and country. Be of good heart, and when you stand in the trenches in France think only of killing the evil Hun. Do not worry about my welfare and the hardships that I must endure. I place my trust in your parents and grandparents to care for me till you return. May the Good Lord be with you! The coachmen may not enlist until I have been returned to Hardcastle Hall.'

Sixty-eight men and boys were marched out of Barleybridge that day, and when the war was over twelve of them marched back.

In 1919 the tenancy of the Hardcastle Arms was awarded to Sgt George Swires. Readers may recall how heroic service on the field of battle has led to the elevation of common soldiers in days gone by. George Swires's elevation to the exalted station of landlord was of this kind and occurred in the following manner. Colonel Sir Percival Hardcastle was inspecting a parade of sanitary orderlies at Folkestone in 1917 when shrapnel from a stray bomb, dropped during the zeppelin raid on harbour installations, blew off his hand. The airborne appendage was seized in full flight by the regimental mascot, a wolfhound of great bulk and voracious appetite. Without a thought for his personal safety, the Colonel's loyal batman, Sgt Swires, seized the ceremonial sword which had fallen from the grip of the rapidly departing hand and sliced off the wolfhound's head before the still-twitching fingers could pass down its gullet. The Hardcastle hand was interred in the Hardcastle vault at Barleybridge, therein to await the eventual arrival of the owner. While the slaughter of regimental mascots by serving soldiers is not normally encouraged in HM forces, the special circumstances involved were taken into account. Sgt Swires was offered a commission in the Colonel's regiment or the tenancy of the Hardcastle Arms: he sagely chose the latter.

When Stoat's Cripplegate Breweries purchased the Hardcastle Arms at The Sale the firm also acquired an aged sitting tenant in the form of George Swires. Not long after Sir Cecil's death the Cripplegate Breweries were taken over by Puddle's Instant Sunshine Ales and Lagers Ltd. George Swires was still in residence.

The management of Puddle's had long since discovered that their only viable marketing strategy was to control a vast network of public houses. Their ales and lagers are brewed in London and shipped in decommissioned oil tankers to various provincial ports, where they are injected into pressurised kegs and freighted to the outlets. The ales and lagers are marketed under the slogan of 'Natural goodness, uncorrupted by hops or barley', although the actual composition is a closely guarded trade secret, known only to the brewers and to National Chemical Industries, their suppliers.

Readers may have noticed that brewers' perceptions of their clientele are encapsulated in their television commercials. The Puddle's commercial is screened several times a day throughout the year and twice hourly during the Christmas drink'n drive season. The shooting script runs as follows:

Scene: Foot of Mount Sinai. Moses descends towards the people of Israel bearing the two tablets of the testimony. Two skinheads wearing the all blue, and the red, black and white livery of famous football clubs leap out from behind a boulder. They kick Moses up in the air, throw away the tablets of the testimony and shout: 'We don't want this! What we want is Puddle's!'

Cut to new scene: A stable in Bethlehem. Enter three kings bearing gifts. Skinheads leap down from hayloft. Put boot into the Magi and chant: 'We don't want gold, we don't want frankincense, we don't want myrrh! What we want is Puddle's!'

Cut to new scene: The shores of the Sea of Galilee. Apostles distributing baskets of loaves and fishes move amongst vast crowds of extras. A boat runs aground. Out spring two skinheads and run amok; toss apostles into the sea. Shout to crowd: 'Who'd rather have a pint of Puddles?' 'We would!' reply crowd in unison – all depart for Puddle's Inn in Galilee.

Voice-over: 'Are *you* man enough to be a Puddle's man?'

Not everybody in Barleybridge is a Puddle's man, and those switching from Stoat's Old Particular to Puddle's ales may experience severe withdrawal symptoms. 'I can't stomach this 'ere recycled beer,' grumbled Amos Raw when the ales and lager were first made available to the locals in the Hardcastle Arms. In the week following the launching of the new beverages the sales figures were as follows:

Puddle's Instant Sunshine Ales and Lagers	4 pints
Stoat's Old Particular	2,667 pints

While these figures show that the 400 parishioners of Barleybridge were patronising their local inn keenly (though some much more keenly than others), Puddle's regional manager, Mr Ridley, was not delighted. He was party to a plan of longstanding that would result in the unforeseeable closure of the Stoat's brewery in Cripplegate because of 'unanticipated technical difficulties' six months after its purchase by his firm. The clientele of Puddle's houses would then be given the choice of drinking PISALL products or the spirits which the company sells to its pub managers at prices 266 per cent higher than those which George Swires was furtively paying at the Cripplegate Cash-and-Carry.

Consequently, Mr Ridley devised a special development plan for the Hardcastle Arms along the following lines: (1) get rid of George Swires; (2) improve the physical appearance of the Hardcastle Arms; (3) improve the social appearance of the Hardcastle Arms, particularly by getting rid of the locals.

Phase 1 of the plan was accomplished with a strategy specially designed to overcome a sitting tenant with absolute security of tenure. A sorrowful Mr Ridley visited the Hardcastle Arms bearing the sad news that, as a result of unforeseeable accountancy difficulties, the brewery was regrettably obliged to sell the Hardcastle Arms. 'I've got a few pund in t' bank, tha knaws,' said George, grasping at the prospect of spending his last days as the owner of the pub that he had tenanted for more than six decades. However, when Mr Ridley had ascertained the amount of George's considerable nest-egg he confided that the brewery was expecting to obtain more than twice as much on the open market.

Thus the Hardcastle Arms was closed pending its purchase and George Swires left to live with his niece in Keighley. Numerous prospective publicans tried to approach Mr Ridley with a view to buying the inn, but he was always found to be unobtainable. With Mr Swires installed but rapidly declining in Keighley, the decision to sell was surprisingly reversed and the Hardcastle Arms was re-opened under the management of 'Fast' Frank O'Grady, transferred by the brewery from the Lockpicker's Arms in Bradford.

Improvements to the inn's physical appearance were accomplished in a more customary manner, with the dispatch from London of a container holding a Puddle's Individual Character Conversion Kit. Each of these identical kits contains the basic decor needed to give a Puddle's house its distinctive appearance: antique roof beams of oak-look plastic; light fittings with plastic candles tipped with pointed pink bulbs; rolls of self-stick lead-look diamond-panes-in-a-jiffy paper for the windows; 'Wanted: Dick Turpin' day-glo posters; and 'Yeomen' and 'Wenches' signs for the lavatory doors. The installation of these improvements took longer than expected. When the Elizabethan oak roof beams in the Hardcastle Arms were removed, steel joists had to be inserted before their oak-look plastic replacements could be fitted. Also, the lead-look paper was difficult to stick to the real leading on the diamond-pane windows originally provided by Josiah Hardcastle.

Naturally the name had to change. 'When we create a traditional old English pub then we create a traditional old English name to go with it,' explained Mr Ridley. In this way the Hardcastle Arms became 'The Merrie Scampi of Olde England'. This, Mr Ridley believed, would underline the olde worlde character of the hostelry. An artist was specially commissioned to paint a sign depicting Robin Hood and Friar Tuck fishing for scampi in the Pither. It was also felt that the new name would help to promote the Merrie Scampi Fries which would feature on the Traditional Pub Grub menu, along with the Chicken in a Medieval Basket, Friar Tuck's Favourite Hamburgers and Tudor Toasted Sandwiches.

The third phase of the strategy, getting rid of the locals, could, 'Fast' Frank advised, be achieved quite simply by imposing a ban on black wellington boots. In the course of the conversions the old public bar became 'Maid Marion's Kitchen', complete with traditional microwave oven and sandwich toaster. The saloon bar became 'King Arthur's Pantry', while the tiny back snug, previously reserved for BUAC meetings and Mrs Farrar's assignations, became the only part of the inn to which wearers of black wellies were still admitted. The improvements were crowned by the demolition of George Swires's pigsties and their replacement by an olde worlde beer garden. This provided members of the new clientele, many of them 'Fast' Frank's old patrons at the Lockpicker's Arms, with unrivalled opportunities to throw their glasses at villagers laying wreaths in the adjacent churchyard.

Fearful that there might be a link between drinking and the mysterious eruption of a plague of jollity amongst his staff, Josiah Hardcastle provided the Barleybridge Institute as a counter-attraction to the Hardcastle Arms. It was the most curious of his buildings, built to a circular design inspired by a painting that he had seen of the Round Tower at Windsor Castle. Three years after its completion the exact nature of its use remained unspecified, and the discovery that villagers were using it as a dovecote helped to clarify Josiah's thinking. It was, he declared, a reading room. The circular form made the installation of the requisite bookshelves rather difficult. For two years it remained unused, the uplifting volumes on the shelves untouched. This in turn led to the discovery that the villagers were, by and large, illiterate. Compulsory classes in reading were inserted between the Sunday church services.

The Institute then enjoyed its finest years. Books were borrowed and read, the horizons of the village expanded beyond Holmesmead, beyond Cripplegate, to the furthest corners of the expanding Empire, while every Saturday the Hardcastle's agent left Barleybridge to recover missing volumes from the secondhand book vendors of Cripplegate. Successive Hardcastles supported their Institute with characteristic patronage. Each morning the previous day's issue of *The Times* was deposited in the Institute, with any potentially subversive passages cut out and any socially significant contributions framed in red. Particularly favoured were those articles which enjoined the poor man at his gate to be content with his lot and not to envy masters who had to shoulder heavy burdens of responsibility. From the point of view of the average Barleybridgian, however, anything that *The Times* might have to say paled into insignificance in comparison to the reports of fat stock prices in Cripplegate market, as reported in the *Pitherdale Messenger*.

With the passage of time, the literary pursuits of the village declined, and with the arrival of television they disappeared. It was only the eruption of a reborn enthusiasm for ferreting which persuaded Sir Cecil Hardcastle to agree to a request that a billiard table be installed in the Institute. His agreement was conditional upon the understanding that all ferrets be removed from the village forthwith and that participants should play billiards and not snooker, which was, he contended, a game for cads. Many an evening thereafter he would leap from his telescope with a cry of 'Coloured balls!' and despatch his chauffeur with instructions to lock up the Institute until further notice.

If the truth be told, the Institute, being small and circular, is not ideally suited to the conduct of a game played upon a large rectangular table. Shots played from positions at any corner of the table can only be accomplished by players who lie upon the third curving bookshelf from the bottom (or the fourth shelf in the case of shots played with heavy 'stun' or 'side'). Naturally members of the Barleybridge Snooker Team are the most accomplished bookshelf players in England, possibly in the world, and they always seek to maximise their home advantage when playing in the Stanley Moreton Pitherdale Snooker League. In Barleybridge a good snooker shot is not one which pots the black or snookers the white ball behind the pink but one which lands the cue ball on the very lip of the corner pocket. (Having lost their last twenty-five consecutive away matches at Barleybridge, members of the Holmesmead team practised their corner game from a set of curving bookshelves which were specially manufactured for the purpose, but even after practising each evening for seven weeks they were quite unequal to the subtleties of Barleybridge corner play.)

Before the billiard table was installed the centre of the Institute was occupied by a pot-bellied stove. Each winter evening village elders who were too poor to patronise the Hardcastle Arms would assemble round this source of warmth, huddled in their black greatcoats like beetles round a glowing beetle king. Here the most scandalous episodes in

Barleybridge past and present were recounted, embroidered and savoured as pipes tapped out a tattoo on the cast-iron stove and spittle sizzled on the coals. The installation of the billiard table brought an end to such gatherings, and the Hardcastle Arms acquired a clientele of old boys who could make a half of mild and bitter last all night.

Before the venue was moved to Barleybridge School, the Institute was the meeting place for the Parish Council. The councillors were all ambitious members of the snooker second team, and following the installation of the billiard table the frequency of the parochial meetings increased from an average of three per annum to two per week. Miss Bliss, the parish clerk, was posted in the little lobby to intercept onlookers and her shrill cry of 'Good evening, Mrs Hetherington-Cohen, the councillors are just debating the barn situation', would be followed by scuffling sounds from within. Cynical members of the community claimed that the councillors were using their meetings as a cover to practise their corner shots and to monopolise the facilities. When members of the first snooker team threatened to offer themselves as candidates in the forthcoming Parish Council elections the council meetings were moved to the school and their frequency returned to three per annum.

Since the Institute failed to fulfil its early promise, the cultural side of life has become the province of the mobile library. Provided driver Ackroyd has successfully negotiated the competing hostelries of Pitherdale, the van arrives outside the Emporium ten minutes after lunch-time closing at the Pack Horse on alternate Tuesdays. The van is noticeably smaller than the renowned libraries of ancient Alexandria, of Oxford or London, but it does have one virtue lacking in these other centres of learning: a whole shelf stack devoted to the particular kinds of literature favoured in Barleybridge. It is only fair to add that these shelves are bare of works by the likes of Tolstoy, Leibnitz or Engels. Where the German theologian and philosopher Harnack is concerned, 94 per cent of the villagers have not heard of him and the remaining 6 per cent think that he is a brand of lavatory cleaner (Mr Addyman drank something similar and went clean round the bend). Yet if the villagers' taste in books is not highbrow, at least it is broad. Mrs Braithwaite, the librarian, consulted her records and reported to the public lending right authorities that Barleybridge readers regularly consulted the following books in descending order of popularity:

1. *Ferreting: An advanced Guide*, A. Noakes.
2. *How to Get Ferrets Out of Kitchen Fittings: A Housewife's Guide*, A. Noakes.
3. *An Edwardian Lady's Wellington Boot Sketchbook*, Jemima Aston-Somerville.
4. *Outdoor Sports for Centenarians*, Vol.III, *Skiing*, Cripplegate WEA.
5. *How to Stuff Your Cat*, M. St J. Haddock.
6. *Making a Ferret-Proof Cage for Your Gerbil*, A. Noakes.
7. *A Busy Housewife's Guide to Tractor Repairs*, National Farmers' Association.
8. *Amanda Cheshire's Lake District*, Amanda Cheshire et al.
9. *100 Things You Can Smoke in Your Pipe*, S. Moreton.
10. *The Collected Writings of Dalesbred Tup*. Dalesbred Tup.

Once the van has ceased to weave and has come to a halt, the literary enthusiasts pile in and half an hour of communal gossiping is followed by half an hour of book selection ('You'll enjoy that, Mrs Reeth, the postman did it'), and then the villagers troop away in little bunches. This formula was followed faithfully for years until the day after Mrs Addyman's cat, Sammy, came a close second in a fight to the death with one of Sam Pullan's lurchers. Mrs Addyman became so engrossed in M. St J. Haddock's *How to Stuff Your Cat* that she was oblivious to the departure of her neighbours. When the van started with a jolt she was cast to the floor and her sticks skidded away to lodge under the outsize books. Undaunted, yet too timorous to disturb the librarians, she put her confinement to good use. Armed with her handbag and knitting she practised cat stuffing all the way to the next stop, outside the Pick and Shovel up on Heathhowe Moor.

Fortunately she obtained a lift back to Barleybridge on the trailer of Tim Robinson's tractor, and by the time she saw the lights of home twinkling from the Summerthwaite road she had mastered all the most intricate techniques of cat stuffing. Such was the breadth of her accomplishment that she bought a herring from Mr Barraclough and stuffed that too.

So now Sammy and his herring survey the world from Mrs Addyman's mantelpiece, treasured mementoes of a day when misfortune was turned to advantage. Moreover, after news of Mrs Addyman's achievement spread round the village, M. St J. Haddock's learned tome leapt to number two on the Barleybridge literary hit parade. Soon the households teamed with stuffed ferrets, sheep, slugs, goldfish and – most demanding of all – hedgehogs. No sooner did an animal bid the world adieu than its warm corpse was seized by one or other of the ardent stuffers and preserved for ever more. A new class, 227B, was proposed for Barleybridge Show: 'The best saddleback sow; entries restricted to amateur taxidermists and locally-raised subjects'. Eventually, however, the book was filched from the shelves and destroyed by Joshua Pickersgill, gravedigger, who feared that any extension of the taxidermist's art into the human arena might undermine his trade. Already Mrs Lowcock was muttering that when her Albert's time came he would make a very nice hatstand.

While the library caters for the demands of Barleybridge minds, the villagers can entrust their souls to the church of St Eric and St Brian. If the Institute is Pitherdale's most curious building, the church is certainly its most striking. In pre-Hardcastle times the village lay in Holmesmead parish but was served by a small late-medieval chapel of ease with the low nave and narrow tower so characteristic of the 'Pennine Perpendicular' ecclesiastical architecture of the region. This homely building fell far below the standards required by Josiah Hardcastle, who, while not exactly an expert on the competing claims of the Gothic and Classical styles, knew what he liked. When difficulties of communication between Josiah and Sir Boothby Pagnell, his architect, threatened to produce an impasse in the dialogue, Sir Boothby produced a copy of Burton Leonard's *Mediaeval Churches of Britain*. 'I want that, that, that and that,' announced Josiah, stabbing a stubby finger at the preferred illustrations.

Sir Boothby envisaged no difficulties in replicating the nave and chancel of the church at Heckington in Lincolnshire. The western end of the church posed greater challenges, for Josiah's finger of favour had pointed to the fifteenth-century church tower at Wrington in Somerset, the crown tower of King's College chapel in Aberdeen and the broach spire at Olney in Buckinghamshire. Sir Boothby reconciled the unique architectural difficulties in a design which placed the incurving arches of the crown tower at the top of the Wrington-based tower, where they could serve as flying buttresses to support a miniaturised reproduction of the Olney spire. To sustain this singular structure, foundations were sunk to a depth of 25 feet. Unfortunately Sir Boothby did not allow for the severity of the autumn gales which blast down Pitherdale from the north-west. Six weeks after the completion of the church, the crown and spire blew down across the graveyard and beyond to demolish the disused wart hog house. A lesser man than Josiah Hardcastle might have been disheartened by this catastrophe, which arrived close on the heels of the difficulties associated with the family museum, arboretum and zoological gardens. But, resourceful to the last, he commanded his workmen to gather the fragments of fallen masonry, ecclesiastical and zoological, and reassemble the crown and spire in the form of an imposing monument to cover what would then become the Hardcastle family vault.

The unusual dedication of the church to St Eric and St Brian has aroused considerable curiosity. St Eric is a shadowy figure of the tenth century whose spirit still lingers over Pitherdale. According to a twelfth-century *Life of St Eric*, he was a Viking convert who wandered round the Northern dales preaching against the iniquities of the age. It appears

61

that Pitherdale was unique in the breadth and intensity of its iniquities and so attracted Eric's special attention. In the course of a particularly intensive mission to Barleybridge he was martyred by drowning when suspended in an ancestral vat of Old Particular. Onlookers are said to have been impressed by the expression of saintly contentment on the face of the corpse and sought to emulate his martyrdom.

St Brian is a rather more controversial character. Josiah Hardcastle was convinced that his uncle, Brian Heptonstall, was, at the very least, a saint and that possibly his presence on earth represented the second coming. Uncle Heptonstall was a lay preacher of immense passion and a man who only permitted the flogging of his mill workers as a very last resort. For the last thirty years of his life he existed on a diet of skimmed milk and watercress, wore a suit of black sailcloth and campaigned relentlessly against nakedness in the animal kingdom. His mills in Rochdale finally collapsed owing to their inability to find a market for their range of three-piece suits and tail-length dresses for dogs and cats. Thereafter he lived in a cave above Settle, refusing all offers of support from his nephew and devoting his last days to pursuing sheep while armed with sheep suits in black worsted.

After his death his nephew devoted his energies and influence to a vain attempt to secure Brian Heptonstall's canonisation. With the construction of the new church at Barleybridge, Josiah mounted the final phase of his quest. An approach to the highest level of the Anglican establishment culminated in the following unwritten accord:

1) The Church of England would graciously accept the gift of 10,000 white cotton surplices so generously provided by the Hardcastle Mills of Oldham.

2) The township of Barleybridge would be separated from the parish of Holmesmead and would become an ecclesiastical parish in its own right.

3) The advowson or right to appoint a vicar would be vested in the patrons of Barleybridge church, the Hardcastle family of Hardcastle Hall.

4) The new church at Barleybridge would be dedicated to SS Eric and Brian. Should members of the Hardcastle family claim that St Brian is the late Mr Brian Heptonstall of

Rochdale and Settle this claim will neither be confirmed nor denied by the establishment of the Church of England.

5) As Ripon Minster was about to be elevated to the status of a cathedral the new diocesan authorities would discuss appropriate contributions to the refurbishment of the minster with Sir Josiah Hardcastle, whose pocket was as deep as his sins were many.

In accordance with article three of the accord Sir Josiah appointed his son-in-law as the first vicar of Barleybridge. The new church was consecrated on St Brian's Day (31 January), the tenth anniversary of the day on which the bodies of Mr Heptonstall and of a Masham ewe wrapped in black worsted were discovered at the foot of Attermire Scar. Landmarks in the ecclesiastical history of Barleybridge were commemorated in the great east window, specially designed for the church by Sir Josiah. The panel at the head of the window depicted St Eric seated in the saloon bar of the Anglo-Saxon equivalent of the Hardcastle Arms. The side panels portrayed kneeling weavers offering their children to Sir Josiah in supplication, while the central panels showed the spirit of St Brian being received into heaven and riding in triumph through the pearly gates on a camel nattily clad in thornproof tweed.

Blobs of red, blue, green and gold light from the great east window dapple the pulpit, an imposing structure of five levels all tiered like a wedding cake. The Hardcastle arms and motto are carved and gilded on the sounding board above the pulpit, causing some members of the congregation to be uncertain whether it was the word of God, Hardcastle or both that was being preached.

The Hardcastles did not have a family pew or a family gallery but rather a family suite, which juts forward like the prow of a great warship from a lofty position on the inner face of the tower. It has a copious hearth, ample dining accommodation, a butler's pantry and a lavatory. Its oak-panelled walls are decorated with sporting prints and its bookshelves stocked with literature of the less demanding kinds. Successive butlers have been instructed to serve sherry as the choir process down the aisle, whisky and soda with the second hymn and port with the sermon.

These family ecclesiastical traditions did not lead, as some might suspect, to inattentive attitudes, for as the vicar of Barleybridge was invariably the son-in-law of the leading Hardcastle, members of the family enjoyed the opportunity to question him about the contents of his morning sermon over the roast beef in Hardcastle Hall afterwards. Over the years a Hardcastle attitude to theology developed which extended beyond the delicate issues surrounding the canonisation of St Brian. They believed the church to be a very good thing, a cornerstone of society, helping people to understand why they should be content with their lot and providing useful opportunities for charitable acts. So long as it did not try and dabble with religion it would not go far wrong. These attitudes, which crystallised in the middle years of the nineteenth century, are still upheld by countless rural congregations and so they remind us what far-sighted people those Hardcastles were.

From the Yorkshire Gazette, *5 April 1977*
Pitherdale Gleanings by 'Dalesbred Tup'

The churches and chapels of Pitherdale are the very hubs of our little communities. It is well known that I serve as organist and choirmaster at one of Cripplegate's finer churches, while I periodically offer my services to the congregation of my local church of Saints Eric and Brian quite free of any charge. Readers will therefore appreciate that the problem posed by the woodworm in the organ loft of Barleybridge church is a matter close to my heart. The parochial church council is now in receipt of an estimate for treatment by Rentokil – and I might add that the sums would be much less if the problem had long ago been treated at source: in Mrs Fawcett's wooden leg. I might also add that I strenuously deny her claim that the pests have emanated from the mahogany frame of the photograph of myself being introduced to Archbishop Fisher which I hung above the keyboard.

Pending more permanent treatment, bales of straw have been placed beneath the organ loft and various fund-raising events are in progress. At the recent bazaars held in Barleybridge School the 'Guess the age of Mrs Fairclough' stall raised £27.75. No prize was awarded because of a discrepancy between the birth certificate and royal telegram of 1972 on the one hand and Mrs Fairclough's claims on the other. Both documents suggest that she is 105, though she only acknowledges being 97. Ladies are renowned for being coy about their ages, but I do feel that the organisers should have chosen a less controversial participant. The 'pin the tail on the donkey' competition raised £13.17 after the deduction of 53 pence for a bottle of iodine. Mrs Morag McPhee, who is currently biding in Pitherdale, kindly attended the bazaar in her capacity as 'Gypsy Rose Lee' and her fortune-telling booth contributed £15.25. Nonetheless one must question whether it is prudent to raise the expectations of the village maids and spinsters in the way that she does. Ladies thus distracted do not make the best cooks! Mr Tinkler confides that his Martha is now refusing to muck out the pigs and served him a starched collar amid his bacon on Sunday. As this was his only such collar he was unable to attend matins.

I think he should tell Martha that there is no history of royal marriages involving Pitherdale brides – and meanwhile Mr Beckwith should make it quite plain to his Emily that Mr Mick Jagger would be a most unsuitable choice, even if he does arrive at Hartstone Farm in a white Aston Martin, as predicted.

Returning briefly to the topic of Mrs Fairclough, I feel that the matter could have been resolved quite smartly if the organisers had consulted her elder sister, Miss Charlotte Fairclough, who was quite close at hand operating the Aunt Sally stall. Later I saw her competing with the cricketers at the coconut shy – and a very good account of herself she gave. In a brief flight of fancy I imagined that she would have made a useful left arm pace bowler with a deceptive late away swing. However, such musings should not be encouraged, and where cricketing matters are concerned the lady's place is in the tea hut. This reminds me that the season will soon be upon us – and it should remind members of the Barleybridge Cricket Club that roller squad training takes place this Saturday at 9.30 a.m. prompt.

6

In which we meet the villagers and enter the mysterious world of Amos Raw's privy

The population of Barleybridge divides into three groups: the native villagers; the Pitherdale Garth community; and the 'social oddments', such as the Vicar, Mr Gavestone and 'Fast' Frank. The natives understand each other pretty well but are completely unable to understand anyone else; they are warm and kindly but resolutely refuse to admit that they are. They love to gossip about each other and yet they treat each other with genuine respect. Within the tight community rogues are not despised and persecuted; they are simply ignored. Barleybridge vices, such as they are, comprise longevity and a somewhat undeserved local reputation for tightfistedness. One school of thought, current in Holmesmead, holds that no Barleybridgian will die while there is still money left to run in the gas meter. Another, circulating in Bishopgate, claims that, thrifty to the end, dying Barleybridgians will use their last energies to rise from their deathbeds to switch off the lights or oven.

If there is a distinctive Barleybridge trait it is a preoccupation with the more trivial aspects of an issue, the form of thinking employed in the village being more tangential than lateral. When the *Titanic* sank ('Cripplegate Man Drowns' trumpeted the *Pitherdale Messenger*) the village quickly dispensed with the larger aspects of the tragedy but devoted three months to an intense debate about the proportion of an iceberg that lies unseen beneath the water. This issue was only resolved when the contents of the ice house at Hardcastle Hall were furtively purloined, carted away, and dumped in the Pither at Ramsbottom Deep. A popular tribunal of thirty-four villagers observed the experiment, half of them standing on the river bank and the other half adopting submerged positions. As a result the *Titanic* death toll was increased indirectly by three.

In the past, agriculture was the lifeblood of Barleybridge. Gone are the days when the Hardcastle home farm employed twenty carters, ploughmen and labourers, but farming still dominates the ethos if not the employment of the village. There is no such thing as a typical Barleybridge farmer (the most common denominator being membership of the Parish Council). Even so, Amos Raw is worth a second glance. Thus far we have only seen him in his pomp, delivering the speech which opens the Barleybridge Show and contributing to the heady debates of the Parish Council. As he has only just passed pensionable age he is a relative youngster by Barleybridge standards, yet already he can look back on life with a certain satisfaction. His great-grandfather was a joiner who also ran a few sheep on Barleybridge Moor. His grandfather and father had been the humble tenants of a Hardcastle farm, but after The Sale Amos had become a prosperous freeholder. The Common Agricultural Policy had stuffed his pockets with green pounds and the sale of barns which were about to collapse for five- and even six-figure sums made him a welcome guest at the bank whose missives once filled him with fear.

For all his affluence we should not expect to find Amos dining at the Hotel Imperial in Cripplegate, nor basking in a solarium at Riddings Farm. Chances are that we will find him seated above the westernmost of the two openings in the elm seat inside the privy behind Riddings farmhouse. He is a victim neither of faulty plumbing nor of what is known locally as 'the skitters'. He simply likes his old privy very much.

As soon as their bank balance began to swell Mrs Raw insisted that Riddings Farm should gain its first bathroom, WC, piped water and mains drainage. Victim of a morbid, rather Hardcastlian fear that an alligator might surge from the WC and attack his exposed portions, Amos has never patronised the Ideal Standard fittings. Instead he spends long, contemplative hours in his old privy, sometimes gazing whimsically at the vacant space to his left and recalling simpler, more homely times.

After breakfasting early on porridge and fatty bacon Amos dons his gaiters, boots and black greatcoat and heads for the privy with the *Daily Express* (plus the *Pitherdale Messenger* on Fridays) tucked under his arm. Through the heart-shaped ventilating hole in the green privy door he can see the clouds moving, gauge the wind and the weather to come. Via cracks in the door boards he can glimpse the bantams pecking in the farmyard, while behind, peacock and small tortoiseshell butterflies flutter amongst the thistle heads. The walls of the privy are festooned with nails. To the right of the seated Amos is the six-inch nail on which the *Express*, once read, is spiked for impending future use. To his left the nails on the wall support his memorabilia and filing system: yellowing articles torn from the *Pitherdale Messenger* which report the openings of Barleybridge Show, meetings of the Parish Council or the progress of barn conversions. Unfortunately a moment of absent-mindedness, provoked by a rare attack of Barleybridge skitters, deprived Amos of a cherished feature on the new houses at Pitherdale Garth.

These days his agricultural activities largely consist of ambling round the fields and yard prodding sheep, bullocks, sows and heifers with his blackthorn walking stick and spitting tobacco juice at the cockerel which retaliates by crowing raucously each morning at 4.30 a.m. His son, Bertram, left the farm at the age of eighteen, heading for London to become a ballet dancer. When Bertram saw his first ballet troupe at the Mercury Theatre he was shocked to discover that the gentlemen in tights were not at all squat and bow-legged like himself. Shelving his aspirations for the moment he obtained a job as a telephone operator and is currently applying for posts as an air steward with Qantas. Amos approves of this career venture and, in the solitude of his privy, he sometimes dreams – perhaps optimistically – that one day Bertram will inherit Riddings Farm and stock it with golden merino sheep, brought back from his flights to the outback.

The real work at Riddings Farm is accomplished by Jim Clough, abandoned as a child by itinerant 'tattie scratters' and employed on the farm ever since. Jim lives in a tied cottage down the lane from Riddings Farm and devotes his spare time to the cultivation of prize-winning potatoes. Perhaps he nurses the subconscious hope that one day his long-lost mother and father will materialise amongst the King Edwards at tattie-lifting time?

Amos and Jim have not spoken for seventeen years. The break in verbal communications began one September evening when Amos was returning from a cricket match against Holmesmead. Sitting with the other wounded Barleybridge players in Robinson's van, he glimpsed his own little grey Ferguson tractor emerging from Holmesmead Hollins Farm. Jim Clough was driving and behind him was a steaming load of horse manure. Since Amos says very little at the best of times his companions did not realise that this sight had left him dumbstruck. Not only does Amos believe that the cattle and pig manures matured at Riddings Farm are unsurpassed, but also he oft-times boasts that Jim Clough's perpetually prize-winning potatoes are an irrefutable public testimony to the efficacy of the product.

When he got home Amos limped round his farmyard lashing with his stick at any passing fowl that intruded on his anguish. Then he decided to hobble down to the Hardcastle Arms and confront his perfidious farmhand.

'Tha's 'umiliated me!' he bellowed. 'I saw thee, tha turncoat, sneaking out o' t' 'Ollins farm – an' t'think tha's led *their* muck wi' *my* tractor! As'll sell t'beggar the morrow an' thas'll be off an' all.'

Jim struggled to explain how he had always sworn by Amos's pig-and-cattle blend but how he liked to leaven the heady mulch with a smattering of well-rotted horse muck.

'It's like 'am and eggs, Amos, tha needs a bit of bread to help it down.'

'Is t'saying that my muck is 'ot?' thundered Amos. 'Ot is it! Well, I'll be blowed! Then tha can go and wuk at t'Ollins farm and 'ave as much 'oss muck as tha wants! 'Am and eggs be blowed!'

Deeply wounded by these threats of eviction and dismissal, Jim went home and plotted a terrible revenge. In the dead of night he loosened the boards low down at the back of the privy. At dawn he concealed himself amongst the thistles and rusting harrows behind the little green shack and began his vigil. At 8.30 a.m. he heard Amos stumping from the farmhouse, still muttering, ''Am and eggs be blowed!' Then the latch rose on the privy door, a rustling sound indicated the unspiking of Saturday's *Daily Express* and a heavy thud marked Amos's contact with the polished elm seat. In a flash Jim pulled back the loosened boards and thrust upwards the bunch of fresh nettles grasped in his gloved hands. From within there was a screech such as might be made by a leopard sat upon by a buffalo, instantly followed by a hollow *bonk* as Amos's head hit the top of the privy, and then another leopard noise as his exposed portions, descending, re-established contact with the nettles.

Shortly afterwards Amos could be found prostrate upon the farmhouse table as Mrs Raw applied calamine lotion to the sago-in-strawberry-blancmange patterns on her husband's tortured rump. The medical administrations were accompanied by a firm lecture on how Jim Clough was the best farmhand in Barleybridge, how her husband was a 'caingy owd fooil' to have tried to sack him in the first place, and she would hear no more of this muck twaddle.

Even so, Amos never spoke to Jim again. Since Mrs Raw refused to act as a go-between, Amos was obliged to develop a new and sophisticated system of communication. For example, one day we might see Amos heading for the privy. This is the signal for Jim to receive his orders for the day. He takes a station to the side of the shack (the rear of which is now prudently armoured, rhinoceros-like, with a plating of old tractor seats and harrow discs). Amos taps three times with his pipe on the elm seat and then a handful of barley flies through the ventilator towards the scratching bantams. Next he kicks twice on the privy door and taps twice more with his pipe. Jim can now commence his duties fully conversant with the tasks concerned. The three pipe taps signify the third field and the form of chicken feed thrown denotes the crop – Jim is to walk down to Longlands field and check the progress of the barley. Similarly, the two kicks denote bullocks, which Jim must move to field number two, Old Intake.

The full code which has evolved allows discourses on most subjects short of the crystallography of the DNA molecule, but basic agricultural topics are dealt with in the following manner:

Fields – tapping with the pipe.
Cereal crops – grain thrown to the bantams.
Root crops – rolled up balls of newspaper of different sizes tossed through the ventilator.
Grass crops – different lengths of walking stick showing beneath the privy door.
Livestock – combinations of kicks on the privy door.
Poultry – feathers poked out between the privy boards.
The weather forecast – puffs of pipe smoke blown through the ventilator.
Farm vehicles – flatulence.

With the establishment of this code of agricultural dialogue Amos managed to avoid seeing Jim for thirteen years. When he accidentally caught a glimpse of him barrowing a load of cow-two-to-pig-one down to his potato patch he noticed how grizzled and stooped he had become. And so he secretly contacted Scarsdale and Scarsdale, willing Jim Clough his tied cottage and organising a retirement pension.

Much of Amos's privy time is devoted to daydreams. For many years he has pestered the BASH executive about his scheme for new classes for muck at Barleybridge Show.

'Look at this lot 'ere,' he proclaims, gesturing grandly to the exhibits in the great marquee. 'Wi'out muck there'd be nowt to exhibit! Tha want t'think on. We could brek new ground, that knaws! Whativver tha says there's no other muck classes i' Pitherdale, not even i' t'North Yorkshire Show at Cripplegate.'

Thus far Amos has failed to excite the imagination of an executive not noted for its pioneering vision, yet he still has one trump card to play. In the future his delivery of the Show opening speech will be conditional upon the inclusion of a new spectrum of classes for muck in the Show catalogue.

Hanging on one of the nails on his privy wall is Amos's

71

old school slate, and inscribed upon the slate are detailed notes which describe the proposed classes and provide notes for judging. There will be four classes: cattle, pig, pig-and-cattle blend and (grudgingly) horse. Each entrant will submit one cubic yard of material for scrutiny by the judges, the entry to be contained in rigid wire mesh boxes specially manufactured for exhibition purposes. The judges will take due account of consistency (which should be even) temperature (low); worm content (high, active, small and red); straw content (low and well-rotted); odour (scarcely discernible); colour (rich, like Old Particular); and texture (friable but moist, like Christmas pudding). Amos would love to judge the classes, but fears this would deprive him of his right to compete. He has already bought a highly polished Regency sideboard and longs for the day when it will bear the four great silver Amos Raw trophies: Best Cattle; Best Pig; Best Pig-and-Cattle Blend; and Best Muck in the Show. The design of the last-named trophy is already roughed out on the back of Amos's slate. It is of solid silver, more than three feet tall, and depicts Britannia forking muck with her trident.

Given Amos's enthusiasms for privies and farmyard muck, psychiatrists might entertain certain diagnoses. As usual they would be wrong. By the standards of Barleybridge Amos is of average sanity; by the standards of Slough and Pinner he is remarkably sane and his sanity is not exceeded by a single resident of the London districts of Bloomsbury, Kensington, Westminster, Chelsea and Knightsbridge combined.

The new residential estate at Pitherdale Garth is as foreign to the rest of Barleybridge as Sarawak is to Surbiton. It seems to have a different climate, for the milkman swears that in summer the estate is a good 2°C cooler than the rest of the parish – though strangely milk turns sour much more quickly here than elsewhere. Small birds can be seen flitting amongst the newly planted laurels and cotoneasters, yet they hardly ever seem to sing. A restless melancholy hangs over the dwellings. Some villagers claim that this is due to the preponderance of lay preachers abiding in the estate. Although these grey-faced gentlemen number only three, they seem to have a rota which ensures that one or another is always to be seen plodding, bent and soulfully, around the pavements of the Garth as if borne down by the sins of Man.

The houses, of simulated stone, form an inner and an outer ring with each frontage facing another across the road and open lawns. All the residents live in mortal dread that one of their number is about to buy a bigger and better car, the anxieties building up into collective hysteria as each new vehicle registration letter becomes due. As soon as the Volvo, BMW and Audi dealers of Cripplegate sell a new model to any resident of Pitherdale Garth they immediately despatch urgent orders for a dozen more lavish models, hire extra salesmen and await the deluge.

The leading resident of Pitherdale Garth is Mrs Janice Sherman, a lady of ashen hue and stately bearing who has been compared to the Statue of Liberty (but minus the torch and words of welcome). Having descended upon one of the least spoilt and loveliest of northern villages, she is determined to change it in every possible way. She resents what she terms the feudalism of the Hardcastle era and resents even more the fact that the indigenous villagers seem to have enjoyed it. She believes that the surrounding countryside is dirty, taking every care to avoid it. She would much prefer to see the entire parish transformed into a northern version of her native Letchworth and is desperately anxious to see the aged villagers winkled out of their old stone cottages and installed in 'suitable' flats for the aged. Equally, she believes that the Hardcastle Houses for the Deserving Poor could be gutted and redeveloped as a community centre, while her sole concession to the rural setting is encapsulated in a thought that Riddings Farm might be allowed to survive as a country club.

Mrs Sherman was determined to make her mark initially by dominating every organisation in the village (although she is still the only person in the parish unaware of the existence of BUAC). Since the Barleybridge attitude to public service

73

is distilled in the motto, 'If there's nowt in it for me let some beggar else get on wi' it', her efforts proved fruitful. Soon she was installed upon the parochial church council, the BASH executive, the cricket club sandwich rota, the school governors and the committee of the WI. Endowed with a subtle ability to damn one and all with faint praise ('One might almost describe Mrs Hetherington-Cohen as an English rose, considering . . .', or 'Mrs Robinson makes such interesting sandwiches and it seems so silly to wonder about all those cats she keeps; I hear she went to the optician again last Wednesday . . . '), she is able to pursue a strategy of divide and rule.

Where potential rivals are concerned, Mrs Sherman's comments become much more lethal. One of her denigration strategies invokes her daughters, Despond and Divinity, the teenage twins, and little Faith. Her long-term designs on a Parish Council seat are orchestrated by periodic daughter invocations such as: 'My dear Despond heard that dreadful Mr Raw talking to Mr Beckwith about foot rot in sheep and when she got home she went straight to the bathroom; she said their language made her feel quite unclean.' Similarly, following an unsatisfactory meeting of the school governors she confided to Mrs Hetherington-Cohen, 'I do wish that little Faith would not mix with the Barleybridge children. Goodness knows what that peculiar Mr Gavestone fills their heads with, but after one of those grubby Robinson brats had told her about the murder of Edward II she was sick for three days. "Mummy," she said, "I feel quite unclean."' In fact the cleanliness of Faith is not debated, although Barleybridge lore holds that Sam Pullan's nephew could tell us a good deal about Despond and Divinity.

Janice Sherman's first rebuff occurred when she made her bid for the chairwomanship of the WI. The office should have been hers for the taking. Normally it passed to whoever had not been chairwoman during the last seven years and was too slow to concoct a convincing excuse when the nomination was made. (On the last three occasions Mrs Hetherington-Cohen has escaped elevation to the office by pleading that the wood in the chair used by successive chairwomen inflames her varicose veins: this must be elm of a most virulent type since the veins in question were removed in 1967.) Despite the reticence of some nominees, the office is not a demanding one, requiring only a working knowledge of the words of 'Jerusalem', an ability to forget the name of the visiting speaker and a readiness to terminate guest lecturers just as the speaker is rising to his or her theme, using the imminent departure of the Summerthwaite bus as a pretext.

Mrs Sherman made the mistake of *campaigning* for the chairwomanship. She even produced a printed manifesto. This included offers of a series of reforms: only five minutes at the end of meetings would be reserved for the reading of the London minutes; local meetings would begin with an hour-long debate on 'Topical Matters of Public Concern', and this great debate would be followed by lectures delivered by speakers drawn from amongst the galaxy of celebrities that Mrs Sherman felt sure she could cajole along to Barleybridge. The Barleybridge ladies found the offer of debates on topical matters rather perplexing; it was true that the issue of the submerged proportion of icebergs was still being actively discussed, while the question of how much Holmesmead contributed to building the bridge had not entirely receded. Were these the sort of topical matters that Mrs Sherman had in mind?

'Certainly not,' replied the candidate. 'I was thinking of issues like AIDS or the responsibilities of the Lord Privy Seal.'

Now the ladies were even more perplexed. The few who had heard of AIDS thought that it was something to do with the artificial insemination of ducks and sheep – and thus far from being a fit topic for polite conversation. They also felt that the suggestion that the Lord kept a seal in a privy was both blasphemous and highly improbable. In any event, the intolerable restrictions proposed for the reading of minutes and the prospect of having to *listen* to guest speakers ensured the unanimous rejection of the manifesto.

However, being quite oblivious to the mood of the Barleybridge ladies, Mrs Sherman set in motion a campaign of innuendoes designed to undermine her rivals. It was ridiculous, she claimed, with the National Health Service dispensing artificial limbs of steel and plastic to all and sundry, that Mrs Fawcett should still go stumping around on a wooden leg. 'I'm sure its got woodworm and she is spreading it all round the village. I had her to my coffee morning last Thursday and as soon as she left I called in Rentokil. I'm still worried about my Sheraton dining chairs.'

Mrs Farrar was deemed to be another possible candidate. 'Poor Mrs Farrar,' Mrs Sherman confided to Mrs Holroyd. 'Do you know I found her stuck in Mr Ewbank's hedge last night? Her best tweed suit was a mass of thorns and she just couldn't budge. She said she was trying to reach some blackberries, and, of course, I believed her. It was on Tuesday, that's when Mrs Ewbank goes to stay with her sister in Bishopgate.'

Only Mrs Sherman could have imagined that Miss Bliss was a rival for office. Nevertheless she felt obliged to tell Mrs Armitage that if Miss Bliss really did hope to entrap Mr Gavestone she should not allow herself to be shut up at Parish Council meetings with a load of dirty farmers. 'They don't bother to change, you know. My Despond went to hear them discuss the Christmas tree and she just had to leave halfway through. She said her clothes were beginning to smell of animals. She felt quite unclean.'

Confronted by the terrifying manifesto and the barrage of innuendoes, the ladies elected Mrs Fawcett as chairwoman of the Barleybridge WI. She was only the second lady with a wooden leg to hold this office, but her oaken appendage proved to be a real asset. The agendas of forthcoming meetings were affixed to it with drawing pins, thus saving the cost of repairing the WI noticeboard. Mrs Sherman did not even receive a nomination, and resigned from the WI in a towering rage. Her resolve to make a bigger mark on Barleybridge life now grew to terrifying proportions.

In any village there will be a core of residents who are neither natives nor ordinary outsiders – or 'offcomers' as these immigrants are known in Barleybridge. These are essential aliens like doctors, vicars and publicans, whose specialist services are too important to be ignored. Barleybridge has been remarkably lucky in its vicars. In days gone by, clergymen were the younger sons of families of substance – gentlemen, in fact. The vicars appointed by the Hardcastles were the current or pending husbands of Hardcastle daughters, so the family took great trouble to see that the village was not burdened with a bounder, a halfwit or a keeper of well-fanged dogs, cats or ferrets.

The last vicar of the Hardcastle era was the Reverend 'Potty' Burton-Latimer, who was universally loved by his Barleybridge flock. The prefix 'Potty' bears no relationship to that borne by 'Nutty' Ramsbottom of Holmesmead, who is barking mad. No, it relates to the fact that at any point in time one or several of the vicar's limbs were encased in plaster of Paris.

Rev. Burton-Latimer did not confine his parochial visits to the homes of the wealthy and thus subsist on sherry and fruit cake like so many others of his calling. He believed in visiting his poorer parishioners as they relaxed in their evening haunts – the Old Particular houses of Barleybridge, Bishopgate and Summerthwaite. To facilitate his rounds he purchased a Norton motor-cycle, but long before he had mastered its controls he abandoned it at speed on Oldborough Hill while seeking to repeat the successes of his mission to the Pack Horse at Bishopgate in the Hardcastle Arms in Barleybridge. He emerged from the ditch with a broken right ankle. This reduced his efficiency as a motor-cyclist considerably, with the result that three weeks later his mission to the Woolpack at Summerthwaite terminated abruptly at Hag Wood Bend where he found himself with a broken left arm. Encumbered by plaster casts, the vicar never gained a mastery of his machine or freedom from the diverse riding restrictions imposed by the successive casts.

A sequence of unfortunate accidents during the freeze-up of 1963–4 put all Rev. Burton-Latimer's limbs in plaster, so that he now resembled a great china starfish. Undeterred, he continued to ride, operating a series of strings running from brakes, throttle and handlegrips with his teeth. On landing after the inevitable crash on Clapton Bank he performed an impeccable series of cartwheels – all the way down

Clapton Bank, past the green and Emporium, through the village almost over the bridge, over its parapet and into the Pither. Onlookers say that on seeing his plaster-white saltire form floating on the deep blue water of the Pither they were reminded of the flag of Scotland. The vicar cartwheeled for a total distance of 763 yards and Mr Gavestone was so impressed that he submitted the achievement to the *Guinness Book of Records*. Sadly, the claim was rejected on the grounds that the encasement of limbs in rigid plaster constituted an unacceptable artificial aid to cartwheeling.

Following forty-seven years of devoted service to his parish, the Vicar accompanied Sir Cecil to the crematorium and then announced his retirement. Villagers of all denominations contributed to his parting gifts: a small motor-car and a lifelong subscription to BUPA.

'Potty' Burton-Latimer was succeeded by the first non-Hardcastle appointee to officiate in the church of St Eric and St Brian. The conversion of Augustus Hobhouse occurred in a most singular manner. As a child his interests were strictly confined to a scrapbook of press cuttings pertaining to his hero, Benito Mussolini, and to a large lop-eared rabbit called Hector. This rabbit he cherished even more than his nearest neighbours, the Carringtons, cherished their dalmation bitch, Spotty. Consequently there was concern when Spotty went missing, only to return in the dead of night proudly carrying the tattered and grimy remains of Hector. After a feverish debate Mr and Mrs Carrington decided to wash and groom the stiff corpse and restore it to its hutch before dawn. 'Perhaps the little swine will think bunny caught the Black Death or committed suicide,' said Mrs Carrington hopefully.

As they accomplished their rabbit restoration the Carringtons could not have been expected to know that Hector had died two days previously of lettuce poisoning and been solemnly buried by young Augustus beside his father's asparagus bed. But in the morning when Augustus saw the open grave and the furry body returned to its abode he interpreted the miracle as proof of a resurrection which was about 95 per cent successful. Even today Rev. Hobhouse has Hector's pelt sewn to the inside of his cassock, and during the crises of faith which afflict him from time to time he imbibes a little port and goes to watch the rabbits on Oldborough Hill. Sometimes he is sure that Hector hops among them.

Before he came to Barleybridge the Rev. Augustus Hobhouse had a career history reminiscent of a game of snakes and ladders. Outwardly he had seemed destined to gain the heights of the ecclesiastical firmament. He had a sound public-school background, bachelor status, the voice of a Shakespearian actor and the commanding prescence of a Roman Emperor (not Claudius or Nero). He was a bulwark of conservatism and completely uncorrupted by any deeply religious sentiments. And yet, somehow, unfortunate little incidents had undermined the high expectations. When it was mutually agreed that he should vacate his post of chaplain at St Tracy's College for Ladies and accept a rural living, he embarked on a tour of vacant parishes – or rather a tour of vicarages. Barleybridge Vicarage is a four-storey neo-Elizabethan mansion of eight bedrooms inspired by a visit which Josiah Hardcastle had made to Fountains Hall. Having inspected the conservatory, billiard room, gun room and stables, Rev. Hobhouse was suddenly seized by an irresistible urge to minister to the souls of Barleybridge.

When Rev. Hobhouse assumed his post, the church of St Eric and St Brian had an average Matins congregation of 97, while the 17 members of the village community who were religious straggled up Oldborough Hill each Sunday to attend services at the Bishopgate Methodist Church. A year later the same 17 villagers were still making the ascent to Bishopgate, but the Church of England congregation now numbered only 22.

Nurtured by a succession of compassionate and energetic clergymen, the people of Barleybridge were slow to criticise any vicar, yet few could deny that mistakes had been made. Wedding services were not the joyous, ebullient occasions known in 'Potty' Burton-Latimer's day. Rev. Hobhouse prefaces his marriage service with a detailed and pessimistic review of the current divorce statistics, looks accusingly at the bride and groom during the pledges of fidelity and

79

stares long and hopefully around the congregation when inviting any who know reasons why the ceremony should not be consecrated to come forward.

His funeral services, some claim, are marred by an excess of candour. When he buried old Hugh Bacon the new vicar remarked that Hugh's demise would bring relief not only to the widow but also to a host of worried husbands, to the trout in the Pither and to Godfearing people everywhere. Moreover, he continued, since the only people who might have cause to mourn Hugh's passing were the various publicans of Pitherdale, he was surprised that none of them were present at the graveside. He concluded with the thought that while the mercy of the Almighty knew no bounds, the chances of meeting old Hugh in a better place were extremely remote. Thus departed one of the most popular members of the Barleybridge community.

However, it is the christening service which has caused most anguish. Being rabidly anti-Semitic, Rev. Hobhouse refuses to give babies Jewish names. Parents are obliged to submit the intended names ten days in advance of the ceremony and in the course of the intervening days the Vicar conducts a survey to ensure that the name suggested does not feature in any of the Books of the Old Testament. (Thus far Iddo Calvert is the only child to have slipped through Rev. Hobhouse's net, the product of a moment's distraction whilst checking the Book of Zechariah.) Villagers are tolerant of the Vicar's foible of dropping babies, which is caused by a trembling in his hands at moments of ceremonial intensity. No infants have been permanently damaged, although a churchwarden is now stationed on hand to administer the kiss of life should a tumbling baby again land in the font. All, nonetheless, are agreed that the christenings would go with more of a swing if the Vicar placed less emphasis on questioning the parentage of the offspring and would drop his off-repeated observation: 'Here's another one with those shifty Pullan eyes.'

It is not easy to become a controversial figure in Barley-bridge. For example, the general view in the village is that if Mrs Shutt wants to keep ducks in her bath then that is her business (so long as they don't quack too loudly at night). The villager who came closest to achieving controversial status was young Danny Kendal, whose interests lay almost exclusively in the realms of combustion and ballistics.

When his prototype rat-killing device detonated success-fully and not only exterminated its intended victim but also converted all the inmates of Fred Tinkler's battery house into a substance which might best be described as a feather pâté, villagers merely decreed that the design was promising but the explosive content perhaps a little excessive. When his Mark III bird-scaring crop gun launched itself from its crater in the Tinkler cabbage field and zoomed unimpeded for two miles before burying its remains in Holmesmead church tower, even the most critical villagers, while regretting the loss of a promising couple of acres of greens, felt bound to concede that it had scared the pigeons quite considerably.

Real controversy only touched Danny on the issue of the blocked drains at Estate Cottages. The four other families who share the terraced row with the Kendals and the Shutts attributed the blockage to a large white duck of the Aylesbury persuasion which, they believed, had inadvertently been flushed down the lavatory during one of Mrs Shutt's dizzy spells. Could Danny, as a man of science, possibly suggest a remedy, they wondered?

Danny did not let them down. With the methodical approach of a proven scientist he paced out the distance from the manhole to the site of the suspected blockage and then retired purposefully to the cellar which served as his laboratory. Four hours later he emerged, carrying a small keg of his own homemade gunpowder fixed to a tiny wooden raft from which extended a waterproof fuse of the appropriate length.

'Appen tha'll hear a little "pop",' he confided to his mother, 'and then t'drains'll be clear again.'

Fearing that the great unblocking might be accomplished unseen as well as unheard, Danny delayed ignition until he had placed a dustbin lid atop the stench pipe of the Shutt cottage.

In the event these fears were unfounded. The detonation was heard *very clearly* in Cripplegate and was recorded on seismic equipment at the universities of Leeds, Durham and Salford. The offending drain was utterly unblocked. Unfortunately, Danny, while mentioning the time, had failed to notify his neighbours in Estate Cottages of the scientific method adopted. At the time of the explosion Mr Reeth of Number 3 had retired to his lavatory with a copy of *The Mail on Sunday* in hopeful anticipation of the clearance. The diagnosis of the blockage proved correct, and after the dust had settled on Barleybridge Mr Reeth was forced to go to work with mirror and tweezers to remove the quivering white duck quills from his posterior. (The beak proved more problematical and had to be extracted by Dr Brailsford under a local anaesthetic.) Meanwhile, and quite unnoticed in Barleybridge, the dustbin lid had ascended into the stratosphere. It was initially tracked by radar at RAF Gushforth and later shot down over Colchester by a Phantom jet scrambled from the Lakenheath base. It is still quoted by spokesmen of the Atlantic UFO Alliance as the best-authenticated case in their files.

Like Danny Kendal, Rev. Hobhouse did not seek to be a controversial figure. Even after his decision to christen babies only with names of his own choosing, he merely achieved grade I on the eight-point Danny Kendal scale of controversy. (His christening of Julius Caesar Armitage elevated him to grade II, but only because she was a girl.) Nevertheless, he was, like Mrs Sherman, determined to make his mark.

With the possible exception of Sir Cecil Hardcastle (whose royal credentials, one must admit, were rather sketchy, despite all Mr Gavestone's patient scholarship), Barleybridge has produced only one famous son. That man was, of course, Samuel Hardstaff, and it was this same celebrity who provided the Vicar with an opportunity to make his mark.

Samuel, known in later life as 'Hardstaff the Denouncer', was born in 1590, the son of the village ratcatcher. At the age of fifteen, following an arduous night-long session plying his father's craft in the cellars of a distant forebear of the Hardcastle Arms, he saw a strange vision. The face of St Eric appeared, floating to and fro, above a keg of porter.

'Hearken to me, thou catcher of rats, thou slayer of moldywarpes, thou sparrow snatcher,' said the vision. 'Abandon now thy paltry trade. Nay, marry, I say, it matters nought if one cellar be ridden of rats when the whole estate has its windpipes stuffed with evil! Go forth and assail the wickedness of these times. Strike terrible blows until all men be rightly grounded in religion and wrested from the jaws of hell.'

His rat club, called 'Blodger', in his hand, Samuel began his mission the very next day and would soon establish himself as a natural denouncer of the first order. The Catholics, he decreed, were verminous traitors poised to fly at the throat of the sovereign realm. With a nose like a ferret Samuel could sniff out a Jesuit at almost any distance, and many a cowering priest was flushed from hiding, pursued along corridors, behind panelling, down chimneys and over the furthest horizon. Puritans fared no better, being branded by Samuel as braggarts of such audacity that they dared dictate to the conscience of the good Lord Himself. Levellers, Baptists, Independents, Millenarians, Calvinists, Quakers, Presbysterians, Fifth-Monarchy Men and Jews all felt the lash of Samuel's tongue and the crack of Blodger on their skulls.

For ten years Hardstaff stalked the north, denouncing as he went, his conviction being regularly fortified by the visions of St Eric, which always appeared on market days following exhausting sessions of denunciation amongst the cringing patrons of the taverns. Such was the force of his delivery and so refined became the accuracy of Blodger that whole villages would empty at the rumour of Hardstaff's approach. Bands of ruffians and mercenaries were then employed to bar his way to towns after Cripplegate Market had experienced a frenzy of denunciation so intense that thirteen stalls, most of the vendors and a third of the corporation lay jumbled together in the market square in a morass of produce, blood, ale and firewood.

Samuel died within yards of his birthplace. Finding his native village deserted, he took up a station beside the old chapel of ease and began a fervent denunciation of all his former neighbours, their heresies and their livestock. History records that at some point in the torrid exposition between the Papists and the Levellers his pounding heart exploded. Local folklore tells a different tale. It claims that Jacob Ingoldsby, a Barleybridge Puritan, crept up from behind and struck Samuel on the back of the head with a well-aimed cobble. Observing the scene from his cubby-hole in a nearby farmstead was Father Carlos, who dashed forth to administer the Last Rites to the stricken Denouncer. However, seeing that the victim was on the point of recovery the good priest administered the *coup de grâce* with a handy bottle of Communion wine. Hardstaff's dying vision was of crucifix and rosary swaying gently in the breeze.

Legend also tells that Blodger, flying from the hand of the falling Denouncer, stuck and then rooted in the ground, from whence it grew into a blackthorn bush which never bore fruit nor flower. This bush was more than three centuries old when it was felled to make way for the Hardcastle tomb.

Latterday historians have written many a learned treatise on Hardstaff the Denouncer. Their subject left the clearest record of the kinds of theology that he despised, but nobody has been able to discover the forms of devotion that he favoured. However, when Rev. Hobhouse stumbled upon a history of Samuel Hardstaff he felt an immediate sense of kinship with a man whose ecumenical outlook was entirely in sympathy with his own. 'How shameful,' he thought, 'that a churchman of such stature should have no monument in his own birthplace – and what a splendid opportunity for me to make my mark!' When his thoughts turned to the form that the monument should take he instantly rejected a statue, as that would smack of popery. Instead he favoured a gigantic black marble monolith, reminiscent of Blodger, bearing the simple inscription: 'Here died Samuel Hardstaff, a tireless upholder of the Anglican faith'.

Since Sir Cecil had bequeathed his modest remnants

of the Hardcastle fortune, amounting to £50,000, to the church, the funds for the monument were readily available. All that remained was to commission the mason and get rid of the Hardcastle tomb, which intruded on the spot where the Denouncer had fallen.

Villagers heard of the plans with horror. The Hardcastles were still revered by people steeped in the myth of noble lordship. Honest, thrifty Barleybridgians recoiled from the notion that Hardcastle money would now finance the desecration of the Hardcastle tomb. Most outraged and outspoken of all was Sam Pullan. Since he and his forebears had hastened the entombment of several Hardcastles, he took a proprietorial interest in the mausoleum, regarding it in rather the manner that a grizzled hunter might view his trophy room. Even so, the Vicar found that a judicious firing and replacement of churchwardens helped to smooth away the local difficulties and he discovered a forceful ally in the statuesque shape of Mrs Sherman. Being a servant of progress in any form it cared to take, she loathed the feudalism of the Hardcastle era and the ingrained conservatism of the villagers at large. Moreover she despised Sam Pullan on sight, believing him to be a vulgarian whose uninhibited discourses on country matters had oft times made her daughters feel unclean. She despised him even more when his cat, Claws, caught and devoured her pet chihuahua.

Villagers like Sam Pullan, Hector Ewbank, Amos Raw and Jim Wharton who felt most strongly that something must be done were surprised that Mr Gavestone, normally a fount of helpful ideas, seemed detached and distant from the great debates. In fact, his historian's mind was ranging from archive to stack and from bookshelf to binder, retracing dusty paths through the debris of time.

A new site was chosen for the Hardcastle tomb amongst the clammy shadows on the northern side of the church. The first stage in its removal involved the deconsecration of the ground beneath the yew trees on which it stood – and this required the services of the Bishop.

Recognising the green ink and bold capitals on the envelope, the Bishop pushed the letter under the toast rack: he was not going to let Hobhouse ruin another good breakfast. As the remains of the kedgeree and the kidneys were cooling on the table he toyed with the letter, sought a moment's solace in the obituary column of the *Daily Telegraph*, took a deep breath and opened it: ' . . . monument to an outstanding Anglican . . . churchwardens all in agreement . . . funded by generous donation . . . a small matter of deconsecration . . . ' 'This seems harmless enough,' mused his Grace, recalling previous letters from Barleybridge vicarage, which had dealt with matters such as the excommunication of a Mr Pullan, the pagan origins of cricket and a refusal to bury suspected Wesleyans.

When the episcopal Daimler arrived at Barleybridge church the Bishop saw Sam, Hector, Amos and most of the roller squad standing with linked arms around the Hardcastle tomb and his heart sank down to his gaiters. And then, for a moment, his attention was caught by a tall, dishevelled yet scholarly figure who emerged from the shadows of the lychgate, pressed a paper in his palm and then retreated amongst the tombstones. Distractedly he unfolded the paper and found it was a photocopy of a seventeenth-century pamphlet.

It was *A Treatise on the Church of England* by Samuel Hardstaff. Dominating the text was an engraving of a goat, mitred like a bishop and with a crozier in one hand and the Devil's trident in the other. In his efforts to explain why the Anglican faith was the most treasonous and poisonous of all the heresies the author explained that though men of good faith had swept the Pope out of England, the Devil had replaced him with twenty-seven new Popes all in the guise of bishops. George Abbot, the Archbishop of Canterbury, was, Hardstaff declared, the first Puritan Abbot and the first murderer to dominate the national Church. (He had killed a man in a hunting accident in the year of his Archepiscopal appointment.)

After scanning the remaining, less restrained contents of the pamphlet the Bishop folded the paper thoughtfully. After asking the Vicar briefly to remind him of the inscription on the proposed monument, he tossed a benediction in the direction of the villagers surrounding the tomb, turned back to his Daimler and was last seen rummaging for his pack of Settlers in the recesses of his vestments.

From the Yorkshire Gazette, *15 May 1985*
Pitherdale Gleanings by 'Dalesbred Tup'

On Thursday last I attended a meeting of Barleybridge Parochial Church Council, deputising for Mrs Fawcett, whose leg now appears to have contracted death watch beetle and ticks in the most distracting manner. We heard a proposal from Mrs Sherman that the Hardcastle suite in Barleybridge church be converted into a refuge for battered wives but a detailed exploration of the problem failed to identify any battered wives within our parish. There is, of course, the case of Mrs Shutt, who trapped her tongue in the mangle, but she did this completely unaided. However, a number of battered husbands were identified. Mr Percy Laycock is beaten mercilessly about the head with a stuffed porcupine each night when he returns inebriated from the Woolpack at Summerthwaite. Since he drinks to take his mind off the beatings we seem to be encountering a vicious circle effect, which the establishment of a refuge would do little to ease. When Mr Beckwith tactlessly enquired about the fate of the late Mr Sherman the whole proposal was withdrawn.

As a consequence of a difference of opinion concerning the (subsequently abandoned) Hardstaff monument, Mr Tom Stott retired as church-warden. He attended this meeting to receive a packet of pipecleaners to commemorate his eighty-two years of former service to the church. Until asked to leave by Rev. Hobhouse and Mrs Sherman he regaled the meeting with his recollections. Apparently the organ bellows were originally powered by a donkey and treadmill. On one occasion, as Mr Stott relates, Mr Jack Pullan suspended a bunch of carrots above the treadmill and the donkey galloped with such vigour that the entire organ began to ascend, just like the organ in the old Cripplegate Odeon used to do.

This reminiscence directed attention towards the current organ loft fund, which now stands at £188.13. Rev. Hobhouse rejected a proposal from Mr Beckwith that we introduce fund-raising housey-housey (or 'bingo' as it is now called) based on the numbers displayed on the board giving the order of hymns. The Vicar reminded the meeting that it is not his wish to have members of his congregation shouting 'Bingo!' at the start of 'Morning has Broken'.

Rev. Hobhouse then drew the attention of the meeting to the latest statement by the Bishop of Middlesbrough, in which His Grace proposed that the Prime Minister should personally pay the funeral expenses of all those who have died as a direct result of the National Health Service cuts. Our vicar deplored the involvement of the Church of England in political matters, and added that the simple fact that the heavens are blue demonstrates that God is a Conservative. He intends to write to the Prime Minister pledging his full support for current policies. He will also propose the reintroduction and privatisation of the hanging service. Mrs Sherman suggested that the Parochial Church Council could lend its practical support for such an initiative by providing the free-enterprise hangman with one of our bellropes – preferably the one with the red, white and blue braiding round the grip, which always looks so patriotic. At this point Mrs Hetherington-Cohen left the meeting and expressed a wish to join the Quakers.

Judging for the Best Kept Village competition will take place during Saturday and Sunday next. Let us hope that Mrs Shutt will keep her dog indoors this time.

7

In which Barleybridge is not a Best Kept Village, but everyone goes to the seaside nevertheless

One soft summer morning, when bees buzzed earnestly amongst the arching sprays of catmint and furtive robins flew a fast-food shuttle service to their nest in the ivy-clasped fence, Mrs Fawcett sat waxing her wooden leg. In the restful seclusion of her back garden she remembered fondly how Mr Bacon had carved it for her from a bough of finest Pitherdale oak. She smiled as she recalled the day when a younger Danny Kendal had removed the brass ferrule from its tip and substituted a detonator from a mortar bomb. The moment she had left the yielding gravel of her garden path and set stump on the pavement outside, the explosion had rocketed her back over the garden gate – and over the clothes line too. Mr Gavestone measured the height of the clothes line at the point of clearance at 6 feet $11^1/_2$ inches and suggested that a new pogo stick jumping record might well be claimed. And then prised her from the marrow patch where the descending leg had impaled a ripe specimen of the custard white variety. 'Such lovely marrows,' she mused.

On this warm and gentle morning she had meticulously treated all the little tunnels with woodworm killer, plugged the drawing-pin holes with plastic wood, burnished away the splinters with glasspaper and was about to impart a high beeswax sheen. Suddenly, and greatly to her surprise, a pair of hornrimmed glasses, a spotty face and a clipboard were thrust above the garden fence. 'Don't worry about me, sweetheart,' said the face. 'I'm just doing the judging for the Best Kept Village competition.' Though normally able to crush a spider at twenty paces, alarm and humiliation took their toll of Mrs Fawcett's aim. The leg missed the judge, sailed beyond the back lane and severely concussed one of Mr Tinkler's best Friesian cows.

In Barleybridge the clipboard is a phobic object of the first magnitude. A man with a clipboard was present when Mrs Shutt's domestic rates, set at five pence per annum by the Cripplegate Rating Department's computer and paid without question for thirteen years, were increased a thousandfold. Back in 1962 another bearer of clipboards had been responsible for Mr Beckwith's reluctant and costly appearance before an Egg Tribunal. A few years earlier yet another clipboard man had materialised just as Mr Robinson was preparing his 'thoroughbred' Aberdeen Angus bullocks for market by applying black boot polish to their subsidy-denying patches of white hair. And so it is that the mere act of walking down Barleybridge High Street with anything resembling a clipboard is sufficient to promote collective hysteria in a community normally noted for its stolid composure.

While the kindly ex-churchwarden was administering mouth-to-mouth resuscitation to Tinkler's cow, Amos Raw was enthroned in his privy and dreamily wondering if his new scheme for a class for merino manure would ever come to fruition at Barleybridge Show. Seeing a shadow cast on the dust at the foot of the privy door he quite reasonably assumed that Jim Clough was in attendance and awaiting his briefing for the day. With pipe, boot, wheat and goosefeathers he communicated his instructions, the message culminating in a loud emphatic order about moving the tractor and collecting the combine harvester from Mr Beckwith. No sooner had the echoes died than a middle-aged, middle-class female face appeared at the heart-shaped hole in the privy door, mouthing enquiries about directions to Barleybridge, where judging in the Best Kept Village competition was due to take place.

As Amos Raw sat huddled in the corner of his privy, shaking with shock beneath the greatcoat he had pulled over his head, odd deeds were afoot at Westgarth House, the home of Major 'Buffy' Hetherington-Cohen, MC, RA (retd), and his wife Celia.

For most of us the war is thankfully part of our past, but the Major had a particularly gruelling war. At a crucial stage in the North African campaign he was alone in a forward observation post outside Tripoli with only his binoculars and the pith helmet, inherited from his Indian Army grandfather, visible above the dunes. Unfortunately they were also visible to the crew of an 88 mm anti-tank gun and the ensuing explosion completely entombed poor Buffy in the sand. Only the tip of his helmet now intruded on the naked desert. For three scorching days the Major endured the heat and thirst, though on the fourth day he was able to capture some providential rainfall in his headgear. Two days later a patrol of the Long Range Desert Group noticed what appeared to be a mine, and when a corporal was sent to defuse it the device proved to be a helmet with a lobster-red Major directly beneath.

Buffy was invalided out of the service and his harrowing experience has plagued him ever since. On many a night when the torments recur most intensely Celia will rise from the sweat-sodden bed to find her dear husband sitting in the cat litter tray with a saucepan jammed down on his head. Experience has shown that the effects of the 'Tripoli Terrors' can only be exorcised in one way. Celia gives the gardener a day off and then proceeds to dig a large hollow in the sand pit behind the delphiniums. Then Buffy, seated in a wheelchair and wearing a chamberpot on his head, is installed in the excavation and covered in sand by his devoted wife until only the base of the potty remains on view. One hour later she turns on the garden sprinkler and Buffy catches the drops in his pot. After a further twenty minutes Celia leads their five labradors in a frantic chase round and round the garden shouting, 'Come on doggy darlings, we must find Daddy'. Once Daddy has been ritually located, a rope running from the wheelchair is hitched to the little tractor which normally pulls the lawn mower – and Buffy emerges from his torments at high speed in liberating clouds of sand. When properly performed, this therapy normally effects a cure which lasts until the next anniversary of the original entombment.

On the day in question, however, Celia had just engaged the tractor motor when she saw three strangers with clipboards standing on the lawn.

'Do excuse us,' said their leader. 'Best Kept Village competition, don't you know? I'm sure you won't mind us saying so, but we do think that big sandcastle spoils your garden. Quite out of place. Afraid it's going to cost you three points.'

Now more shell-shocked than her husband, Mrs Hetherington-Cohen released the clutch with such violence that the tow-rope snapped and the tractor and driver careered into the depths of the carp pond. Seven hours passed before the distraught and quaking lady was capable of summoning the gardener to come and assist at once. Under the circumstances her alibi did her credit but as gardener Reeth mentioned later, 'That's nivver quicksand. Iffen t'Major had really lost a contact lens then 'ow come he allus weared glasses? 'Ow can you search in sand if you're sat in a wheelchair? And any road, who wears a pee pot on their 'eads these days, except for Mrs Horner? It's a rum do if tha asks me!'

In the realms of grocery the Pitherdale Emporium conjures visions of a paradise lost. The air within is spiced with the tang of smoked bacon and fresh-ground coffee, while acid drops, warm loaves, pickles and sheep dip each impart a subtle addition to the heady vapours. Apart from supplying all the materials essential to life in Barleybridge, the village-store-cum-post-office dispenses other equally vital services. Postmistress Reynard offers a funerary hotline to Messrs Moreton and Pickersgill which includes free use of a tape measure, allowing essential dimensions to be telephoned through on the special dial-a-box service. She also dispenses free medical advice and remedies and will offer dispassionate judgement on the relative merits of oak, pine and walnut as applied to casket-making on those rare occasions when her medical opinions have gone unheeded. And last but not least, the Emporium is the hub of the local communication system, providing a venue for communal discussion and a clearing-house for gossip. This is particularly evident on pension day, when the senior citizens jostle for seats in the post office alcove of the store. Sometimes conversation is wide-ranging, embracing bridges, icebergs, operations, roller technology and royal babies. On other days it is finely-focused and pension books may remain unstamped for hours until the sages have explored every trivial undercurrent of some pressing issue.

Never, however, have the discussions been more focused and passionate than on the morning that the Emporium opened after the judging of the Best Kept Village competition. Farmers abandoned their farms to zip to the store and dash the rumours that the Parish Council had anything to do with entering Barleybridge for the competition. As a result the bridge-to-store Land-rover record was broken three times before the school clock struck ten and was raised in stages from the existing 27.3 m.p.h. record to 84.7 m.p.h. When Mrs Sherman suggested that the Women's Institute might have been responsible, the efforts of the full Parish Council were needed to restrain Mrs Fawcett from clubbing her with a leg still defaced by matted tufts of cow hair. In the course of the day the debate spilled out of the store and down the High Street. When the policeman from Holmesmead arrived to clear the road of gesticulating villagers, Mr Gavestone suspended classes and the debaters crammed into the school. A decision was reached in time for classes to reconvene the following afternoon.

An Action Committee headed by Mrs Fawcett, Mr Raw and Mrs Hetherington-Cohen was formed, with Mr Gavestone promising to assist in his capacity as an honorary Barleybridgian of greater than normal intelligence. Mr Raw encapsulated the feelings of the committee when he explained that there is 'gawping and there is *gawping*'. If outsiders wanted to visit Barleybridge the villagers had always treated them kindly. But if they stuck their noses into private gardens and farmyards and tried to tell people when to paint their gates or where to plant their cabbages, then this was something else.

'Best kept for who?' demanded Mrs Fawcett. 'I like Barleybridge the way it is, and I'm one as lives here. I don't go round Cripplegate with a clipboard telling folks to wash their curtains, or polish their prams, or clean their cars, so why should they come here? This is our village, not a peep show.'

'Any road,' added Amos Raw as an afterthought, 'Holmesmead's won it for t'last three years, so that shows 'ow daft it is.'

Mrs Hetherington-Cohen, who had stayed silent thus far, then mentioned that her dear husband had kindly offered to put £1,000 at the committee's disposal. This offer provided the solution to a plan which Mr Gavestone had quietly been hatching.

In the course of the weeks that followed, delegates from Barleybridge arranged furtive visits to the leading residents of neighbouring villages. They bore the tidings that the judging day of the next year's Best Kept Village would coincide with judging the 'Worst Kept Village in Pitherdale' competition. Moreover, while the BKV winners would get only a temporary plaque and a few lines in the *Pitherdale Messenger*, the WKVIP winners could expect rather more. The organisers would win a free coach trip to Scarborough in time for the cricket festival, with all expenses and refreshments provided. The owner of the scruffiest lawn would be chauffeur-driven to Harry Ramsden's fish and chip parlour and have the lawn restored to its former glory by Mr Reeth as soon as the judging was over. Meanwhile, the owners of dirty windows, smelly hen-houses, weedy gardens and ramshackle vans could all expect to be recognised and rewarded.

As May melted into June the face of Pitherdale was transformed. Groundsel grew where groundsel had never grown before. Thistles appeared amongst the aspiring prize-winners in Mr Farrar's marrow patch. Amos Raw's privy, painted in a discreet shade of corporation green since time immemorial, acquired a new (but temporary) hue of day-glo orange. As judgement day approached, tips were scoured for broken gates, dead cats changed hands at prime beef prices, burnished brass door knockers turned green and Austin vans jacked-up on bricks appeared in every High Street.

The competition was intense. When the first BKV judges were sighted in Holmesmead, 'Nutty' Ramsbottom was released to perform, as predicted, his animated discourse on 'pig slaughtering in days gone by' before arbitrators not yet recovered from their encounter with 'Flasher' Voles, also paroled for the day. In Summerthwaite, where the whitewash was still wet on the church wall graffiti, villagers were seen lifting paving stones at the roadside in the course of burying a horse which had apparently dropped dead in the shafts of a coal cart.

'We allus do this,' explained a man with a shovel proudly. 'It's in t'intrests of 'ygene, tha knaws. Ayup! We can't bury it there, that's where we buried Sam Bower's donkey fower week back.'

Not to be upstaged, Bishopgate had evolved its own strategy. Not a soul could be seen in the overgrown gardens; every cottage was deserted; dead rats lined the gutters and in the door of the Pack Horse was pinned a sign, 'Closed for the Duration of the Plague'.

Barleybridge opted for a broad-based strategy. As the judges approached the village from Summerthwaite they became aware of cricket being played in what appeared to be a hay meadow. Only the heads, shoulders and maroon caps of the Barleybridge players could be seen, moving like strange seabirds cruising on a shimmering sea of green. The view down the High Street was screened by washing spattered with pigeon droppings which hung on lines stretched across the street from house to house. Pigs wallowed and rooted in the school playground beneath a placard which proclaimed 'Privatise and Profit!' Progress along the High Street was impeded by the recent passage of Amos Raw's muckspreader, which had imparted stipple patterns of dung and straw to the road and all the roadside scenery.

The view from the bridge on the Pither offered no more reassurance. Housewives beating out their washing on boulders were apparently oblivious to the sign 'Typhoid, No Swimming', standing on the river bank and equally unmoved by the bloated carcasses (from Pullan's yard) which bobbed on the waters like buoys. Clasping their clipboards to their heaving chests the judges hastily departed from the nightmare. They went past the hummocky and ash-covered meadow with its sign 'Fred Tinkler, Alternative Undertaker, Cremations to Order', past the clusters of muddy, drunken brawlers, avoided most of the turnips that they hurled, and paused for breath outside Amos Raw's farm gate, which was now luminous in slanting bands of emerald and scarlet as though attired for the piste.

Close on their heels came the WKVIP judges, one member from each competing village. Never, since the Scottish raid of 1318, had the valley been so united – and even the Holmesmead delegate was ready to concur that Barleybridge had won.

The victory outing was a day of unsullied bliss. United in song and good fellowship en route, the villagers divided in Scarborough, the menfolk bound for the cricket, the ladies for the shops and beach. Still weary from his exertions and celebrations, Amos Raw hired a beach hut for the day. There he sat and dreamed of days gone by and show days yet to come, absent-mindedly issuing instructions about tractors, seed drills, harrows and combines to nobody in particular. On the sands nearby Mrs Fawcett gambolled with her grandchildren. As lively as an April lamb, she hopped around on her wooden leg making chains of peg prints in the sand. And when Sally, Susan and Jimmy joined up the dots they made pictures of Mickey, Goofy, Donald and Mrs Sherman.

Not far away, and for the first time in public, Mrs Hetherington-Cohen covered Buffy in sand. There he lay in a golden mound, indistinguishable from a dozen other sand-enveloped hubbies. And when the tail of a passing donkey was placed in his hand and he burst forth from the sand at a canter, none of the other beach folk even noticed. This public emergence finally cured his Tripoli Terrors. Buffy was so delighted that he placed a block booking for the Boxing Day performance of *Puss in Boots* at Cripplegate

Theatre, inviting villagers from all the WKVIP entrants to attend. Within a few days of the contest Pitherdale was again just as spruce and wholesome as its inhabitants wished it to be. But clipboards and judges have not been seen again.

From the Yorkshire Gazette, *8 June 1986*
Pitherdale Gleanings by 'Dalesbred Tup'

Many readers may be surprised to learn that this year's Best Kept Village in Pitherdale competition was won by Low Bank, the suburb of Cripplegate which contains the gasworks, and little else.

I have read with interest the recent remarks by Councillor Kit Jackson concerning the need to stimulate the tourist industry in the Dales by reviving old crafts and customs. Curiously his statement coincides with the publication of *The Traditional Crafts and Customs of Old Pitherdale,* by Nancy Jackson, published by Masham Press, price £2.95. It is fascinating to learn that Pitherdale developed its own regional form of 'wheelbarrow' in the fifteenth century. Unlike the conventional barrow with its two legs and a wheel, the Pitherdale variant had three legs and no wheel. It is believed to have been as stable and commodious as the standard barrow, but much more difficult to move. Apparently attempts to improve its efficiency by fitting springs to the ends of the legs gave the Pitherdale barrow a marked superiority when streams had to be crossed, but also made the vehicle inclined to shed its load.

Some Easter customs have survived into modern times; one thinks of the Bacup coconut dancers and the 'Plough Stots' of Sleights, who performed on Plough Monday. Mrs Jackson tells us that Barleybridge once had its own 'frog dancers'. Draped in waterweed from the Pither, the frog men would dance through the village each Good Friday. At every door they would pause and sing:

A penny, a farthing, a guinea or crown.
Give us a fat toad or we'll burn your house down.

97

The custom began in Norman times and persisted until 1787. Over the years various houses were burned down by disappointed frog men, but the custom appears to have lapsed when the dancers realised that they had no earthly use for any of the fat toads that they received. The demise of the ancient ritual seems to have been a relief to all concerned.

8

In which conservation and consternation march arm in arm and cows change colour

From the Yorkshire Gazette, *27 April 1987*
Pitherdale Gleanings by 'Dalesbred Tup'

Last week we lost Jeremiah Wigglesworth at the age of only eighty-one. A lay preacher of my acquaintance attributes this untimely death to Jeremiah's infatuation with the Devil's music, but I prefer to blame the No. 23 bus which struck him as he was jogging home from a pipe-smoking contest at the Clog Maker's Arms in distant Colne. In any event, thoughts of his demise reminded me of the custom of village dances held in the Barleybridge school on Saturday nights commencing at 8 p.m. and continuing until dawn. Music was provided by the late Wigglesworth twins on fiddle and accordion, Mr Bacon on euphonium, Mr Kershaw on piano and Mrs Fairclough on drums. Dancers from the furthest farms in Pitherdale would arrive by pony and trap and return to their outposts in time to rinse their faces, snatch a cup of coffee and begin the milking. And what good times were had by all! The last such dance was held in 1957, after which the advent of television and a stricter interpretation of the licensing laws brought the festivities to an end.

In those times the almost universal garb for the hill farmer included a cloth cap, gaiters and an army surplus greatcoat. Consequently many a husband was mistaken when the dances ended in the thin light of dawn. Oft-times two tractors would meet in a remote Pitherdale lane and the conversation would take the following lines:

'Na'then Jack, 'ast' got my Meg?'

'Aye, Cedric, 'ast' got our Annie?'

'Aye lad. If tha's goin' to Masham market next Seterda' 'appen we can swop 'em ower, like?'

''Appen. Either there or Skipton t'week efter any road. Meantimes tha'll find Megs a'reet wi' t'dashery an' she meks good funeral cakes but doan't let her mek bannocks, they're like river cobbles.'

Over the years this column has helped trace a number of missing persons, and now we must rally to this cause once more. On Saturday Mrs Umpleby of Summerthwaite attended the Spring Flower Show at Cripplegate, having arranged that her husband, Mr Albert Umpleby, would collect her with his car at the bandstand at 4.30 p.m. Mr Umpleby arrived on time, saw a number of ladies in attendance at the bandstand, but was unable to remember which was his Martha. With great presence of mind he returned home to refresh his memory by consulting the photographs of their holiday in Filey. But by the time he returned to the venue at 6.10 p.m. the place was deserted.

Poor Mr Umpleby is quite distraught and has been obliged to call in his sister from Otley to cook his breakfast. We cannot provide a detailed description as Albert is still unable to remember what his wife looks like. The Filey photographs reveal a lady in her middle years holding candyfloss and wearing a 'Come to Primrose Valley' tee-shirt. However, Mr Umpleby fears that she may no longer have the candyfloss and tee-shirt so not too much importance should be attached to these clues.

Mrs Umpleby is the third lady to be lost from Pitherdale in this manner since Easter and it is high time that some system of identification was introduced. Perhaps something on the lines of the 'dog tags' worn by soldiers might suffice? Meanwhile Mr Umpleby tells me that the washing is piling up and he is sick of fish and chips for supper. Should any Cripplegate reader spot 'missing Martha', please hang on to her until Albert comes to town to place his bet for the 2,000 Guineas on Saturday morning.

As the last in line of a now threadbare dynasty, Sir Cecil Hardcastle bequeathed his money to the village church and his remaining property – the Hall, its park and gardens and the village green – to Conserving Our Nation (CON).

Members of the Council of CON were not even remotely grateful to their new benefactor. As their Secretary, Sir Hamish Aston-Somerville, pointed out to them, the public would insist on believing whatever was published in the CON magazine, hand-outs and newsletters – and would then perversely assume that the organisation was concerned with the preservation of fine countryside and architecture. As all members of the Council knew perfectly well, CON exists to allow impecunious members of the aristocracy to continue to occupy their ancestral homes without being pestered by bailiffs or tax men and with the disturbances by day trippers reduced to an absolute minimum. The jewel in the CON crown is Hogswallow Hall, where the penniless twenty-third Earl of Ravenser still shoots his own venison, pheasant, grouse and keepers and is only troubled by CON members and other visiting proles on the third Tuesday in January, during leap years.

'Hardcastle! Hardcastle!' trumpeted Brigadier Twyning-Green, 'Upstarts! Nouveau Riche! Bloody drapers, that's what they were!'

'Wouldn't have a Hardcastle in my house,' boomed Lord Mercia, a man of such a long and impeccable pedigree that he regards the royal family as German parvenus and Lord Montagu of Beaulieu as a used-car dealer.

'It's a perfectly beastly Neo-Gothick rabbit warren, it's just so utterly horrid I positively shiver every time I think of it,' whimpered Gervaise St John Stoops, the Council's art historian. 'And it's in the *North!*'

'We couldn't put Lady Wick-Rissington in a dump like that. Far too far from Ascot,' added the Brigadier. 'Perhaps we could use the stone to build that aeroplane hanger that Lord Mounteagle keeps asking for?'

'No, we're stuck with it,' announced Sir Hamish. 'I've just received a report from the Department of the Environment. It's full of codswallop about a fine monument to Victorian industrial entrepreneurship and patronage. Exceptional collection of estate buildings ... unique assemblage of public architecture . . . embodying the spirit of an age of paternalism, and so on. It's all here!'

'Well,' said the Brigadier, 'if we're stuck with it we might as well make some money out of the bloody place. Then perhaps we could do something about that water garden that "Squiffy" Ravenser keeps asking for.'

In days gone by the Council of CON would gladly have filled Hardcastle Hall with battery hens and used the proceeds to buy man-traps for the Hogswallow estate. Of late, however, the press reports on CON properties have included a few less-than-enthusiastic examples. There was the awkward case of the nature reserve in the Chilterns, which had been leased to the local foxhunt. Then there had been all the regrettable ballyhoo surrounding the covert installation of the cruise missile base in the great park of Russell Towers. And when Crimplebeck Hall collapsed during the excavation beneath it of a nuclear fallout shelter for hereditary peers and members of the CON Council, matters did rather come to a head. *Guardian* readers were reminded that the hall and garden had only been open on three days during the ten years following the public subscription of £5 million for its restoration. Somebody even wrote to *The Times*. And so the Council decided that a drastic change of policy was required. They hired a new publicity officer.

Reluctantly CON assumed control of Hardcastle Hall. CON properties of the commercial rather than the residential type are placed under the custodianship of a passed-over major. These majors have the right sort of background, a staff of gardeners and assistants to bully, too little intelligence to allow them to become a nuisance to their employers, and army pensions which permit CON to pay them minimal salaries. The majors are obtained from the P-OM Agency in Kensington, which supplied Major 'Pongo' Bloodlust to Barleybridge. He was allowed to pass round the sherry as members of the northern regional council of CON gathered at Hardcastle Hall to assess its commercial potential.

'I'll tell you what the stupid punters want,' proclaimed Cedric Clifford-Chambers, the properties advisor. 'They want four-poster beds that Queen Elizabeth slept in. They want suits of armour. They want dungeons and torture chambers. They want minstrel galleries. They want to eat their filthy packed lunches in a Capability Brown park. And I'll tell you something else: there's none of that here!'

'Heritage with horns on,' murmured Chairman Eustace Cock-Bevington, following a long and reflective silence.

'What?'

'Heritage with horns on. The punters will pay to see anything old-fashioned and they'll always pay to stare at animals. So let's give them old-fashioned animals and they'll be crawling over themselves to get in. And if we can milk the damn silly creatures then we can charge them top whack for Heritage Ice Cream, Antique Cheese and Tudor Yoghourt. We'll graze the animals in the park, turn the ballroom into a dairy parlour, put the cheese shop in the trophy room and sell milk shakes in the banqueting hall. And when the bloody animals drop dead we'll put them in the freezer and serve them up at medieval banquets for the Round Table crowd.'

The sward in Hardcastle Park had never felt the bite of the plough. On warm March days, while the grass was still short, Mr Gavestone would explore the preserve with his class in tow, pointing out the circular traces of Bronze Age dwellings, the low domed mounds where the ancient chieftains of Barleybridge were still entombed and the hollowed tracks worn into the slopes by the numberless flocks of Delacroix Abbey. Since the unfortunate wart-hog incident the parkland turf had been grazed only by deer and rabbits. Herbicides and pesticides were banned on Hardcastle land so that in summer the park was spangled with wild flowers and all a-flutter with butterflies. In June the children would return to gaze in wonder at the most northerly colony of the green-winged orchid and jostle to flick through the pages of Mr Gavestone's butterfly book. These were the days that they would savour as they stumbled painfully along the last rocky stages of life's highway, recalling the tang of wild thyme, the vigour of young legs, the brilliance of light and the vibrancy of an unspoilt valley.

'You couldn't graze a camel on this,' said Fred Sheppard, the CON agricultural officer, swiping a clump of cowslips with his stick. 'Spray it with herbicide. Plough the lot up. Spread some fertiliser. Sow it with rye grass. Then spray it again and keep on with the fertiliser. The more fertiliser, the more grass; the more grass, the more livestock – and the more fools who'll pay to come and look at them. And you don't want all those damned oak trees dotted around doing nothing and shading the rye grass. Get them down. Then you can shoot the deer and gas the rabbits and you might be getting somewhere.'

If there is one thing that a CON official cannot abide it is a conservationist. At CON headquarters in Blackshirt Hall a censor is constantly at work eliminating any mention of conservational issues from the texts of CON countryside books and guides. An administrative trainee was once thrown bodily from a second-floor window in Blackshirt Hall when she was heard to use the word 'ecology'. (Actually she had said: 'Ah! Scones for tea', but it proved too late to remedy the misunderstanding.) Of all the conservationists CON people dislike, the ones who chained themselves to the gates of Hardcastle Park during the ploughing, re-sowing, shooting and gassing rank highest on the list of the loathed. Major Bloodlust inspected them along with an old chum from Special Branch. Several suspected hunt saboteurs and CND members were recognised, along with Mrs Fawcett, who became only the thirty-seventh female wooden-legged pensioner to be listed in the Special Branch files. Shortly afterwards her grandson, Billy, was surprisingly dismissed from his post as a junior clerk in the Ministry of Health.

During the season that followed, the silent, treeless park acquired a dense mat of bottle-green rye grass. Then the animals began to arrive in an antediluvian avalanche of half-forgotten farm stock: lowing longhorns, dainty dexters, black cows from Kerry and South Devon giants. Check-by-jowl they munched the lush, nitrate-laden turf, while the goats looked on from their pens. And then coaches from Blackburn, Gateshead, Nottingham, Salford and everywhere began to arrive. The village looked on with an interest which bordered on amazement as each coach disgorged its goggle-eyed cargo at Hardcastle Hall.

The Parish Council met to formulate its lack of opinions on this and that, and afterwards the talk turned to the events in the park. 'Tha's telling me that folks are warin' good brass to gawp at coos?' queried Reg Barker in disbelief, but the other farmers confirmed that this was so. The following afternoon Fred Tinkler was accosted by an American couple as he drove his Friesians to the milking parlour.

'Say, how much is it to watch a traditional cow milking?' enquired the strangers.

'I usually charges a pund,' replied Fred with all the quick-witted astuteness of a Barleybridgian who has scented cash. After milking Fred charged his visitors 50p to see the chickens being fed, £2 to scratch a pig, and 20p to walk round the muck heap. He was finally rewarded with a £5 tip for his efforts.

The tidings of easy pickings flashed round the farming community like wildfire. Each farm had a roadside frontage on one or other of the approaches to Hardcastle Hall and each owner set out to join the gold rush. At Riddings Farm Amos Raw had resisted the Friesian tide and still kept a herd of Ayrshire cattle, loving their rich milk, so heavily larded with butterfat. Soon the herd was installed beside the Barleybridge road, where the stately nursery-book cows with their red-on-white markings and upswept horns grazed beneath a hastily painted sign: 'Ancient Milk Cows of Olde England. Hay to feed a Heritage Cow £1.50 per bundle. Be photographed with a cow of your choice, £2.50. Top Grade well-rotted Heritage Cow manure £7.50 per tractor load delivered, or £1.20 per souvenir matchbox full.'

Reg Barker hired his brother's small herd of stocky dairy shorthorns and the dappled beasts were soon penned nearby beneath an equally prominent hoarding: 'Dairy shorthorns, the traditional cattle of Pitherdale. Sponsor a cow and save a rare breed from the knacker's yard. Your name engraved on a manger for £20.'

For many years Tim Robinson had wielded a bootblacking brush with such dexterity that Irish bullocks of dubious parentage were bought at auction and converted into passable members of the Aberdeen Angus fraternity. Now, however, he added blanco to his arsenal and a herd of rare belted Galloway cattle materialised in his field; when the white-banded beasts were aligned along the hedgerow they produced the effect of a gigantic zebra crossing. This image and the remarkable popular success of the belted Galloway project encouraged Tim to convert his daughter's pony into a zebra. But this shortlived enterprise was swiftly denounced by his fellow farmers, who feared a cheapening of their ventures and reminded him that zebra stripes do not run horizontally but vertically.

Until a century ago each farmhouse in Pitherdale produced its own Pitherdale cheese, creamy and tangy, rather like the Swaledale cheese which still just survives. Then a local dairy began buying-in the milk to produce Wensleydale cheese in bulk and when it closed and supermarket Cheddar flooded the Cripplegate stores, almost all memory of the Pitherdale product was lost. Granny Beckwith could just remember how it was made, and her copper kettle, sieve and 'chesfords' or vats still lay in the dust of the loft. When she saw shorthorns grazing once more in Barker's pasture she recalled the summer cheese-making days. And when she heard the prices that visitors were paying for sour slivers of gift-wrapped Heritage Cheese at Hardcastle Hall, she shot into the loft like a rat up a drainpipe. Soon the Barleybridge men were out scouring all auctions between Bedale and Kendal for dairy shorthorn heifers and cows; copper cheese kettles were unearthed from the depths of barns and byres, scoured, burnished and put back to work. A little later roadside stalls selling Pitherdale cheese had erupted at every junction – and it quickly emerged that the cheese derived from shorthorns grazed on old Barleybridge buttercup pastures was far more marketable than the CON product with its undistinguished flavour of plastic, cow cake and fertiliser.

Left aloof from the cheese bonanza, Amos Raw discovered, meanwhile, that his Ayrshire milk would yield a rich and buttery ice cream. Only the flavourings remained to be decided, but when he proposed turnip, marrow and

106

cow-and-pig mix, Mrs Raw intervened with an array of real-fruit natural recipes. Thereafter any coach bound westward for Hardcastle Park had first to negotiate Amos's farmhouse ice-cream stall and his Ayrshire display, Reg Barker's 'Save a Shorthorn' campaign, Tim Robinson's ever-growing collection of rare (hand-painted) cattle – now including 'Lincoln reds', 'Devons', 'red polls' and 'Welsh blacks'– and then at least three Pitherdale cheese stalls. Very few succeeded in reaching their original destination.

In all directions Hardcastle Hall was hemmed about by cottage heritage industries, some traditional and others less so. For £5 you could stop at Frank Cockburn's workshop and buy a hand-turned leg of Pitherdale oak, just like Mrs Fawcett's. For the same price on rainy days you could shelter in Tim Robinson's barn and help him to re-blanco the belted Galloways or re-stain the Lincoln reds with gravy browning. On Wednesdays and Fridays there were sheep-dog trials at the Beckwith farm; for £10 you could take control and whistle commands to your heart's content – and wise old Jem would ignore it all and pen up the sheep for you anyway.

Meanwhile, the heady diet of force-fed rye grass and the lowing nearby of so many ravishing shorthorn heifers proved too much for the rare bulls in Hardcastle Park. One by one they tried to batter through the drystone walls of their prison. At first so many cracked their skulls that the Hall freezer overflowed and medieval banquets were scheduled twice nightly to reduce the beef mountain. But as the walls weakened and crumbled, so bulls of the rarest breeds and fanciest pedigrees became commonplace in Barleybridge High Street, where an unseemly scramble was likely to develop between Sam Pullan's slaughterhouse truck and the cattle wagons of the farming fraternity.

Sam Pullan was reluctant to see his stake in the heritage bonanza restricted by the vagaries of bovine escapology and the speed of his ailing truck. The tourist market for his traditional cow tails was flat and even his 'pin a cowtail on the vicar' competitions did little to revive the trade once Rev. Hobhouse had become hypersensitive to the sound of children approaching on tiptoe from behind.

107

It was a chance meeting with a taxidermist in the Wool-pack at Summerthwaite that put his business back on the rails. Instead of exposing his clients to the undiscriminating palates at the Cripplegate steak house, Sam had members of the more unusual breeds stuffed and mounted on wheels. Now the intending visitors to Hardcastle Park had a new temptation to negotiate. 'Pony Trekking with a Difference', read the sign at the end of the Pullan track. And different it certainly was, for nowhere else in Britain could one pay a modest £4 to be towed in convoy along the Pitherdale High Road by an antique Fordson Major tractor while viewing the world from the back of a rumbling longhorn bull.

The longhorn was also suited to visitors of a more solitary and adventurous disposition. The widespread horns made excellent handlebars and a rudimentary form of steering could be achieved by brake cables running from the handlebars to the right and left sets of wheels. Oldborough Hill has some of the characteristics of the Cresta Run and top speeds of 93 m.p.h. can be achieved during the breakneck descent from Pullan Lane End to the stuffed bull recovery station at Barleybridge bridge. (This speed was confirmed by traffic police, whose radar-supported testimony failed to secure prosecutions at Cripplegate magistrates' court owing to the revelation that the vehicles concerned were not covered by any of the traffic statutes.)

Nowhere can one encounter more stalwart upholders of the principle of free enterprise than amongst the members of the CON National Council. If Brigadier Twyning-Green had his way then the National Health Service would be reduced to a privatised euthanasia unit created to accommodate those patients who could not afford subscriptions to a private health scheme. Nonetheless, free enterprise had cast an evil spell over the commercial operations in Hardcastle Park. During the fortnight following the opening of the rare breeds heritage centre the dairy and park had received a daily average of 2,700 visitors. Six months later a visitor total of 63 was recorded over a seven-day period – and this included 42 members of a lost coach party bound for Harewood House. In the banqueting hall the milk shakes stood unshaken. In the Heritage Shoppe the balls of soap, floral cheeseboards, Edwardian country aprons, CON country books and Humphrey Rabbit tea towels lay untouched and unwanted.

The number of visitors had declined to a point where expenditure on fertilisers, wall repairs and bull replacements exceeded income. Faced with the drain on their funds, the members of the Council of CON closed the gates on Hardcastle Hall. Nobody was more delighted than Gervaise St John Stoops, who had been harried, kicking and squealing all the way, into compiling an architectural appraisal of what his report describes as '. . . a really quite dreadful expression of parvenu vulgarity which leaves the onlooker limp with horror and craving for the restrained classicism of an architectural haven like Hogswallow Hall, there to purify the spirit of Northern insensitivity and forget the tragedy of the Gothic Revival'. Throughout his inspection of the exterior of Hardcastle Hall Gervaise had been pursued by a passionate nanny goat of the Toggenburg type, a goat which had plainly mistaken his amorous orientation on at least two major counts.

In the weeks that followed, the entrepreneurs of Barley-bridge became rather bored with their successes in the heritage industries. The village and its approaches were clogged with day-trippers, while north of the Pither one walked in constant fear of being impaled by a runaway stuffed longhorn. His artistic instincts jaded by the repetitive conformity to breed standard colour coding, Tim Robinson was beginning to produce ever more bizarre cattle in the liveries of MCC touring teams, Harlequin rugby players and Bradford City FC. Amos Raw, tired of filling souvenir matchboxes and seeing his daily milk ration disappear into the ice-cream machine, began to yearn for the quiet con-templation of the lost privy days of yore. And Sam Pullan became thin and listless from the daily exertions of pushing stuffed longhorns back up the steep curves of Oldborough Hill, gluing horns back on and summoning ambulances.

Soon the village decided that enough was enough. Down came the hoardings and the stalls; Rev. Hobhouse was able to put aside his backward-seeing periscope; the unsold peg-legs in Cockburn's workshop were sold off as a job lot of skittles, and peace returned to Pitherdale. The only remaining legacy of the gold rush is the revival of Pitherdale cheese. And if you go to Barleybridge and do not gawp or blether too much, then Mrs Reynard just may sell you some at the village store.

9

In which we lose a parish councillor but gain a Country Ned

From the Yorkshire Gazette, *8 March 1965*
Pitherdale Gleanings by 'DalesbredTup'

Much has been written about the longevity of Pitherdale folk, and of Barleybridge folk in particular.

One of the disadvantages of this habit concerns the dearth of funerals. Just the other day Mr Cockburn was telling me that he can scarcely remember when he last enjoyed a good bite of funeral cake washed down with whisky, while, as he points out, decent boiled ham just goes to waste without a funeral tea now and then. February usually promises at least one worthwhile departure, but this year the month passed without incident. There were brief expectations concerning Mrs Bickerstaffe,who fell through ice while skating at Ramsbottom Deep. Despite losing her pension book and royal telegram to the icy waters she recovered quite swiftly, and wishes to apologise to all her relatives who had stocked up with funeral fare in anticipation.

With the failure of February to fulfil its promise, villagers began to discuss the possibilities of an alternative funeral party. Mr Reeth suggested that as the funeral of Mr Zebediah Peacock, who died in 1945, had been a bit of a flop on account of the blizzards, the old gentleman might care to be dug up and given a proper 'do'. However, our Vicar pointed out that Mr Peacock probably appreciated the reasons for the poor attendance and that the Bishop might not be sympathetic to the notion. Then the idea of a funeral rehearsal was suggested by Mr Stott, who made the point that if we did not get some practice in soon, we might forget how to do the job properly when the next time came. This proposal was well received.

Mr Stott offered the services of uncle Gilbert Stott in the role of mine host and so Gilbert was fitted for a coffin by Mr Moreton according to an arrangement by which the coffin was hired for the rehearsal and then stored by Mr Moreton for final purchase at the appropriate time. In the event Gilbert proved to be the life and soul of the party, rising from time to time to recharge his glass and join in the old ballads and dirges before snuggling back to rest awhile in the white satin upholstery. He tells me that if he enjoys his next funeral just half as much as this one then he will be in fine fettle to meet his Maker. Nevertheless he sprang from the coffin with great agility as soon as the 'mourners' began to disperse, fearing perhaps that his relatives might seek to carry the event to a conclusion and thus economise on the ultimate funeral costs.

So fickle is the nature of fate that no sooner had we all completed the rehearsal with Gilbert Stott than poor Mrs Ingilby dropped dead while riding her tricycle to the Plumpton point-to-point meeting. She passed away in the prime of her life at the age of only eighty-nine. Her departure comes as a great surprise, though Mrs Reynard maintains that her badminton game had declined noticeably of late. Nonetheless, Mr Moreton, who is noted for his fine sense of anticipation, was caught completely unawares at a time when seasoned oak is hard to come by. This notwithstanding, the rehearsal with Mr Stott stood us all in good stead and I am pleased to report that the funeral was a great success. Personally I feel that black formica will prove to be the casket-making material of the future, and I was so impressed that I placed an advance order with Mr Moreton, who assures me that it is completely resistant to woodworm.

In the first warmth of spring, flower buds burst and the blackthorn hedges no longer hem the fields darkly but fringe each close in wedding-white frills. In summer the blue-black sloes fill the places where the blossom had danced. And in winter the berries sustain some birds, while

112

others starve and perish. As long as there have been people in Pitherdale there have been times to laugh and times to mourn. During many a distant winter Dalesmen bearing wicker coffins would ford the rushing Pither, gently lower their burden in Holmesmead churchyard and with it shed the anguish of bereavement. Struggling for life and coping with death were always part of the Pitherdale way.

And so it was when Reg Barker fell into his combine harvester. 'Local Farmer Reaped' grieved the headline in the *Pitherdale Messenger*.

'I'd ha' come quicker . . . ', explained Mr Moreton, as he unpicked the bale containing the mortal remains of Mr Barker, ' . . . but t'missus maintained it were a misprint.'

At the funeral the surviving parish councillors served their old friend as pall bearers. Then, while Rev. Hobhouse was briefly distracted by little Danny Beckwith, who flitted betwixt the tombstones with cowtail and pin, they performed the ancient local ritual which goes back beyond the days of St Eric. Each broke a pitchfork across his knee and tossed the pieces down to clatter onto the casket. And then the gloom lifted like a morning mist and the long ranks of slumbering Barleybridge Barkers welcomed a new spirit into their throng.

As Mrs Barker passed round the sandwiches of home-cured ham, the whisky, parkin and fruitcake, she explained to the jovial mourners at Hag Wood Farm that, rather than stay to be haunted by all the happy memories, she would be joining her widowed sister in Cripplegate and starting a new life as a vendor of Pitherdale cheese.

Seldom before had the sages of Barleybridge had two pressing topics to debate at one and the same time. Rising to the testing occasion, postmistress Reynard divided her office with a plank and trestles. The vacancy on the Parish Council was discussed in the eastern sector, beneath the fading Colorado Beetle poster, while the auction of Hag Wood Farm could be debated in the western section in the heady vicinity of the coffee grinder.

Dealing first with the Eastern Question, the village elders found themselves perplexed. The system of logic that they adopted ran as follows: 'We are a farmer short on the Parish

Council. Farmers and parish councillors are the same thing; always have been, always will be. So if an offcomer buys Hag Wood Farm we will have an offcomer on the Parish Council. But we don't want an offcomer on the Parish Council. So what can we do?' Since Mrs Reynard wanted to be fresh and lively to celebrate her imminent ninety-eighth birthday she closed the Post Office at 11 p.m. and put the matter in the scholarly hands of Mr Gavestone. He wrestled with the problem without sleeping for two days and nights, and on the third day the following proclamation was pinned to Mrs Fawcett's leg and the tidings paraded round the village.

Results of Research Concerning the Vacancy on the Parish Council

1. No non-farmer has served on the Barleybridge Parish Council since its creation in 1894.
2. The same is true of the Parish Councils of Bishopgate and Summerthwaite.
3. Four of the seven members of Holmesmead Parish Council are non-farmers.
4. We all know what we think of Holmesmead.
    Signed: *P. Gavestone*, BA, F Ed II S (Headmaster)

For once Mr Gavestone had been unable to assuage the anguish in the village. It deepened profoundly with the discovery that the Vicar had nominated Mrs Sherman to fill the vacancy.

Perhaps quite wisely, the good people of Barleybridge deplore elections. In Hardcastle times everybody prudently voted Conservative – all except Gideon Lofthouse, who voted Labour and was much missed by his neighbours when Colonel Hardcastle found out. But no Parish Council seat had ever been contested, and before the Lofthouse and Raw tenancies were amalgamated the membership of the Council was not determined by votes, but by acreage.

With society in turmoil the debate spread from the post office to the Institute and from the Institute to the cricket pavilion. It rippled through BUAC and was even discussed in an interlude between the London and local minutes at the WI. Eventually a consensus was reached, which ran

114

as follows: (a) Sam Pullan is not a farmer, but he *does* have a smallholding; (b) Rev. Hobhouse and Mrs Sherman detest Sam more than they detest anyone else in Barleybridge; (c) therefore Sam Pullan should stand for election.

And so it came to pass that a delegation of elders toured the inns of Pitherdale until Sam was discovered holding court in the Pick and Shovel high up on Heathhowe Moor. His reaction to the nomination was at first forthright and not encouraging. In desperation Mr Farrar broke the habits of a lifetime and told a lie.

'I 'ear as 'ow t'parson and Mrs Sherman were seen measuring up t'Hardcastle tomb last Friday back. 'Appen she'll be able to get it shifted for 'im once she's elected like,' he claimed.

'Reet,' said Sam, slamming down his glass. 'You're on!'

Mrs Sherman threw all her formidable energies into campaigning. She knocked on all the doors in Barleybridge, including many that she hoped to see demolished to make way for OAP flats, marriage guidance centres, nurseries and prep schools – and each cringing inmate pledged their support. Meanwhile Rev. Hobhouse prepared to denounce Sam's candidacy from the pulpit. He scoured the Old Testament for apt denunciations of the proprietors of knackers' yards, but found nothing. And so he prayed for divine guidance – and then invented one.

'Place not thy trust in the slayers of old nags,' he bellowed across the little congregation. 'For it is written that if thou shouldst welcome such a butcher of beasts into the bosom of thy house then shall he biteth like the adder and stingeth like the serpent. And it is graven on the stones of Hebron that he shall not slay thy weak and ailing beasts. Nay, thy best and most fruitful cattle, only them shall he slay.

'And I say unto you that shouldst thou harbour such a man, yea, and in the fullness of time render unto him high office, then shall the foulness of his mouth cause thy daughters to feel unclean. And those that were cleanest even they shall feel most unclean. And all the waters of the Tigris shall not make them clean again. Mark not the scrolls to favour any vendor of cow tails and pricker of holy priests lest thou shouldst join him in the fiery furnace of damnation. Jeremiah 53, 32-33.'

Sam pursued a different strategy. Not wishing to be reproached by the electorate for any future misconduct, he decided to do his worst on the eve of polling day, so that the electors would know just what they were getting. Thus it was that he careered wildly into the Merrie Scampi wearing illicit wellies and mounted on his last remaining longhornmobile. With 'Fast' Frank pinned to the bar by the 'handlebars' of his steed he proceeded to grill slabs of tripe in the Tudor Sandwich Toaster and sample the rows of spirits. Warming to the occasion he then substituted a cowtail for the chain in the 'Wenches' lavatory, evicting 'Fast' Frank's daughter whom he then chased round the beer garden, desisting only when she showed signs of wishing to be caught.

Twenty-four hours later the votes were counted. With the support of the Vicar and 'Fast' Frank, Mrs Sherman had achieved three votes, the remaining 295 being cast in favour of Pullan, S., Independent Humane Termination candidate.

The sale of Hag Wood Farm was handled most cannily by the agents, Softly, Softly, Leer and Smarme of Cripplegate. Realising that each neighbouring Barleybridge farmer would like to expand into the Barker holding, they sold the land in four separate lots and reserved the farmstead, a couple of pastures and Hag Wood for sale by separate auction. As the CON consultant involved in the shooting and gassing in Hardcastle Park, purchaser Ned Withershins (aka Nigel Voakes) had already experienced the charms of Pitherdale.

Known to television viewers as 'Country Ned, the Molecatcher Man', Ned's squashed-tomato face and rumpled tweed suits epitomise the urban image of rural life. In the countryside the image is less plainly defined.

''As t'seen yon offcomer as bought 'Ag Wood?' queried Amos Raw.''E looks like summat as got run ower on t'way to t'grouse shooting on 'Eath 'Owe Moor.'

Ned began his rustic career as Nigel, a used-car salesman of Bristol. With the onset of war and conscription he hastily obtained a reserved occupation as a farm mechanic in the Vale of Evesham. His first media success came after he overheard some farmworkers talking and rushed to the BBC with their nutritious and patriotic recipe for hedgehog pie. The wartime listeners warmed to his West Country burr and asked to hear more of it. As his post-war fame grew he cultivated the art of mimicking rural accents broadcast on *Down Your Way*. Now his dialect swings easily between those of Cornwall, Somerset, Hampshire and Norfolk, though nobody seems to notice the changes. With the dawning of the television era, Ned, as he had now become, toured the game fairs acquiring a wardrobe to fit his carefully cultivated image. Deerstalkers, plus fours, moleskin weskits, shepherd crooks and Bond Street brogues were all grist to his rustic mill.

The countryside which Ned has created for his metropolitan admirers is a peculiar place, packed with vicious vermin all eager to be trapped, hounded or otherwise disembowelled.

'So when you've caught the ol' weasel just give 'e a lil boit on the back of his head – loik this. Then into the pot with 'e. Moi ol' granny, Rosy Withershins of Bourton-on-Windrush, used to swear by weasel kidneys. They eased her spasms no end. Gawd luv us they did!'

He receives generous retainers from various hunts following his spirited defence of their perversion.

'Oi remembers when oi wuz a lil' lad on moi dad's farm in the Vale of Pewsey and the hounds couldn't hunt on account of the swine fever then in they parts. Well, the ol' foxes missed the hunting so much they wuz throwing fits. Then they troid to hunt *each other*, but in the end they all went mad and bit themselves to pieces. The fields wuz all covered in fur and dead foxes. Oh Ar, they luv being caught by hounds. Gawd luv us they do!'

Ned's greatest success came with the televising of the series *Men and Moles* in which leading molecatchers from all parts of the realm competed for the *Men and Moles* trophy. Since most of the action took place underground and out of sight of the cameras, all credit was given to Ned's lively, countrywise commentary.

'Now the ol' mole's a vicious beast. Eats twenty times his weight in rabbits each day, e' do. And if you corners 'e – woi, 'e'll floi straight for your throat. So when you catch 'e just give 'e a good tap with the spade. That's what 'e loiks. Then into the pot with 'e. But keep his skin for to make britches and weskits. Moi ol' uncle, Walter Withershins of Piddletrentithe, swore by moleskin britches. They did wonders for his palsy. Gawd luv us they did!'

Viewers know that Ned's inseparable companion is his springer spaniel, 'Trusty', and, after filming, Trusty returns to kennels and Ned changes into a Savile Row suit and false beard and retires to his Bloomsbury flat. On completing the fifth and final series of *Men and Moles*, Ned's producer, Timmy Dollimore, discussed future programmes.

'Now listen, Neddy sweetheart,' he cooed, 'the viewers want to know so much *more* about you. They want to meet you at *home*, killing all your horrid vermin, chatting about country matters with your neighbours and picking all the pretty flowers. *At Home with Country Ned*, that's what we'll call it. Of course, the company will help you buy a suitable place, but you'll have to keep Trusty, you know. Anyway, you keep being recognised in Bedford Square and it's bad for the image. There'll be a book to go with the series so there'll be all those lovely royalty-poos. So do be a sweety and let's not argue. Bye-ee!'

And so it was that Ned, with mixed feelings, moved into Hag Wood Farm and Trusty into its pigsty. As he expected, he took an instant dislike to the villagers. None of them recognised him, for when townsfolk are immersed in *Men and Moles* all rural sets are turned to *Coronation Street*. Consequently there were no autograph hunters for Ned to insult – and if there is one thing a media star hates more than recognition it is a lack of it.

The villagers became aware of their new neighbour when barbed wire was slung across all the footpaths leading to Hag Wood. A gatehouse, closed-circuit camera and infra-red sensors which triggered a set of floodlights bought from Leeds United FC completed the anti-intruder precautions.

Safe from the gaze of reporters and roving admirers, Ned could then leap out of his tweeds, don smoking jacket and Gucci slippers, retire to his computer room in the former wash house and juggle his stocks and shares.

The first edition of *At Home with Country Ned* was devoted to conservation. It began with Ned explaining how he had left his old farm in the Cotswolds because he was advised by Aunty Withershins of Stow-on-the-Wold that the northern air would relieve the pain of his molecatcher's knee. He then described how Nature got herself in a terrible pickle if she was left alone, so that environmental stalwarts like himself were needed to impose a harmony.

'The adult grey squirrel can destroy fifty hacres of proime oak wood in a day,' said Ned. BANG! went his twelve-bore, and down plopped the squirrel. 'Now the jay is an evil bird. Steals your shoes and picks out the oies of babbies.' BANG!

In the course of a programme with a soundtrack reminiscent of the battle of Ypres, Ned described the amazing depredations of the lesser spotted woodpecker, the bank vole and the pygmy shrew, leaving viewers in Glasgow, Manchester and London relieved that there were men such as Ned to protect them from vermin and sort out Nature's imbalances. Subsequent programmes covered county sports like stag hunting, deer stalking, grouse shooting, beagling and hare coursing and they were interspersed with useful tips on how to remove bloodstains from Harris Tweed, how to despatch a lame beagle or cook a fox pie.

It was while Ned was away filming hare coursing in Cheshire that Sam Pullan ambled at dusk towards Hag Wood with a spot of mild poaching in mind. He ducked under the newly strung barbed wire, sidestepped a mound of dead owls and squirrels and headed for the gate in the wood wall, just as he had headed so many times before. However, as his fingers touched the latch a powerful electric charge shot up his arm, the countryside was blindingly floodlit and loudspeakers slung from the trees trumpeted a selection of Wagner's greatest hits.

Collecting his tortured senses Sam headed at speed for the haven of the Woolpack, leaving the seat of his cord britches in the foaming fangs of the leading guard dog.

His calm returned with the fifth glass of Horse Trough Ale and he recalled his former escapades with the Hardcastle keepers. Nonetheless the draughts which wafted through the vents in his thermal long johns served a chill reminder that his youth was but a memory and that his new found dignity as a parish councillor had been severely dented.

As Sam was rummaging in drawers and tea-chests for that elusive other pair of long johns that he was sure he had once owned, Country Ned and Timmy Dollimore were attending to their filming expenses in the gourmet restaurant of the Grand Hotel at Chester.

'It's a Country Ned special, sweety, to celebrate the 100th anniversary of CON,' explained the producer. 'And it *must* go out live. No use grumbling, Neddy-dumpling. If you want that OBE then this is the sort of cross that you must bear. Anyway we'll get some of those lovely Fortnum and Mason hampers on expenses like we always do. And I just *know* that the Duke will be watching. Neddykins OBE – I can feel that you won't let us down!'

'The big hampers?' queried Ned.

'The biggest, fattest, fullest, cuddliest hampers you have ever seen,' gushed Timmy in relief.

He then explained that this Country Ned special would be a good chance for Ned to introduce the viewers to some of his fascinating country neighbours.

'They're a load of mad yokels,' grumbled the star. 'There's an old idiot who spends his time talking about pig muck, a crazy school teacher and a daft old bat with a wooden leg – and from what little I've seen the rest of them are all barking mad.'

Still convinced that Pitherdale must be packed with colourful rustic characters, Timmy did the rounds of the local inns. It was in the Pick and Shovel that he noticed a red-faced gentleman clad in a loud check jacket, a yellow waistcoat and a strange pair of britches crudely tailored from potato sacks. The initial visual promise was emphatically confirmed in a conversation which ranged widely from maggot baits to roller technology and taxidermy.

'O' course,' boasted Sam, 'I'm t'last lad i' these parts as can still do t'rabbit calling, tha knaws.'

'It's just super-duper-do,' beamed Timmy, as he explored a new hamper with Ned back at Hag Wood Farm. 'Rabbit calling – it's a television first and it's live! Just picture Gabby Ploughman's face over on Channel 4. This will knock his stoat-sniffing programme into a cocked hat!'

The day of the rabbit-calling epoch dawned glumly, with Ned and Timmy arguing about whether Trusty could be allowed to appear on a live programme.

'Now Neddipoos don't be all gruff and lumpy, you know the viewers love to see your faithful dog at your side – but we must give her a bath and a decent meal first or there'll be sacks and sacks full of horrid letters.'

Eventually the crew assembled at the warren in Hardcastle Park which Sam Pullan insisted was ideal for the demonstration of rabbit calling. They were joined by Lord Mercia and Cedric Clifford-Chambers representing CON, and when Sam arrived in a new pair of cords provided from the facilities budget Trusty bounded over and eyed Ned suspiciously from between Sam's knees. Sam winked at her and she nestled snugly against his cords.

As the opening theme of 'A Farmer's Boy' faded in his headphones Timmy signalled to Ned and the programme began.

'Noo moi dears, Oi've got sumpin' vorry special for you orl today. Oi want you to meet my good ol' chum Stan Pulman. Noo Stan and oi goes back a long way and Oi can remember how we used to pick zider apples together on Uncle Withershin's farm in the vale of Taunton when we wuz both knee hoigh to a grasshopper. That wuz when ol' Stan here used to go out a-rabbit callin' and 'e's here today to show uz orl how 'tis done. Gawd luv us 'e is!'

Sam knelt down at the mouth of a burrow and called, 'Coney, coney, lettuce and kale, come out now for carrots and ale'.

Then he pressed his ear to the ground and stretched a long arm down the mouth of the burrow. His fingers touched the catch on the lid of the wicker fishing creel that he had placed down the burrow at dawn that morning. He reached in, extracted a rabbit and withdrew his arm. He held the quivering creature up to the cameras triumphantly, patted it on the rump and away it scampered. Then he repeated the remarkable feat and turned to address his first audience of millions.

'Nathen, as I recall from our 'appy days in t'cider orchard owd Ned 'ere worra knacky rabbit caller an 'all. So c'mon Ned, pretha, and let's see thee lakin' at t'rabbit calling lark.'

Ned took up his station at the mouth of the burrow. 'Coney, coney, lettuce and kale, come out noo fur carrots and ale!' Nothing happened.

'Nay, Ned lad, thas'll 'ave to do better nor that,' said Sam. 'Do as I did and stick thi gob reet dahn t'oil.'

'Coney, coney, lettuce and kale, come out noo fur carrots and ale,' bawled Ned down the burrow.

At this moment, Trusty was seized by an irresistible urge to sink her jaws into the prominently displayed rear of the owner of the cold, dirty pigsty in which she had passed the summer.

The sudden surge of pain caused Ned to shoot forward into the burrow. His head jammed into his deerstalker hat and the brim of the hat lodged firmly and immovably against the sides of the hole.

All this was quite unfortunate since the live programme had a further twenty minutes to run. There was no alternative but to sink a microphone into the warren and allow Ned to continue his commentary from his semi-subterranean position.

'Noo the rabbit's a most fearful form o' vermin,' echoed the disembodied voice as the last remaining rabbit in Sam's creel marked its territory on Ned's big red nose. 'Oi've seen a single buck rabbit kill a full-grown ram with one blow of its claws – and then eat six hacre of clover for supper. When oi wuz a nipper in the Vale of White Horse moi ol' Dad would hunt rabbits with a pack of bull mastiffs. They just loves to be hunted with mastiffs! Noo, when you've cornered and catched Mr Rabbit just give 'e a good thump with your rabbitting stick. That's what 'e loikes. Then into the pot with 'e. Ol' grandad Withershins down at Maiden Bradley swore by rabbit ear broth. It eased his carbuncles no end. Gawd luv us it did!'

122

Ned continued in this manner for some time after the camera crew had packed and departed.

'There may be an unexpected vacancy for a presenter in our Countryside unit,' said Timmy to Sam.

'Not interested,' replied Sam, 'but I'll keep t'bitch if I may?'

'Yes,' said Timmy. 'We won't be needing Trusty any more.'

From the Yorkshire Gazette, *7 May 1977*
Pitherdale Gleanings by 'Dalesbred Tup'

Two decades have passed since the arrival of television in Pitherdale. I must say that I regard the entertainment as a very mixed blessing. Ever one to broaden my mind, I have lately feared that I may have been subverted by the Marxist gentlemen associated with the Open University programmes that I used to watch. For a moment I began to feel some strange sympathy for some unemployed gentlemen in Newcastle, but a telephone call to my Party's agent soon put me straight on that one. (I fear that his weakness for gin and tonic has robbed the nation of a statesman of the highest calibre.)

In Barleybridge some households receive their programmes from Yorkshire Television, others from Tyne Tees. This has given rise to a most active debate about whether the episodes of *Coronation Street* transmitted by the former network are identical to those screened by the latter. The first attempt to establish the facts was inconclusive. Mrs Reynard, who receives the Yorkshire transmission, placed her set in the shop window and went to the call-box outside to converse with Mrs Armitage, who takes the Tyne Tees programmes. However, Mrs Reynard's blow-by-blow account of the events on *Coronation Street* was periodically interrupted by the need to insert 2p coins, so that the continuity of her commentary was totally flawed. Then, after an overheated debate between the Yorkshire and Tyne Tees factions over what Annie Walker had really said to Elsie Tanner-that-was in the Rover's Return, the Parish Council intervened. With Sir Cecil's permission, two television sets were installed in the school, one tuned

123

to Yorkshire and one to Tyne Tees, and the villagers were invited to watch. Unfortunately there was only one aerial socket available, so that Miss Bliss had to dash between sets, and with all the connection and re-connection involved, the results were again inconclusive.

Following this frustration the debate intensified. One faction argued that events in the Street are covered by two sets of cameras manned by the different networks. Another faction claims that one set of cameras serves both networks, but there is little support for Mrs Shutt's firmly held belief that there are two quite distinct and separate Streets in different parts of the country.

Coronation Street is believed to lie in a suburb of Manchester called 'Wetherfield'. When the dispute reached crisis proportions Mr Arthur Beckwith boldly volunteered to lead a commission of inquiry into the land of the Red Rose. Mrs Fawcett, Mrs Reeth and Mrs Farrar joined him in his Land-rover. Having safely negotiated the Lancashire border the commissioners passed without incident through Nelson, Colne and Burnley. Now deep in alien territory, they paused in Oldham to ask directions to Coronation Street, Wetherfield. However, while the local people reportedly seemed quite friendly, the members of the Barleybridge delegation were completely unable to understand their dialect. Mr Beckwith relates that the world of Oldham and Rochdale reminded him of Mr Chamberlain's description of Czechoslovakia as 'a faraway land' which was populated by 'people of whom we know nothing'. It was in Rochdale that the nerve of our observers finally cracked, and so the mystery remains unsolved.

All hope has not been abandoned. Mr Gavestone tells me of a machine called a 'video recorder' which can, in some obscure way, preserve television programmes. Should any of my many readers have knowledge of such a device then I am sure that I speak for the whole of Pitherdale in saying that all relevant information will be gratefully received. Perhaps with the aid of two of these contraptions we could establish the facts and return to more peaceful times.

10

In which there are loud noises and Barley-bridge attempts to join the Warsaw Pact

It was a blissful June morning in Barleybridge. Dawn showers had freshened the leaves and pastures, but now flimsy mists of vapour were rising in the warmth of the climbing sun. A shaft of sunlight streamed through the ventilator in Amos Raw's privy, illuminating the yellowing cuttings recalling half-forgotten village shows. Rooted on his perch of sturdy elm, the ageing farmer's daydreams slipped gently into slumber. He dreamed of a vast flock of golden merino sheep spread out across the grazings of Hollins Farm – and Bertram in the braided uniform of a Qantas Air Marshal pirouetting amid the fleecy host, selecting the prize-winning entrants for Barleybridge Show. Outside the air was so still that one might almost hear the butterflies as they alighted on the opening thistle heads. But in an instant the stillness was rent by a screaming thunder. YEEEOW! The corrugated iron of the privy roof quivered and tugged against its nails; the wooden walls throbbed, and Amos was launched from his seat in an involuntary spasm of fear of such force that he flew right through the privy door. As he rose from the dust beyond he glimpsed the fast-diminishing dot that was a Tornado of the RAF.

Across the valley Fred Tinkler was winding the church clock. This is a clock of some magnificence and was donated by Sir Marmaduke Hardcastle in 1892 in memory of his niece, Emily, following her fatal encounter with a hippopotamus as she attempted to export Christianity beyond the river Congo. Ever since the installation of the clock and its encircling motto, 'Only the slothful count the hours', the

125

task of winding has been entrusted to the head of the Tinkler family. This awesome responsibility is compensated by the right to hunt wild geese in the churchyard (should any ever land there, which is most unlikely). The perk of the job is modest considering that winding can only be accomplished after the ascent of a cast-iron ladder which zigzags its way uncertainly towards the belfry.

Fred accomplished the weekly winding and was hopefully scanning the churchyard in search of geese through the little lancet window below the clock face when his world exploded in a cacophony of sound. YEEEOW! The tower shook, the ladder rattled and Fred's goose gun fired its first shot, the heavy pellets blasting through the rusting bolt which bound the ladder to the wall. Fred flew headlong into space, but as the paving slabs at the base of the tower came closer and closer, his flailing arms embraced the red, white and blue bindings of the bass bell rope. DONG! tolled the bell and up went Fred. DONG! it tolled and down he came. DONG! DONG! DONG! DONG!

As the slow, remorseless tolling rattled the willow-patterned china on her kitchen dresser, Mrs Fawcett reviewed the options. There was certainly no village funeral scheduled, so either the monarch had died or Britain was at war again. Preparing herself for both eventualities she pulled a black garter on her wooden leg, grabbed the kitchen poker and headed for Hardcastle Hall along with the growing throng of village elders.

When they reached the gates of the Hall the sages remembered that there was no longer a Hardcastle there to tell them what to do, and so they scuttled back down towards the source of the tolling.

After a damaging session of trial and error it was demonstrated that if Mr Farrar stood on Mr Reeth's shoulders and grabbed Fred Tinkler's descending legs, and if Mr Wharton then grabbed Mr Reeth's legs as the trio ascended in line astern, then the result would be a tangled heap of disgruntled villagers and a continuation of the tolling. Peace was finally restored after the arrival of Sam Pullan, who placed the bin containing the discarded churchyard flowers in the place communally predicted for

Fred's return to terra firma, picked up the fallen fowling piece and discharged its second barrel at the bell rope. In the event Fred missed the flower bin, but was grateful nonetheless.

When the *Pitherdale Messenger* materialised that Friday all the worst fears in Barleybridge were confirmed: 'TORNADO SQUADRON MOVES TO RAF GUSHFORTH. PITHERDALE DESIGNATED A LOW FLYING ZONE'.

Responding to overwhelming popular demand, the Parish Council called a special meeting. For four of the five members the meeting was fraught with internal tensions. For years the farmers had been conditioned to offer no observations on any matters unconnected with the barn situation or Holmesmead Parish Council – and now they were being pressed by the electorate to formulate opinions on a new issue that was only one week old. Arthur Beckwith preserved a chairmanlike impartiality. Councillors Raw, Pullan and Tinkler resolved that something had to be done. Councillor Robinson, however, could not bring himself to form an opinion and, being virtually deaf, he was unable to understand what all the fuss was about. He moved that the Council should proceed to discuss the barn situation and finally, in desperation, he suggested that they should defer any decision, or indecision, until a medium could be employed to discover the late Councillor Barker's opinions. There then followed two hours of debate on whether parochial funds could legally be invested in the hiring of mediums. A further half-hour was then absorbed in an inconclusive discussion about whether the plural of medium was mediums or media. Eventually, as the cocks began to crow at Hollins Farm, it was decided by a majority of three to one that the Parish Council would form a delegation to RAF Gushforth.

'Wheel them in, then,' ordered Group Captain 'Tufty' Beamish, hastily removing his ear plugs, slipping his officer's guide to public relations under the blotter and placing his English–Dales-talk dictionary close to hand.

'Is t' boss 'ere, pretha?' asked chairman Beckwith.

'Privy?' enquired the group captain. 'There's a toilet in the corridor, turn right, third door.'

'Privy be blowed! 'E said *pretha*,' barked Amos Raw.

'Pretha?' enquired Tufty, grabbing his dictionary. 'Pash . . . Pleean . . . Pretha. Ah! Prithee or pray thee.'

'Pleean, that's reet! We're 'ere to pleean abaht t'racket o' yon airyplanes.'

'Aye,' said Amos, 'I fair 'weeaked when they jathered jemmers on t'privy door.'

'Pretha?' queried the group captain.

'Privy!' barked Amos Raw.

'Permission to speak, sir?' enquired Airman Perkins, who had just arrived with the coffee trolley (and who had gained an acquaintance with Dalestalk in the course of supporting his Prime Minister's enthusiasm for free enterprise by selling War Department supplies to local farmers from the back of an RAF Land-rover).

'Please sir, he says that he really shouts with fright when they rattle the hinges on his privy door.'

'Does he really? I see.'

'Aye!' interjected Fred Tinkler. 'And I were nowling t'bell till me oxters tenged and snirped.'

'Until his armpits were stinging and aching, sir.'

'Sit down, Perkins, you may be here for quite a while.'

Much later, when the Barleybridge councillors had provided a full account of their problems and Perkins had translated, the group captain leaned forward and beamed at his guests in the approved PR manner.

'Now, gentlemen, I have listened very carefully to everything that you have told me and naturally I sympathise with your point of view. But now I must explain that my Tornadoes are all that stands between you good people and the Russians. Low-level training is the essence of air strategy – and there is nothing we can do to change that! So I want you to tell all the chaps in Barleybridge that whenever they hear one of our aeroplanes they should say a little prayer of gratitude that we are here to keep the Russians at bay. And now I must bid you all good day.'

The next day the delegation reported back to a packed village meeting at Barleybridge school.

''E said as 'ow t'Roosians is aht to get us,' explained Arthur Beckwith.

'We've nivver done nowt to no Roosians,' muttered the assembly.

There then followed a long debate about whether Mrs Poireau from Holmesmead Stores, her that ran off with Sam Pullan's cousin, was a Russian – and whether Mrs Armitage's remark about the quality of the cabbage that she sold could have precipitated the diplomatic crisis. Initially it was agreed that she was French and that anyway as the cabbage incident had taken place some twenty years ago it was unlikely to have been responsible.

'They browt 'er back from Cherbourg in a Green 'Oward's waggon underneath a pile o' kit bags,' recalled Sam Pullan.

Quite a lot of time was then wasted in exploring the question of whether Mrs Poireau could have been a Russian *masquerading* as a French woman. Had anyone actually seen her eating frogs? No. To staunch the doubts Sam Pullan left to phone his cousin, now living in Middlesbrough. Half an hour later he was able to report that Mme Yvette Pullan (née Poireau) did occasionally buy tinned snails from a delicatessen on her shopping trips to Newcastle, and so a wave of relief lapped across the assembly.

By this time Mr Gavestone was beginning to worry that the school might not be available for the Edward II pageant rehearsals scheduled for the following day.

'I would like to propose that we placate the Russians by declaring Barleybridge a nuclear free zone,' he announced. He then spent the following hour explaining what a nuclear free zone was.

''As thee got any nooclear missiles up at Riddings Farm?' demanded Mr Beckwith of Mr Raw, accusingly.

'Missiles be damned!' replied Amos.

The rounds of accusation and denial rumbled on and culminated in an inspection team being sent to High Green Farm, where it was found that the suspicious structures were, as Fred Tinkler claimed, cow feed silos and not missile silos.

Once every aspect of the crisis had been explored Mr Gavestone drafted the following letter:

To the First Secretary of the Communist Party
The Union of Soviet Socialist Republics
The Kremlin
Moscow

Comrade First Secretary,
    We, the Parish Soviet, peasants, kulaks, artisans and industrial workers of Barleybridge extend fraternal greetings to the Soviet people. We wish to proclaim that Barleybridge is now a nuclear free zone and that we pose no threat to our comrades in the Soviet Socialist Republics. Members of your Presidium are welcome to inspect any suspected missile installations in this parish at any time of your choosing (including Comrade Tinkler's cow food silos).

Yours fraternally
Arthur Beckwith, Chairman
Barleybridge Parish Council

PS. Just in case Mme Poireau *is* Russian Mrs Armitage would like to apologise about the cabbage.

A fortnight of shock and thunder followed as the Tornadoes practised low-level interception of A10 'tankbusters' from the USAF station at Laconsby in the skies over Barleybridge. Mrs Batty found that the problems were eased a little if she clipped earmuffs fashioned from a pair of Rhode Island reds over her ears, but then the clucking kept her awake at night. The gloom only lifted when Mr Beckwith received the following letter from the Soviet Embassy in London.

    Fraternal greetings to our comrades in Barleybridge! The people of the Soviet Socialist Republics return the hand of friendship. I am instructed to inform you that any missiles which *may* have been targeted on Barleybridge have now been removed from our arsenals. With this comradely gesture we trust that all

130

barriers to further co-operation between our two great peoples have been removed.

> Yours fraternally
> Vladimir Rostov, 2nd Air Attaché
> London Embassy of the Union of Soviet Socialist Republics

PS. It will not be necessary for members of our Presidium to inspect suspected military installations in Barleybridge. However, I would personally be honoured to receive Pitherdale cheeses and woollen garments of local manufacture.

'That's capped it then!' exclaimed the jubilant Arthur Beckwith. He hurried to the Cripplegate copy shop to duplicate the peace documents and posted the photocopy to Group Captain Beamish, along with a covering letter which explained that the RAF presence was no longer required and which also suggested that the squadrons might like to transfer to Cyprus, where Mrs Reynard had had a very good holiday, in spite of the beer. He was so cock-a-hoop with the way that the Parish Council had been seen to solve a thorny new problem that he broke with all Barleybridge traditions and sent the letter first class.

News of the diplomatic triumph flashed round the village like wildfire. Mrs Farrar returned the chickens to their coop and laundered the egg yolk from her pillowcases, while Amos Raw hung a wreath of thanksgiving upon his privy door.

For the first time in its history the church clock had stopped, for all attempts to wind it were fraught with hazard so long as the Tornado threat lasted. Now, however, with the peace proclamation being paraded round the village on Mrs Fawcett's leg, Fred Tinkler again assumed his duties. He placed his old rick-thatching ladder beneath the belfry, shouldered his goose gun and ascended. With the clock re-set and wound he peered through the lancet beneath.

131

His eye was caught by a distant V-shaped formation. As the geese came closer he could hear their honking. As they drew closer still the leading gander let the air spill out from under his wings, stretched out his feet and descended. Feeling secure in the apparent solitude of the churchyard it began to nibble the flowers on Reg Barker's grave. With trembling hands Fred, still unseen, gently extended the barrel of his goose gun further and further through the lancet. Slowly but surely he took aim, then . . . YEEEOW! YEEEOW! YEEEOW!

As the Tornadoes began their simulated attack on Barleybridge church Fred jerked his gun upwards to strike the top of the window. BANG! went the gun, back toppled Fred, hurled into space by the force of the recoil. Out stretched his arms. DONG went the bell. DONG! DONG! DONG! DONG! DONG! This time he missed both the dead-flower bin and the pile of hassocks, but he was grateful to his neighbours nevertheless.

Within days half the population of Barleybridge could be seen with chickens clamped over their ears (the Rhode Island reds being much softer and more soundproof than the white leghorns). Chicken prices rocketed, as did the laundry bills, but egg yields plummeted. Barleybridge had become an angry and resentful place. No longer could one relax confidently in the seclusion of a garden or breathe in the peace of a riverside walk, while the RAF's repeated violations of the understanding with the Soviet Union heaped insult upon injury. The Parish Council wrote a letter of complaint to the District Council, which referred it to the County Council, which forwarded it to the Air Ministry, which referred it to NATO headquarters, which did not reply.

The village now had to look to its own resources, and what emerged was the Barleybridge and District Committee Against Tornadoes (BADCAT). The leading members of the committee were Sam Pullan (Diplomacy), Mr Gavestone (Intelligence), Danny Kendal (Technology) and Amos Raw (Communications).

Given that Amos Raw says as little as possible and prefers to communicate in a code that only Jim Clough understands, he might seem an unusual choice for village communications supremo. However, in war as in business, contacts are all-important and Mrs Raw's brother, Malcolm Fothergill, lives midway between Barleybridge and Gushforth, directly beneath the flightpath used by the Tornadoes. Thus the highly sophisticated early warning system was put into place. As soon as Malcolm recovers his senses after being overflown by a flight of westbound Tornadoes he phones his sister. Hilda Raw immediately opens her kitchen window and throws a lump of coke at the privy. Amos then tugs at the length of clothes rope passing through the ventilator which raises a red banner (actually an old pair of Amos's flannel long johns) up the nearby telegraph pole, whence it can be seen throughout the village down below. When the villagers hear the cry 'Red Flag at Raw's' they know that they have five minutes in which to catch their chickens or dash to the crypt. Later, two rings on the Raw telephone denotes that the alert is over and the planes are returning to the base. Hilda then hurls two old potatoes at the privy and the beacon is lowered.

This system proved extremely effective, save only for the one occasion when a woodpecker attacked the privy wall and Amos became hopelessly entangled with clothes-line as he tried to keep pace with the rapidly changing signals. Meanwhile the banner shot up and down the telegraph pole like a frog in a pump.

Despite the excellence of the early warning system, Mr Gavestone felt bound to point out that this did not constitute a defensive capability. Moreover, the stresses imposed by the continuing Tornado menace were causing the local chickens to moult, reducing their sound-proofing coefficient by a factor of three. He suggested, therefore, that Mr Pullan should write to their new Soviet allies requesting the immediate despatch of a fraternal consignment of SAM missiles, for which Barleybridge would pay with cargoes of Pitherdale cheese, Masham fleeces and malting barley. Amos Raw added a footnote to the effect that Soviet farming would not be in such a pickle if more attention had been paid to the use of natural fertilisers: 'Tha weean't get muck frae a tractor, that knaws'. A fortnight later the following reply was received.

Comrades,

Be assured that we in the Union of the Soviet Socialist Republics deeply regret to learn of your continuing provocation by the imperialistic adventurist forces of the so-called NATO alliance. Moreover, we are regretfully obliged to reject your application for membership of the Warsaw Pact organisation owing to your lack of a common border with any other pact member. Unfortunately, under the terms of the SALT agreements we are unable to fulfil your request for 'two gross SAM heat-seeking missiles complete with warheads'. However, I am instructed to advise that my government is most interested in the supplies of cheese, fleece and barley that you mentioned and we would be pleased to despatch a mission to Barleybridge. Would you consider exchanging said agricultural produce for a consignment of 10,000,000 abacus-type calculators and 200,000 valve-type radios?

Fraternal Greetings
Igor Bukharin, 2nd Air Attaché
London Embassy of the Union of Soviet Socialist Republics

PS. We regard the use of cow and pig-based fertilisers as a degenerate capitalist form of land 'improvement' designed to undermine the exploited fertiliser producers of the developing world.

PPS. Thank you for the cheese and the jumpers in the excellent wool of the Swaledale Soviet. In future please do not forward such tokens of your fraternal solidarity to me at the Embassy address but c/o the Cambridge University Former Students Association in Hampstead High Street. Cde Rostov has been seconded to our Embassy in Papua New Guinea.

With the arrival of this letter the people of Barleybridge knew they stood alone. Consequently the members of BADCAT formed a sub-committee on Defensive Armaments, Static, Tactical and Retaliatory Divisions (DASTARD). Sam

Pullan was placed in charge of the static defences, the tactical and retaliatory divisions being combined under the leadership of Danny Kendal.

Sam's first act was to disinter the chain of kites which had proved such a surprise to Sir Cecil. The original cartoon was furtively overpainted and in its place appeared the forthright message:

BARLEYBRIDGE NUCLEAR FREE ZONE.
DO NOT ENTER THIS AIRSPACE WITHOUT PERMISSION.
TO REQUEST PERMISSION RING S. Pullan Tel. CRIPPLEGATE 552114
BEFORE 7 p.m. (NOT SUNDAYS).

More unusual was Sam's development of a static defence system inspired by photographs that he had seen of the London barrage-balloon network. His bovine clients were skinned, the skins then being sewn back together along the seams and the seams sealed with glue. A tractor tyre valve was then inserted in the udder, allowing the skins to be inflated with helium from Danny Kendal's laboratory. The kite chain was raised to a height of 1,200 feet and then anchored to a tree-stump on the eastern limits of Barleybridge parish, directly in the flightpath favoured by the approaching Tornadoes. Within the frontiers of the parish were the twenty bovine barrage balloons (BBBs), stacked at heights ranging from 2,200 to 800 feet and secured by ropes and by wires borrowed from Holmesmead's telephone system to features like the church spire, the cricket club roller and the bridge. (Amos Raw claimed that his privy was a Grade A target and thus required its own BBBs, though he changed his mind when the unexpected lifting power of the balloon threatened to uproot this by now much-abused structure.)

Strangers to Pitherdale regarded the tethered airborne cattle as rather odd and rumours soon circulated that they were associated with a television commercial for low fat butter. Those more familiar with Barleybridge and its doings merely shrugged and continued on their way. 'Nutty' Ramsbottom deduced that the balloons were launched by Barleybridge's farmers attempting to escape the wretched summer. He argued that by uprooting their parish and having it borne southwards by the northerly winds the wheat and barley crops would ripen more swiftly. As a result of this speculation an emergency meeting of Holmesmead Parish Council was convened. While having no observations to offer on the imminent disappearance of Barleybridge parish they were determined that the long-disputed half-acre on the parish boundary must remain *in situ* until United Nations' arbitrators had resolved the dispute.

While Sam was engaged in the inflation and tethering of BBBs, Danny Kendal was researching retaliatory systems. At an early age he had realised that if he removed the mainsprings from those devices used to launch clay pigeons and then substituted heavy-duty springs salvaged from the suspensions of tractors he could create weapons of great power. They would fire metal discs filched from disc harrows a distance of four miles at speeds of up to 650 m.p.h. However, the trajectory of the missiles could only be predicted approximately. This shortcoming, rather than any deliberate intent, was responsible for the decapitation of a very promising row of Mr Farrar's sweet peas, the release of a tethered BBB and the severing of Mrs Fawcett's wooden leg. The BBB was sighted by members of the Atlantic UFO Alliance at Warminster in Wiltshire and later discussed as the second most impressive case in their files. Mrs Fawcett's leg was expertly spliced together again by Mr Moreton, but sadly the sweet peas were to prove a great disappointment.

Danny then experimented with large rockets launched from drainpipes and he developed a remarkable semi-solid fuel propellant based on a combination of sulphur, saltpetre, charcoal, Puddle's bitter and Raw's grade one pig-and-cattle blend. The drainpipes were bound in a cluster which was mounted on the moving arm of a JCB commandeered from the Holmesmead roadworks. They produced an effect which reminded Mr Reeth of the German multiple mortars he had faced in Normandy, though the homegrown product frightened him considerably more.

And so it was that when Flight Lieutenant 'Bingo' Brewster led his Tornado flight in a mock attack on Barleybridge school his cockpit radar suddenly warned

136

that he was being pursued by a gaggle of hostile missiles. Instinctively he armed his own missiles, threw his aircraft into a mind-numbing turn, and as soon as his blackout began to clear he fired on the first hostile that shimmered into view. This proved to be the BBB tethered to Barleybridge Institute. The missile passed straight through the bovine balloon, the helium of which ignited in an explosion of Kendalian proportions. Meanwhile and undaunted, the missile continued on its way, neatly removing half the second floor of the Vicarage. The two remaining members of the flight witnessed the airborne explosion, assumed that poor 'Bingo' had 'bought it' in a surprise attack by Soviet Foxbat intruders, looked for the nearest hostile and shot each other down.

Their leader headed at top speed for RAF Gushforth and was surprised and relieved to find that the airfield had escaped destruction in the Soviet first strike. He leapt from his Tornado and described to an incredulous Intelligence Officer how his flight had been bounced by a superior Foxbat force, how 'Chalky' and 'Biffo' were 'flamers', but how he had 'bagged at least one bandit'.

Only his lightning reactions, honed to the highest pitch of readiness by the cow-tail incidents, saved Rev. Hobhouse when the floor of his Vicarage vanished from beneath his feet. He was left hanging grimly to the chain of his lavatory, gazing down into the dust-covered interior of his gun room two floors below. Strangely the same villagers who had striven so hard to save Fred Tinkler from similar plights seemed immune to the Vicar's misfortune and cries for help. Instead of mustering beneath with hassocks and flower bin in the accepted manner, they all sped towards the church, its spire and parapet now festooned with the parachutes of Chalky and Biffo. Both pilots were returned no more than bruised, each elated and anxious to lodge his claim for one Foxbat definitely destroyed.

When a rope materialised in the space to his left, Rev. Hobhouse assumed that it had been lowered by rescuers from the roof above. He swung to and fro on his creaking chain and just succeeded in clasping the rope as the cistern broke free from the wall. As he sighed with relief and began to shin down it Sam Pullan unhitched the free end of the rope from the tow bar of his van and the Vicar ascended into the wide blue yonder clinging grimly to the tether of a BBB.

'Ta ta for now, Vicar,' said Sam.

Six hours later, Rev. Hobhouse was rescued by the massed membership of the Atlantic UFO Alliance, which had gathered on Battlesbury Hill near Warminster in anticipation of another amazing UFO sighting.

'The Alternative Society of the Planet Earth bids you welcome, o alien being,' proclaimed Sid Tosh, while the alternative assembly hummed the communication theme from *Close Encounters of the Third Kind*.

'I'll burn down his bloody knacker's yard!' replied the Vicar.

'A strange greeting from an intergalactic traveller,' thought Sid to himself. 'Perhaps he got stuck in a time warp.'

Realising that this time they might have gone just a little too far, the BADCAT committee members hastily dismantled their DASTARD systems. Holmesmead people noticed a distinct upsurge in their quality of life following the restoration of drainpipes, telephone links and JCB, and in both parishes life began to return to normal. Nevertheless the recent events could not be overlooked and they were directly responsible for the meeting convened between the Bishop and Col. Sir Malcolm Swaffham-Prior, MP for Cripplegate and Pitherdale.

Hitherto Sir Malcolm had been more than content to leave Barleybridge to its own devices. Nearly all the villagers voted Tory because they had always done so; this corner of the constituency took care of itself, freeing Sir Malcolm to concentrate his attention on the grouse on Heathhowe Moor. Until the time came for their MP to blast them out of the sky each grouse was cosseted, nurtured and guarded. No bird could hope for better representation in Parliament, for of the ten questions tabled by Sir Malcolm during his long career no less than eight pertained to grouse. He viewed the Falkland Islands as grouse moors of immense potential and offered to send his two best gamekeepers with the British expeditionary force. Now, however, he was obliged to take account of his human constituents.

'I don't know what the RAF thought they were playing at,' snapped the Bishop. 'Repairs to the Vicarage will cost £60,000. The Church Commissioners are furious. They were just waiting for old Hobhouse to retire to sell it off as luxury apartments.'

'I'll sort something out with the Air Ministry chaps,' promised Sir Malcolm. 'Incidentally, I hear that your vicar was blown more than two hundred miles away and still escaped unharmed. How on earth did he manage that?'

'God knows,' replied the Bishop.

Faced with the loss of two incredibly costly aircraft, embarrassing questions in both Houses and a hostile press ('Fighter Ace Zaps Unmarried Vicar in Raunchy Village of Fear', the minister announced that low flying over Pitherdale had been suspended 'owing to geological difficulties'.

Sadly, however, the matter was not allowed to rest. The contacts between BADCAT and the Soviet Union had not failed to escape the attentions of MI $6^7/_8$, the most secret of the security services. As soon as it was realised that Soviet fighters were not involved in the Tornado incident and the NATO retaliatory attack was cancelled then MI $6^7/_8$ began its own investigation. (I confess that I would never had known of the existence of this organisation had I not attended the same Lodge as Jimmy Arkwright, who tells me that he joined MI $6^7/_8$ after failing his stoker's examination in the Merchant Navy. Fortunately for him, a Winchester and Oxford education still counts for something, in certain quarters at least.)

The first hint that something strange was afoot emerged when Sam Pullan shot a crow. He had noticed it perched immobile on the same branch above his yard for ten days, and fearing that it was a victim of amnesia and must shortly die of hunger or boredom he peppered it with his 16-bore shotgun. The outcome was not a puff of feathers and gore but a noisy flash and a shower of transistors.

'I 'ope they doan't start mekkin' pheasants like yon!'
he muttered.

Meanwhile bugs had been installed in the cracks between
the planks of Amos Raw's privy.

'Listen to this,' said Agent Black, starting the tape
recording.

'Disgusting old devil!' replied Agent Orange.

'No, I think it's in code.'

For six months MI $6^7/_8$ attempted to crack the code by
which Amos communicated his instructions to Jim Clough.
Even the Pentagon computers were unable to unravel the
messages. Eventually the investigations were called off, the
entire resources of MI $6^7/_8$ being redirected to Bideford,
where a group of pensioners were suspected of attempting
to organise a boycott of South African grapes. Nonetheless, a further three months elapsed before Mrs Fawcett
discovered the micro transmitter secreted in her wooden
leg by Agent Blue, who thought she might be stumping in
morse. And Barleybridge is still scanned by a closed-circuit
television camera mounted high in the church spire. Few
but Danny Kendal know that the pictures which reach MI
$6^7/_8$ headquarters in Cheltenham have been rerouted via
satellite dish and a distant cousin and reveal panoramas of
life in Jubilation township, Wisconsin.

From the Yorkshire Gazette, *10 September 1978*
Pitherdale Gleanings by 'Dalesbred Tup'

How fortunate are we in Pitherdale to be represented
in Parliament by a gentleman of the calibre of Col. Sir
Malcolm Swaffham-Prior, MC, MP. Of late I have noticed that
constituency associations have selected some very curious
candidates: estate agents, merchant bankers and property
speculators – those sorts of people. One of the current
Conservative MPs was even associated with a union for
airline pilots, and a very odd bird he looks too! A gentleman?
I doubt it! He reminds me more of Mr Moreton, the Pitherdale
undertaker.

Last week Sir Malcolm demonstrated the courage which made him a legend in the messes of Naples and Rome. Plans are afoot to re-open the Grey Scar quarries, but because of fears that the noise of blasting might create a disturbance, a trial blast was arranged on Thursday last. We gentlemen of the press assembled to observe the event from a cordoned area 200 yards from the quarry face. Arriving hurriedly from the adjacent grouse moors, Sir Malcolm inserted his shooting-stick beside a red flag which he presumed had been erected to mark his observation station. He then ordered the quarry manager to stop flapping about and get on with things as there were still birds waiting to be shot on Heathhowe Moor.

The explosion was indeed tremendous, and when the dust had settled we saw Sir Malcolm still perched resolutely on his shooting-stick but partly buried in rubble. He was not at all pleased by the course of events, and I fancy that the quarry will not re-open.

Once extracted, Sir Malcolm made directly for the Pick and Shovel. Concerned, as ever, to discover the views of his constituents he enquired the landlord's opinion of the quarrying issue. Mine host, a gentleman of questionable stock, had the audacity to inform Sir Malcolm that the racket of grouse shooting was far more annoying than any noise that ever came from the quarry. A lesser gentleman than Sir Malcolm might have had the scoundrel beaten on the spot, but he simply instructed the landlord to attend to his customers and then noted down his name. I have little doubt that when Sir Humphrey Stoat is informed of the incident we shall see a new landlord installed in double quick time!

I see that the 'popular press' is still making a meal of the little affair involving Sir Malcolm and the hang glider fellow. The tabloid journalists all miss the point that this man was *disturbing the birds*. Under the circumstances Sir Malcolm's reaction was perfectly understandable: he did not shoot to kill, and a near-complete recovery is not ruled out. I am not at all surprised that PC Clapperton refused to investigate the complaint against Sir Malcolm – and the Keighley police should have left things to the local bobby. They had no business on Heathhowe Moor and if Sir Malcolm says he mistook them for poachers, that is good enough for me. As soon as Sergeant

141

Lowcock is released from hospital the entire issue should be forgotten. Had the national press covered the story in a dispassionate way, they would at least have given Sir Malcolm due credit for the twenty–two brace of grouse he bagged that day. I rest my case!

11

In which we meet the Black Dog and its fellow travellers, while graves are dug in unlikely places

Autumn slips gently into Pitherdale. By mid-October the oaks in the riverside pastures are amber. Bright amber. This is a sweet but soulful time. It could be the finest season of the year, but it is stalked ever closer by the looming spectre of a winter which is long, bleak and reluctant to relinquish its grip despite whatever the calendar may command.

The autumn following the vicarage incident brought fieldfares, redwings and Sid and Janice Tosh. The amber of the oaks, the reds of the dogwood and guelder rose and the yellow of the horse-chestnuts could scarcely rival the psychedelic swirls which enlivened the Tosh dormobile as it jolted to its appointed anchorage outside one of the empty chalets in Arthur Beckwith's meadow. Sid and Janice had come to pursue research for their forthcoming book *God's Spaceman is Here!* This deals, of course, with the miraculous arrival of Rev. Hobhouse on Battlesbury Hill and, more important still, the first third of the £20,000 advance from Pentagram Publishing is already nestling sweetly in the Tosh bank account in Jersey.

As many will already know, Sid and Janice are the leading prophets of Ufology, the occult, alternative archaeology, geomancy and a host of other potty but lucrative fields of psychic study. They first captured the impressionable imagination with their book *Divine Starlight*, which proved quite conclusively that God resides on the planet Mumbo in the Crab nebula and that apostles visit the Earth regularly in flying saucers. Their second book, *Earthforce Theology*, demonstrated no less conclusively that God lives in a cavern six miles beneath Glastonbury Tor and manifests his benign powers along a radiating network of ley lines. It was eagerly devoured by the same 50,000 readers who had already invested in *Divine Starlight*, each of whom accepts every sentence, phrase and comma of both books and sees no contradiction between the two theses on offer.

Subsequent works of Tosh scholarship have shown beyond doubt that the dinosaurs were all exterminated by a blast of cosmic energy released from a stranded UFO; that the stones of Stonehenge were transported from Surbiton and erected on Salisbury Plain by the powers of telepathy transmitted by druids; that the London underground system utilises burrows dug by mystical Martian mega-worms; that God inhabits a disused gasometer on the outskirts of Weybridge and exterminated the dinosaurs in a fit of pique; and that the Loch Ness monster travels by underground tunnels to Fewston reservoir near Harrogate whenever scientific investigations disturb its home waters.

What is the secret of the Toshes' literary and scholastic success? One factor appears to be a total disregard for sterile, mind-constricting facts. A second is the frequent use of the phrases 'could it not be' and 'it has been said' to preface any claims which the narrow scientific mind might regard as preposterous and unsupportable. The third Tosh talent is described by Sid (who claims to be a reincarnation of Windy Bison, a Red Indian wigwam contractor and soothsayer) as 'mind over matter'. In more prosaic terms this involves using the imagination rather than tedious research to discover the hidden truths. A demonstration of the Tosh powers of deduction and communication is encapsulated in the following passage from *Divine Earthforce*.

Silbury Hill near mystical Avebury is the largest artificial hill in Europe. When we clambered up to its dark towering summit at the dawning of the winter solstice, once more to celebrate rebirth of the world with a ritual meal of mushrooms gathered from the Andean plains of Nazca, we were seized by a strange psychic power. Little Tarquin Geronimo Tosh was violently sick, and though onlookers blamed the mushrooms, we knew

144

better! It has been said that at the moment of the sunrise the earthforces converge on the legendary summit and strange beasts, like orang-utans and bandicoots, materialise from the morning mists. Janice was sure that she saw an aardvark, but it had metamorphosed into a golden labrador by the time my camera was ready (see Plate XVI).

Silbury Hill lies on a ley line linking Stonehenge and the village of Lydford Millicent – the same village where Tarquin Geronimo was sick in the dormobile on the way to the Feminist Witchcraft festival on Whitehorse Hill. And this is also the *very same* village where Janice experienced a cosmic awareness that the petrol pump attendant was a reincarnation of Sitting Bull, Chief of the Sioux nation. Plainly the location of Silbury Hill is of the greatest psychic significance. Moreover, it lies almost midway between the Uffington White Horse and Battlesbury Hill, a site famed for many UFO sightings and the selfsame place where Tarquin Geronimo had a psycho-gastric experience during the Alternative Muesli Eat-In there.

In *The Tunnels From Space* (Pentagram, 1982) we explained how the dragon power earthforce travels in tunnels beneath the ley lines, tunnels which were excavated by gigantic moles transported here telepathically from the planet Venus (the same moles which excavated the London underground system). As we stood there that midwinter morning in the rising dawn, celebrating Tarquin Geronimo's latest gastro-paranormal event and spying for aardvarks, the truth was suddenly implanted in our minds by a divine power. Could it not be that Silbury Hill is a mega-molehill erected at the convergence of the dragon power tunnels – a cosmic molehill which yet endures as a timeless monument to the Venusian moles? The so-called 'archaeologists' in their ivory towers of Babel may deny this psychic truth – but what sane womun [sic] or man-person could seriously question the facts recorded here?

(Reproduced by kind permission of Pentagram Publishing)

Those who are not discomforted by Sid's penchant for Red Indian costumes, hallucinogenic mushrooms and herbal cheroots may find him to be quite a jovial fellow (indeed, it was he who suggested using horse liniment diluted in holy water as a treatment for woodworm in the organ loft. This proved quite efficacious, for clearly the woodworms liked the smell no better than did the congregation.)

Janice Tosh is more of an acquired taste. Her conversation is largely limited to certain incantations, mainly of a feminist nature. She relies upon her vocation as a self-employed witch for social impact, and in her principal stamping grounds of Chelsea, Cambridge and Glastonbury this is most effective. Recordings of these sessions reveal that the following types of encounter are commonplace:

> *Janice*: Hi! I'm Janice, Witch and Womun-psychic.
> *Emma/Charlotte/Sara*: Wow! Far out! Gosh! I can't believe it! Damian and Diana, come quickly, there's someone you've just *got* to meet. This is Janice, she's a real live *witch*! Too much! Yah?
> *Damian/Diana*: Hi, Janice! Have some of these pro-fiteroles, they're really ever so more-ish!
> *Janice*: I'm a vegan witch. I only eat Tibetan rice and Kosher-killed vegetables.
> *Everybody*: Yah? Wow! You absolutely must come to our psychotherapy talk-in on Thursday!

In Barleybridge, however, Janice has found that her vocation inflicts rather less of an impact, and the following conversation was overhead outside the village shop.

'Hi! I'm Janice, witch and womun-psychic.'

'Are you, dear?' replied Mrs Holroyd. 'I'm a Methodist, though my Albert is C of E, but he stopped going after Rev. Hobhouse arrived. Our son-in-law in Cripplegate is a Jehovah's witness, but perhaps that's not the same? Anyway, I do wish that Mrs Reynard would keep her cat out of the carrot bag. Must dash now, I promised Mrs Fawcett I'd get some teak oil for her leg.'

'Are you coming to my feminist teach-in on Thursday?' enquired Janice.

'Sorry dear, Thursday is bath night and if I'm not there to squeeze the blackheads in Albert's back he'll say he itches all through the weekend,' replied Mrs Holroyd. 'Ta-Ta!'

Once Sid and Janice had convinced their editor at Pentagram that readers would flock in thousands to discover the facts surrounding Rev. Hobhouse, the astronaut, they then grudgingly accepted that the 'mind over matter' technique should this time be supplemented by research of a more mundane nature. Sadly, the Vicar proved to be uncooperative and reticent regarding his space adventures, mentioning only his revitalised enthusiasm for the excommunication of Sam Pullan. When Janice was overheard pestering the gravedigger, Joshua Pickersgill, for any spare bones that he might happen to dig up, relations with Rev. Hobhouse reached a low ebb. And when she invited the Sherman daughters to join her at midnight beneath the Hardcastle tomb for a spot of devil worship they hit rock bottom.

'Bring a sacrificial cockerel,' she bade, but instead they brought their mother. Janice Tosh was caught red-handed, along with a bottle of best communion wine that the Vicar had been storing in the cool of the vestry for future consumption with his Christmas turkey, and also with the bones of Enoch Pickles (1748–1843). Rev. Hobhouse appealed to the Bishop for permission to stage a double excommunication ritual, but he caught the Bishop in one of his ecumenical moods and had to settle for a reconsecration of the Pickles grave instead.

'It's a scandal,' he complained later to an equally indignant Mrs Sherman. 'Instead of letting me get on and excommunicate the two blackguards – and her drug-crazed husband too, for good measure – he prattled on about the need to create a broad church which could embrace all the creeds from witchcraft to shamanism!'

'My poor, dear Despond still feels quite unclean,' replied the harassed mother.

'I nivver kenned them were owd Enoch's bones. I thowt yan o' owd Nelson Beckwith's pigs must've burrowed in to t' churchyard and deed underground. I 'eard tell as 'ow there were plenty o' burrowing pig in t'owden days,' explained Joshua, unconvincingly, to his Vicar. 'An' any road 'e were lucky to get buried in t'churchyard in t'fust place. It were owd Enoch as put that polecat in Mr 'Ardcastle's bedpan. That's t'fust Mr 'Ardcastle, sitha, an' when 'e went . . .

'You're fired,' barked the Vicar.

'Suit thissen. Any road, I'm near deed wi' backwark. I'm ninety-fower, tha knows,' retorted Joshua, shouldering his spade, turning for home and wondering if the Vicar knew that it was really Clifford Spittlehouse who had put the polecat in the Hardcastle bedpan. Or was it Amos Pullan? One thing was certain: if he died and the Vicar had *still* not employed a new gravedigger then he would surely sue. He certainly did not intend to be left hanging around in his coffin just because the Vicar had sacked the best gravedigger in Pitherdale. 'An' he needn't reckon as 'ow I shall get up an' dig it missen,' he resolved.

Despite the Vicar's unecumenical attitude towards the black mass, Sid was proving to be a most popular, if colourful, character. Each evening he held court in the Pack Horse at Bishopgate, buying rounds with gay abandon for a group of companions which expanded as the news of his largesse spread. Only one cloud darkened the horizon, the complete failure of the Hobhouse investigation – and as November advanced, so the cloud grew bigger and blacker. Meanwhile, however, Sid was regaled with tales of sheep dipping, poaching, unofficial angling and many morsels of Pitherdale lore. He certainly felt more at ease amongst his new chums than he had when leading his seminars on UFOs and ley lines in Hampstead or Cambridge.

The first heavy snowfall came early, and once the landlord was satisfied that all the roads to Cripplegate were firmly sealed with snowdrifts he stoked up the fire and broached a new barrel.

'On a neet like this I reckon t'owd Barguest'll be lowpin' down Pitherdale High Road,' said Sam Pullan, tapping his pipe on the fender.

'The Barguest?' queried Sid, wondering if any more guests could be crammed into this cosy little public bar.

'Aye,' said Hector Ewbank, 't'Barguest. T'black dog o' Pitherdale. Ivverybody knaws abaht t'Barguest.'

Sam then explained that the Barguest was a phantom

148

black dog, as large as a bull calf with huge red eyes like dinner plates. Moreover, he proclaimed, the Barguest had stalked Pitherdale High Road since time immemorial and all who saw it were instantly killed and turned to stone. At this point the critical onlooker might have enquired how, if all who saw it were killed, there were so many Barleybridgians around who knew exactly what the dog looked like. Warming to this theme he or she might also have asked what had happened to all the petrified bodies – surely they would have come in handy as fence posts or as pit props for the lead mines on Heathhowe Moor?

Sid, however, asked no such questions, for already his fertile mind was exploring ways in which his commissioned work on the intergalactic parson could be redefined as a definitive and lucrative investigation of the black dog phenomenon.

Fired with new-found enthusiasm, Sid erected an old lavatory tent in the snowdrifts beside Pitherdale High Road and prepared for his vigil. He even gave up his Andean mushrooms, just to be sure that any dogs, snakes or aardvarks that he might see would be real ones. There he sat with his camera for three freezing nights, icicles growing from his nose and headdress, shivering from cold and from mushroom-withdrawal symptoms. But no black dog came by. On the fourth night he sought solace in the Pack Horse, where he confessed that his mission to Barleybridge had proved a failure. Janice had heard a rumour of a giant lobster living in a sewage farm near Basingstoke, so at the end of the month they were off to Hampshire to investigate.

This news, with its forebodings of an end to the free drinks at the Pack Horse, cast a long shadow on the merry band. Sam Pullan summed up the situation admirably for Hector Ewbank. 'No Barguest, no Sid; no Sid, no ale. Think on.' Sam thought on and the answer came to him whilst skinning an Aberdeen Angus bullock.

'It's me, 'Ector, Sam,' he barked down the phone. 'Na' then, 'ave they still got yon Alsatian guard dog, Champ, up at 'Ardcastle 'All? Aye, well, kep t'beggar, will tha, an' bring it ower 'ere.'

149

Sam then gave Champ a good meal of offal and released him at the Summerthwaite end of Pitherdale High Road to see if he would come back to the yard for more. Within a couple of days the Alsatian could be relied upon to return to the knacker's yard whenever he was released. And while Champ practised his homing routine Sam was at work tailoring his black bullock-skin costume with luminous red eyes fashioned from bicycle reflectors.

A blizzard was raging outside when Sam burst into the Pack Horse. 'It's 'owling t'neet,' he announced to the public bar sages.

'Aye,' agreed Fred Tinkler. 'It's a reet lazy wind an' no mistake.'

'Not t'wind, beggar t'wind, it's t'Barguest! It sounded like it were 'owling reet behind me when I come down t' 'Igh Road.'

Sid was off to his tent like a shot.

Meanwhile as Champ plodded along the High Road, thinking of offal and pausing to scratch at the safety pins securing his heavy black overcoat, he became aware of a companion following close behind: a huge black dog the size of a pony with red eyes like headlamps.

Now we all know that dogs cannot talk – in fact they do not need to since they communicate by a form of canine telepathy. Should anyone doubt this simple fact let him ask himself if he ever saw a dog that was not perfectly well aware of what another dog nearby was up to? No. And so it was that high on the ancient snow-lashed trackway the following canine conversation took place.

'Ow do. Ow is t'?' greeted Champ.

'Oh, fair to middlin', tha knaws,' replied the Barguest.

'By 'eck, it's a bit parky t'neet,' added Champ.

'Aye,' agreed the Barguest. 'It's been reet floudby these last fower days. Me paws are fairly dazzened.'

The Barguest then explained to Champ that he had been patrolling Pitherdale High Road for the last three thousand years, though he could no longer remember just why. 'It were a sight better afore t'Romans came, tha knaws,' he exclaimed. 'Stinkin' up t'place wi olive oil an' spaghetti, pokin' their gurt noses into other folk's business

150

an' sikelike. That's where t' rot set in, I'll warrand.' He then proposed that all the talk about turning folk into stone was a load of nonsense created by the sensationalising Victorian press. 'I'd drop into owd Cliff Spittlehouse's place for pie and peas ivvery Friday neight regular till that lot started. Appen I'd take 'im a rabbit or summat. But after yon article in t'*Yorkshire Gazette* it all changed. An' then I got blamed for biting off young Clarence 'Ardcastle's nose when ivverybody should 'ave kenned 'e stuck it in a moletrap – an' now I can't even 'owl wi'out folks start weaking. It's a reet bad job an' no mistake. Any road, Champ, tha looks a reet big girl's blouse i' that get up. Why doan't tha nip off 'ome an' leave t'Barguest lark to t'professional?'

Champ, who had begun to take more than a passing interest in Trusty, was only too pleased to concur, leaving the Barguest to pad alone along the High Road. When he saw Sid's tent he reacted like any normal dog and cocked his leg, but was surprised by the stifled cry from within. Soon, however, the phantom dog and the famous author had established a fine rapport, based in part on a mutual enthusiasm for Andean mushrooms and herbal cheroots. The Barguest howled obligingly into Sid's tape recorder and posed in a spectrum of canine stances. 'Just one more of you scratching,' requested Sid before he departed, leaving the Barguest alone in a hallucinogenic haze.

'I saw it!' shouted Sid as he burst in upon the early morning festivities in the snowbound Pack Horse.

'Aye,' replied Sam. 'I thowt tha would.'

The jovial congregation from the Pack Horse staggered homewards at dawn, the Barleybridge contingent sledging rumbustiously down Oldborough Hill on a door borrowed from Amos Raw's barn. The Barguest, however, spent a more harrowing night huddled up in Sid's tent, his innate fear of ghosts heightened by the evening's psychedelic hospitality, so that he was greatly relieved to dematerialise again at sunrise.

151

Withdrawal symptoms of a different kind were beginning to affect poor Joshua Pickersgill, whose plight we have overlooked amid all the excitement of the Barguest incident. A gravedigger for seventy-eight years and now cast uncaringly into the ranks of the unemployed at the age of ninety-four, it is not surprising that his excavatory urges had become ingrained. At first he had slung his long-handled spade into a corner, but soon he was glancing at it, then sharpening it, and before very long he found himself waiting outside for the store to open.

''As anyone deed, Mrs Reynard, does tha knaw?' he asked hopefully.

'Sorry, Josh, nowt doin' today. Mrs Bickerstaff 'as a touch o' gout but vitinery give 'er some 'oss pills an' e' says 'e's quite 'opeful.'

Joshua then offered to dig Mr Reeth's garden for him, but after elevenses he was obliged to depart. All his talents were for digging downwards, not sideways.

'It woan't do, Josh, it woan't do at all. It's tatties I'm efter plantin', not giraffes,' said Mr Reeth, rolling away the boulders from his cabbage patch.

In the course of the next few days deep coffin-shaped holes began to materialise in many parts of the parish. Of these the most regrettable was the one which appeared at the end of Mrs Fawcett's garden path, so that when she went to put out Tigger both cat and mistress vanished from view. She was followed in rapid succession by the milkman, the postman and the paper boy – and Fred Tinkler's tractor and tow-rope were needed to haul them all out. Amos Raw was the next to suffer an involuntary entombment, disappearing from the scene en route for his place of contemplation. Only by grabbing the tail of a passing bullock was he able to extract himself in time for dinner. The most socially divisive of the excavatory incidents occurred when Janice Tosh descended into the unknown outside the churchyard and landed on Rev. Hobhouse, who had been trapped there for quite some time. Her cries for help took the form of full-blooded incantations to the pagan goddess, Annis, and the louder Janice bawled the louder the Vicar chanted his exorcism ritual.

Eventually Mrs Shutt (whose eyesight is becoming quite a problem) attributed the resonant wailing to one of the periodic cat fights involving Tigger and Claws and hurled a bucket of water in the direction of the clamour. Both parties involved in the subterranean clash of theologies then claimed to have achieved divine intervention and the wailing only increased. It did not subside until 'Fatty' Holroyd also fell down the hole and the rivals ascended to freedom via his braces.

Fatty himself was extracted using a block, tackle and sheerlegs fashioned from Holmesmead telegraph poles. Mr Gavestone was responsible for this engineering feat and for wisely resisting Danny Kendal's offer of an extraction by means of what he termed a 'controlled explosion'.

Native Barleybridgians are tolerant of each other's little eccentricities. They sympathised with Joshua's plight and deplored his dismissal after so many years of good service. After all, most of them had former relatives accommodated in his custom-dug holes, and none of those thus interred had ever complained. Unfortunately, however, the matter came to a head when Joshua's excavatory urges led him to Pitherdale Garth. Mr Hewitt's BMW collapsed into a coffin-shaped cavity and broke its back axle – and when Mr Hewitt replaced it with the latest Volvo a wasteful spasm of car-buying ricocheted round the Garth just weeks before a new registration letter was due. When Mrs Sherman announced her intention of having Joshua certified insane and removed from the community a special meeting of the Parish Council was urgently convened.

Fred Tinkler suggested that should a new epidemic of the Black Death break out then Barleybridge would need all the graves it could get its hands on. However, Mr Gavestone reminded the meeting from the floor that the last outbreak of the pestilence in Barleybridge had occurred in 1537 and that the Council should neither tempt fate nor place its trust in the improbable. Amos Raw generously offered to let Joshua dig all the graves he liked in the stony patch in the corner of Poverty Furlong, but Arthur Beckwith pointed out that the excavations had taken on a random and unpredictable pattern. Sam Pullan argued that the excavatory process was not entirely aimless: Joshua had started studying the obituary columns in the *Pitherdale Messenger* and had been seen taking down the numbers of cars that visited Mr Moreton's funeral parlour.

'Empty 'oles is bad enough, but 'oles wi' folks in as doan't want to be there is goin' too far. It's a rum do an' no mistake!'

And so the meeting rumbled on. Eventually, just as the deliberations seemed in danger of becoming diverted into the quicksands of the barn situation, Mr Gavestone made a second intervention from the floor.

'I have in my hand a crematorium covenant,' he declared, adopting a Chamberlain-like stance and brandishing a large document. He then proposed that all the villagers should sign the covenant, declaring their intention to be cremated. ('No, Mrs Reynard, don't worry, only *after* you are dead.') He also reminded the assembly that there was nothing Rev. Hobhouse liked better than a good burial, and if the Vicar would only give Joshua his job back then the covenant rather than the villagers could go to the crematorium.

So once again common sense wedded to communal action emerged triumphant. Joshua signed a pledge undertaking not to dispose of bones without the written permission of the Parochial Church Council – and both Janice Tosh and Joshua's dog, Patch, were poorer for it. Otherwise the old man was able to return to the churchyard and grumble about his backache and the problems of digging in frozen ground.

'Next 'un 'll be me,' he muttered as he tidied the wreaths on Reg Barker's grave. But Joshua was far from ready to occupy the hole that he had dug for himself on the sunny south side of the chancel, for the next day he was poised and waiting outside the Pitherdale Emporium.

'Owt doin' today, Mrs Reynard?'

'Well, Martha Lewty says 'er grandad's maffly an' showin' no signs o' leetening. T'vitinery say's there's nowt more as 'e can do an' they're thinking on callin' t'doctor.'

'Aye, it comes to us all i' t'end. Let us knaw if Mr

Moreton rings. I just 'ope t'owd beggar can hod out till it thaws.'

From the Yorkshire Gazette, *12 April 1987*
Pitherdale Gleanings by 'Dalesbred Tup'

Pitherdale is in the news again following the recent publication of *The Black Dog Mystery Revealed* by Sid and Janice Tosh. For the last fortnight the ancient trackway known as Pitherdale High Road has been overrun by visitors hoping to glimpse the Barguest. Mr Pullan, a local parish councillor and livestock terminator, was complaining to me bitterly last Thursday about the intrusions on his solitude. But now I see that he has erected a sign, 'Feed the Barguest, £5', outside his premises and is charging customers £7.50 for small bags of offal with which to accomplish the feeding. There are two facts which I feel I should make quite clear. Firstly, visitors tell me that the mistal in which the black, Alsatian-sized beast resides is extremely dark. Secondly, our Mr Pullan does enjoy a certain local reputation for entrepreneurship of the less discriminating kind.

People in Barleybridge are amazed that strangers should be so preoccupied with the Barguest. It has been around for as long as I can remember without provoking a great deal of interest. Frankly I would have thought the phantom camel of Heathhowe Moor to be a much more exotic apparition and I am bound to agree with Mr Reeth that 'There's nowt so queer as folks'.

Competing for space in the Cripplegate bookshops with the Tosh volume is yet another tedious exposé of Freemasonry; again I fail to see what all the fuss is about. With my extensive local knowledge I must take issue with the author regarding what he chooses to describe as 'the Cripplegate cover-up'. There were perfectly good reasons why Chief Inspector Currie was not charged after reversing into the royal motorcade outside the car park of the Square and Compass. His Royal Highness suffered no more than a broken wrist and Superintendent Grimes conducted a thorough investigation, as any member of the Cripplegate force will testify. We should trust in the integrity of our custodians and desist from such muckraking, say I!

This brings me to the contemptible allegations that I am myself a Freemason and have used my column to publicise the commercial enterprises of my fellow masons. I shall treat these slanders with the contempt they deserve, unless compelled to place matters in the invariably capable hands of Messrs Scarsdale and Scarsdale (125 Crown Street, Cripplegate).

As well as sustaining a most active and socially beneficial Lodge, Cripplegate also harbours branches of the Foresters, Lions, Oddfellows, Gibbons and Emperor Penguins. No gentleman with a respectable background in business or commerce has any excuse for failing to take advantage of the stimulating social contacts and opportunities for charitable works which such organisations provide. Certainly ladies are excluded from some of these institutions – far better that they should be allowed to get on with knitting and the planning of menus than be involved in serious matters and conversations that they simply would not understand.

On my last visit to Cripplegate I was privileged to enter a new cake shop on Victoria Street, recently opened by Mr Hubert Apron. The parkin displayed was of an exceptional quality, likewise the yule cake and scones. Mr Apron allowed me to sample his exquisite funeral cakes, and he tells me that these can be ordered at short notice and delivered to the appropriate venue, simply by telephoning Cripplegate 321123. I fancy that competing confectioners must look to their laurels! The Cakestand is at 128 Victoria Street, between Quikchange Tyres and the gents of the Square and Compass.

12

In which lunacy returns to Hardcastle Hall and a whist drive ensues

From the Yorkshire Gazette, *4 September 1953*
Pitherdale Gleanings by 'Dalesbred Tup'

Last week Sam Wharton and Herbert Farrar returned to Barleybridge having completed their National Service with the Green Howards. They will doubtless be delighted to discover that proper standards of military discipline are still observed in their native village. For those unfamiliar with our little ways let me explain that at 9 a.m. prompt the landau bearing Brigadier Humphrey Hardcastle departs the gates of Hardcastle Hall for the Brigadier's morning inspection of the village. By this hour all windows on the estate must be cleaned and all doorsteps holystoned. Village housewives, properly attired in freshly starched aprons, are expected to be on station at their front doors to acknowledge and curtsey to their master as he passes by. The village inspection culminates at the surgery of Dr Earl, where the Brigadier reviews the sick parade. Any tenants suspected of malingering, or those whose services are considered essential on the day in question, are dismissed from the ranks of the infirm and marched back to their duties in the charge of the head gardener, Mr Clifford Umpleby.

As well as ensuring that the village operates according to well-proven military principles, Brigadier Hardcastle is also responsible for civil defence matters in the community. In the event of a Russian invasion it is anticipated that the authorities will inform Mrs Reynard at the Pitherdale Emporium and Post Office. Should the invasion occur on Wednesday half-closing it is hoped that they will remember to contact Mr Swires at the Hardcastle Arms instead. Once the invasion is announced the Hardcastle Hall gardeners must immediately evacuate the contents of the orchid house, pineapple house and orangery into the security of the Hall cellars. Only then will the park gates be opened, allowing villagers to take up defensive stations round the Hall. The gun room will be opened and the more trustworthy servants and tenants will be armed, with small parties being despatched to guard the most strategically significant objectives: the bridge, the vicarage, the cricket club roller and the telephone box. Meanwhile, the Brigadier will co-ordinate operations from his secret bunker beneath the family mausoleum. This will ensure that if an atom bomb falls on Barleybridge he will not have to rely on there being survivors to bury him in the proper place.

Last week Hardcastle Hall provided the venue for the garden party of the Cripplegate and Pitherdale Conservative Association, which was honoured by the attendance of our member of Parliament, Col. Sir Malcolm Swaffham-Prior. A cold collation of peacock, grouse, salmon, heron and widgeon flesh was served, the *piéce de résistance* being an osprey in oyster sauce, shot by the Brigadier himself and believed to be the last of its kind to reside in these parts. The choir of Barleybridge church, clad in new blue cassocks, was graciously allowed to enter the park to entertain the guests with a rendition of 'There'll Always be an England', and pupils of Barleybridge Church of England School were then admitted to perform a modern mystery play in which Mr Churchill replaces St George and Mr Atlee substitutes for the Bragging Turk.

After the conclusion of the festivities morsels were salvaged from the platters, gathered together in a cauldron and heated to produce a most nutritious stew. In keeping with custom this stew was then served to villagers assembled on the green, with Brigadier Hardcastle himself condescending to serve the first ladle. The company sang 'For He's a Jolly Good Fellow' and gave their master three rousing cheers as his landau departed. Owing to the indisposition of his father the speech of gratitude to the now departed Brigadier was given by young Mr Amos Raw, who praised the qualities of natural fertilisers and informed the gathering that he does not believe that the tractor is any more than a passing fancy. Estate workers and tenants were allowed to stay up until 10.30 p.m.

while domestic servants were permitted to attend two church services on Sunday.

The months and seasons following the death of Sir Cecil Hardcastle saw many a crisis come and go, or come and stay. We have described the affairs involving the Hardcastle Arms, the new Vicar and the low-flying aircraft, and those concerning Amos Raw's missing barn, the Vicar's exploding boots and the great Sherman scandal must wait until another day. There is no denying that the normally calm and ordered affairs of the village were stalked by a sense of unease. The epicentre of the unease was Hardcastle Hall, for the house which once seemed to cast a commanding but caring eye across the parish stood cold and gaunt, its great windows blind like the empty eye-sockets in a mouldering skull. Without a Hardcastle to tell them what to do or to keep the rascals at bay the old villagers felt just a little vulnerable and insecure. True, it was good to own one's cottage, to be able to paint the door red if one chose and not to be summoned from slumber at 3 a.m. to join the tenantry in a hunt round the Hall and park for a missing monocle or ear trumpet. It was good not to have to muzzle all your animals for a Hardcastle farm inspection – especially the chickens which were so hard to catch. And it was good not to have to struggle through the snowdrifts in leaking shoes at midnight on Christmas Eve so that the presiding Hardcastle could wish you a Merry Christmas and present you with the time-honoured gift of four currants and a sultana for the Christmas cake (which you had already baked back in October). Even so, the sight of the empty hall on the hill crest was a nagging source of discomfort.

It was a source of greater discomfort to the council members of CON, particularly after they received the estimate for roof repairs.

'Eighty thousand pounds!' thundered Lord Mercia. 'Do you realise how many stag hounds we could feed for that? Dammit, we could buy enough live stags to keep a pack hunting till kingdom come!'

'We could certainly better spend the money on that mobile sauna that Lord Ravenser keeps asking for,' offered Brigadier Twyning-Green. 'I think it's a damnable disgrace if a peer of the realm can't have a good sweat just because we have to maintain a dump built by some upstart cotton-mill oik.'

After the meeting had continued in this vein for a little longer Sir Hamish Aston-Somerville was instructed to investigate the terms under which Sir Cecil had granted his home to CON.

Sir Hamish could hardly conceal his glee when he reported back to the next council meeting. 'No strings, no covenants, no nonsense. It's ours. It's listed, so we can't pull it down. But we can sell it. Let's sell it to some wretched Arab. It was a sheikh that bought that nature reserve from us – they're crazy for stuffed badgers in Dubai. And remember, that's how we got the cash for Lady Wick-Rissington's brain transplant in Cape Town. And her turbo-powered wheelchair, too.'

In the event it was not an Arab who bought Hardcastle Hall but Sir Hamish's cousin Sir Clarence Hemingford-Grey. The price was less than one might have expected – but still sufficient to allow CON to improve the visitor-proof electrified fencing around Hogswallow Hall.

Knighted for his patriotic endeavours, Sir Clarence is a staunch supporter of Mrs Thatcher's health service privatisation policies and he operates a small chain of select hospitals for mentally disturbed gentlefolk. In each of these hospitals he enforces a strict code of patient classification. Class B patients (or 'Barkers') are barking mad and constitute a small minority; Class E inmates are, for whatever reason, an embarrassment to their families, while Class I patients are inheritors – or at least they would be if not certified and confined to one of Sir Clarence's caring institutions. The hospitals are all carefully sited, each being sufficiently removed from centres of aristocratic civilisation like Henley on Thames, Ascot, Cowes, Knightsbridge or Glyndebourne, to be out of sight and out of mind (the last phrase being perhaps an unfortunate choice).

Sir Clarence pursues a strategy of cure through confinement which is based on the premise that patients *may*

160

be cured provided they are completely isolated from all people of consequence, breeding or media connections for a sufficiently long period. However, since none of his patients has yet *been* cured in this manner there is no way of knowing how long the critical quarantine period really is. On the other hand, since very few of the inmates are mad anyway it would be unfair to expect that they could be cured. After fifteen years of operation the medical statistics for Sir Clarence's hospitals are as follows:

Admitted	Cured	Escaped	Recaptured
1,837	0	4	3

The sole successful escapee was a Class B inmate, Humphrey Wildbloode, who soon gained a post as a district organiser for the National Front and is now the director of one of the nation's security services.

Following the repair of the walls round the park, the barring of its windows and the erection of sophisticated security devices, such as barbed wire and watch towers, the Hardcastle Hall Refuge for Unbalanced Gentlefolk was ready for business. The inmates were shipped in sealed coaches, the curtains of which were opened as soon as the South Yorkshire boundary was crossed and the passengers deemed safe from the gaze of any people of consequence. Medical equipment, in the form of a gross of white coats and several crates of powerful sedatives, followed in the armour-plated ambulance driven by the newly appointed Overseer, Dr Gavin Bracegirdle. He is one of only a dozen or so private hospital directors to hold a mail-order doctorate in numismatics from the University of Pocahontas, Arkansas; his academic career blossomed after a dispiriting start when his original doctoral submission was rejected as a consequence of his failure to enclose the required stamped and self-addressed envelope.

The Refuge had been open for only a few days when 'Nutty' Ramsbottom appeared at the gates on a lead and in the custody of his relatives from Holmesmead. 'We've decided to 'ave 'im put away, like,' announced old Horace Ramsbottom. ''E's started bringing back rats agin an' we can't be doing wi' all his pig-killing antics when folks come round efter chapel on Sundays.' Dr Bracegirdle took one look at the gumboots and threadbare clothing of the Ramsbottom Brigade and another at Nutty, now deeply immersed in one of his toad impersonations, and slammed the heavy iron gates.

'We can't have him in here, he's a raving lunatic! This is a respectable mad house. Take him away before he upsets my patients!'

And so the Ramsbottoms trudged despondently back down the hill, apart from Nutty, who hopped in a sprightly manner and had already caught four bluebottles on his tongue by the time they reached the bus stop by the green.

The Barleybridgians were not at all distressed to be sharing their village with the 'loonies'. In fact they were rather relieved to have people of quality re-established in Hardcastle Hall. There was the heir of the Earl of Kensington, the younger brother of the Marquis of Rotting-dean, two self-appointed Lords of the Isles and a throng of titled maiden aunts. Were rumours to be believed, there were even hopes that the royal coat of arms might soon be mounted above the iron gates, and meanwhile there was no denying that several of the most prominent former Hardcastles would quite easily have qualified for admission to Dr Bracegirdle's establishment.

Although relations betwixt the villagers and natives were discouraged – mainly by black-uniformed security guards, who stalked the park permimeter wall with guard dogs – the fraternisation issue was brought into focus by the whist drive organised to raise funds for the woodworm in the organ loft. ('I doan't ken why they want to raise brass for t' woodworms,' grumbled Fred Tinkler. 'There's far too many o' t'lil beggars as it is.') On this occasion misfortune had robbed the community of two of its most resolute whist part-ners: Mrs Fawcett was in a huff after overhearing remarks pertaining to the source of the woodworm, while Mrs Shutt had dislocated her shoulder in attempting to retrieve her second-best Aylesbury duck from a position on the wet side of the U-bend in her lavatory. News of the dilemma filtered through to the Refuge, where two of the inmates expressed a keen interest in filling the vacant places. They were Jervase Fitzallan, who would have succeeded to the Earldom of Melton Mowbray had the Earl not considered him soft on foxes and therefore insane, and Stephen Profit, who was caught by his senior partner and brother reading *Private Eye* at the stockbrokers' banquet.

Their attendance at the whist drive in Barleybridge school was facilitated by Danny Kendal, who organised some modest diversionary explosions while a ladder was slipped over the park wall. The event was well under way before the absence of the two inmates was noted at the 8.30 p.m. pre-sedation roll call. It was not until the whist prize (a Tamworth piglet exquisitely stuffed by Mrs Addyman) was being presented to Jervase and Mrs Armitage that the Cripplegate police burst in upon the rustic gathering. 'You can't mistake them, they are both as mad as hatters,' Dr Bracegirdle had told the sergeant. And so it was that Amos Raw and Mr Gavestone were borne kicking and shouting to the gatehouse of the Hardcastle Refuge, whilst Jervase and Stephen quietly slipped back inside the confines.

As the days rolled by, the presence of the security patrols became increasingly intrusive. Conversations across the park wall concerning vital topics, like how many pigs could be taken to market in a hot-air balloon, whether onions discourage the carrot fly or who invented shoes, were regularly disrupted, along with short-lived plans for whist drives and cricket matches. Matters came to a head as a dowager of impeccably noble birth was just about to impart to Mrs Fawcett the name of the Queen's chiropodist when a Dobermann guard dog made a perfect dental impression in Mrs Fawcett's leg. 'My fault, I suppose, madam, for teaching him to fetch sticks,' apologised the guard. But Mrs Fawcett had resolved that things had already gone too far.

The tunnel began inconspicuously in the graveyard. 'It's for owd Mr Spittlehouse,' lied Joshua Pickersgill to the Vicar. ''E's a big squarish sort o' fellow and 'e asked t' be buried in an 'oss box.' Down and down went the shaft, past ever more distant ancestors of Arthur Beckwith. When it reached the level of Roger de Beckwith (1197–1242) it turned through a right angle and headed towards the derelict ice house on the edge of the park. Mr Reeth was posted on the churchyard steps to intercept the Vicar and divert him away towards Oldborough Hill with tales of a large lop-eared rabbit that had just been seen there. A more challenging problem was posed by the need to dispose of the vast quantities of earth rubble and bones dislodged by Joshua's darting spade. Sam Pullan's dogs took care of the bones, devouring so many of them that Sam swore they were beginning to develop the distinctive Beckwith scowl. The other materials were dumped in the Vicarage cellars, with convoys of wheelbarrows operating a shuttle service whenever Rev. Hobhouse was away on rabbit-watching duties.

Shortly after Joshua broke through the floor of the redundant ice house the tunnel was complete and Mrs Fawcett was able to enter the park, resume her conversation and discover the true identity of the royal chiropodist. Villagers wishing to retrace her footsteps would carry flowers to the grave of Tobias Beckwith (1823–1911), roll aside the grave slab, now mounted on castors from the Vicarage harmonium, and proceed along the tunnel. Inmates of the Refuge making the reverse journey would amble down towards the ice house in a seemingly aimless manner, slip inside and re-emerge in the graveyard.

The system worked admirably until the evening when Mrs Sherman, currently engaged in compiling a report on the state of the churchyard for the Parochial Church Council, was attracted by the fragrant mound of flowers beside Tobias Beckwith's grave. Just as she paused to consider the lillies the graveslab rolled back and the torso of the Hon. Jeremy Pillerton-Priors, clad in his favourite Bengal Lancers uniform, emerged from the grave.

'I just cannot understand it,' said Rev. Hobhouse after he had performed the exorcism ritual and a special cleansing ceremony for a whiter-than-usual Mrs Sherman. 'I could have sworn that there is no history of resurrection in the Beckwith family. They are all such respectable people. Now about that bottle of Mrs Armitage's turnip wine that you won in the organ loft raffle . . .'

This minor inconvenience apart, the Refuge subway system was a great success, though it did result in considerable consternation amongst the medical staff at the pre-sedation roll call. On the evening of the great whist drive for the newly instituted Tobias Beckwith Challenge Trophy the tally at the Refuge was short by eighteen couples. When the Barleybridge CC played a friendly match against an Eton and Harrow Former Pupils XI some forty-three absentees were noted, while during the York races the Refuge was quite devoid of inmates, apart from those in solitary confinement. The villagers delighted in the company of their new acquaintances, but unfortunately the delight was not shared by the custodians.

'The worst thing of all is that the loonies are all turning sane,' confessed the Overseer at his Monday morning staff conference. 'If you ask me, the wall is in the wrong place. It should be around the blasted village. Those Barleybridge yokels are all as mad as hatters.'

Then matters took a further turn for the worse when the Lord Chancellor arrived in a curtained limousine to check on the security surrounding his cousin Giles – the one who knows all about the take-over of the Heatheryburn Distillers by Puddles – and found the relative in question returning from a fishing trip with Jim Badger of the *Financial Examiner*.

Much as the villagers enjoyed their new companions they were shocked to learn about the diet and régime inside the Refuge. As a result, an undercover liberation network was established involving the tunnel, a panel of consultant psychiatrists in Cripplegate and furtive moonlight journeys in the back of Sam Pullan's truck. All the appellants were certified as completely sane, apart from Mr Gavestone who was really only present to help Lady Mangotsfield with her luggage. Within a fortnight of the network being established the patients still present at the Refuge had been reduced to three who were designated as belonging to category B.

Plainly the Refuge could not operate for such a restricted clientele, but relief was at hand in the form of the terrible accident which afflicted the parliamentary delegation to the Hungarian wine producers' co-operatives. With a laudable

165

devotion to their duties the delegates sampled the complete range of Tokaj vintages, drank toasts to the vineyard workers of Scotland, Wales, England, Northern Ireland and the Isle of Man, toasted the barrel-makers, bottle-blowers, corking-machine operatives and label-printers of each respective province of the UK and then their Hungarian counter-parts, before proceeding to inspect the Riesling-producing districts. When the delegation paused for a picnic lunch fortified with Bull's Blood wine on the shores of Lake Balaton, various members, now rendered jaded and emotional by their burdensome duties, were seized of a conviction that they could walk upon water. Perhaps they were mistaken, or perhaps the waters of Lake Balaton are unusual, but in any event it was necessary to call a number of by-elections to restore Parliament to full membership.

With remarkable acumen, Dr Bracegirdle submitted his three remaining 'barkers' to selection committees in the constituencies of Pinner Central, Bournemouth Seafront and New Dockland. When the committees heard the bark-ers' outspoken views on immigration, capital punishment, privatisation and capital gains tax they were each adopted on the spot. All now wear their Hardcastle Refuge Old Boys ties with pride as they stride the corridors in the Palace of Westminster. Harold Sloan, MP, is now a parliamentary spokesman for the Police Federation, the Hon. Nicholas Staughton-Highway chairs the parliamentary committee on race relations, and Quintin D'Eath is a junior minister in the Home Office. The remaining former inmates are all pursuing useful and interesting lifestyles even though their relatives may seem restrained in their praise for the cures effected at the Barleybridge Refuge.

13

In which the future seems bleak and the village stages a Great Debate

Once again Hardcastle Hall stood gaunt and desolate, frequented only by bats, rats, Despond and Divinity Sherman and their current escorts. The kitchens, where hordes of menials had scurried around pickling peacocks and removing the teeth from boars' heads, were silent and dank. The wind gushed through the broken panes in the pineapple house. Moles tunnelled in the once-immaculate asparagus beds. And the ghosts of Hardcastles long passed over searched hither and thither for their missing limbs and portions, vanishing into the ether when the phantom wart-hog clattered through the corridors in its eternal search for the remainder of little Victoria Hardcastle, whose toes had been so very tasty. All night long the iron gates clanged as the gales tugged and twisted at the great 'For Sale' sign that they bore.

When the Hall was eventually sold by agents Gadeling and Misedeparte, Mr Gadeling remarked to his partner that the purchasers had semed much more interested in the park and the village green than in the mansion. The reasons for this became clear when the Technical Services Department at Cripplegate District Council received an application and plans from the Schuster and Shyster Development Corporation. The green was shown transformed into a 'Country Leisure Centre'. The rural aspect was emphasised by the life-sized fibre-glass cows placed at regular intervals round the perimeter of the green, while in its centre was a gigantic perspex dome covering the proposed tropical swimming pool. The dome was encircled by the hills and valleys of what would become England's largest roller-coaster and an aerial walkway encased in perspex ran above the church providing pedestrian access to the car park and amusement arcades in Hardcastle Park, beyond. The land in the western section of the park was portrayed as an estate of dwellings for first-time buyers, all built in stone-look concrete blocks at a density of ten to the acre. Accompanying the plans was a sheaf of explanatory notes which revealed that the developments were ' . . . designed to harmonise with and enhance the rural character of the village and its setting.' And there were yet more bonuses. The leisure centre would provide much-needed employment for some forty car-park attendants, ticket sellers and fun-ride operatives while a small plot in a backwater of the leisure complex was reserved for a village-hall-cum-social-centre.

'This is what progress is all about,' explained the Schuster and Shyster executive to Planning Committee Chairman Kit Jackson, as he topped up his brandy glass.

'Yes, but it will turn one of the few remaining unspoilt villages into a ruddy great fairground,' replied the Councillor.

'Of course it will,' retorted the man in the business suit, 'but look at it this way. If your committee turns it down then we will go straight to appeal – forty new jobs, private housing for first-time buyers, exciting new tourist developments, not to mention the extra rates revenue from the fun park and the hundred new houses. Can you imagine that the Minister would uphold a planning refusal? And can your council afford to fight and lose an appeal against Schuster and Shyster? Anyway, we will be looking for an accountant to handle the affairs of the fun park. You're an accountant, aren't you? Perhaps we could talk it over somewhere a bit warmer – I think that the company yacht is in Miami at present . . . '

Unbeknown to chairman Jackson, the Minister of the Environment, Christopher Smedley, was already well aware of the projected Barleybridge fun park. When the fairground equipment was transferred from Cripplegate Show Field to Barleybridge the old fairground site could be acquired by the Smedley Development Corporation and transformed into

168

another estate of 100 first-time-buyer houses in stone-look concrete built at a density of ten to the acre. Naturally the Minister had no personal interest in this scheme, the directorships of the Smedley Development Corporation being transferred to his wife and sons immediately he obtained his ministerial appointment.

Christopher Smedley is, in fact, one of the most exciting and exemplary products of the enterprise culture. His rise in the world of commerce began when the majority Conservative group on Brightbourne Borough Council decided to privatise the rodent-control services and duly accepted the lowest tender, of £250,000, submitted by Smedley Rodent Operatives. The council labour force of twenty-five full-time rat-catchers was instantly replaced by rodent operative Jim Clegg and his cat, Sambo. While one cannot deny that subsequently there have been a limited number of unexplained outbreaks of bubonic plague in some of the poorer districts of Brightbourne, Christopher Smedley's rousing speeches on privatisation issues always win a standing ovation at Conservative Party Conferences – even at the one transferred to Bournemouth on account of the unforeseeable Black Death epidemic in Towerton, where Smedley Rodent Operatives also enjoy the rat-catching franchise.

From rodent control the Smedley organisation then expanded into the competitive arena of private refuse collection. The far-sighted councillors of Brightbourne again took the bold initiative and soon Harry Maggs, his brush and handcart became familiar sights around the thoroughfares and back streets of the famous resort. Those over-fastidious householders, shopkeepers and restaurateurs who found Harry's monthly collections somewhat erratic could take full advantage of the free enterprise system and convey their refuse personally to the Smedley Free Market Tip for disposal at the modest rate of £1.50 per bag (radioactive materials 50 pence extra). Shortly after the instigation of the Smedley Refuse Disposal Company, Brightbourne was afflicted by an unaccountable plague of rats, a plague of such severity that Smedley Rodent Operatives was obliged to increase its tender to £750,000. Fortunately, however, the company was able to expand its services accordingly, the local animal shelter providing Tibs and Stripey, which both now accompany Sambo in the basket on Jim Clegg's bicycle. Moreover, local rumour asserts that Tibs is due to have kittens, so an end to Brightbourne's rodent problems may yet be in sight.

From the supply of sanitary services the Smedley organisation expanded rapidly. Smedley Post-Operative Stitching Services relieve National Health Service specialists of some of their more tedious duties, Smedley Green Belt Developments fearlessly sponsor many of the more tricky building operations, and Smedley Private Surgical Hospitals have spearheaded the replacement of expensively trained surgeons by robots. Perhaps the greatest triumph for robot-assisted surgery occurred after Junior Health Minister Dame Edith Pepper drove her Jaguar over the end of Towerton pier after a particularly exuberant party fringe meeting. Only her robust head survived undamaged, and it was successfully transplanted onto the body of a coloured gentleman who had carelessly mistaken a third-floor window of a Johannesburg police station for the cloakroom door. Although no longer able to perform her ministerial duties Dame Edith became the first former minister to run a mile in under four minutes. Such was her gratitude to the Smedley surgical services that she insisted that Christopher Smedley be selected as her successor as Member of Parliament for Cheltenham Central.

Christopher then began his meteoric political career. His first departmental appointment gave him responsibility for the privatisation of the fire services. Nobody could fault his efficiency and drive and it was sheer bad luck that the project had to be shelved after his offices burned to the ground during a strike by firemen protesting against privatisation. As a junior energy minister Christopher tackled the thorny issue of the Gustshieling nuclear power station. Every few days the press had carried reports of accidental radioactive emissions from the plant, and passengers on the Irish Sea ferries were periodically falling overboard as they leaned over the guard rails to admire the luminous fishes below. Moreover, if they were not rescued within six minutes of immersion they became luminous too. The resourceful minister solved

170

this problem, firstly by changing the name of the plant from Gustshieling to Jollyfield; secondly by removing all the troublesome radiation monitoring equipment, and thirdly by providing free coach trips to Jollyfield for press and public alike, with hospitality stops at every public house en route. His department also published a booklet which explained all the benefits of exposure to radiation, including a photograph of a Jollyfield worker who was positively glowing with health – to such a degree that he could read his newspaper in the dark and thus economise on the very electricity he was working to produce.

When Minister of the Environment Cedric Harty was found to have made 17,000 successful applications for shares in the newly privatised Royal Navy plc, under a wide variety of pseudonyms, Christopher Smedley was the imaginative choice as his successor.

'You haven't seen me,' said Smedley to Sammy Shyster at their non-existent meeting at the Lancers Club.

'No, I'm not here either,' replied his host.

'Now,' said the Minister, 'if those oafs in Cripplegate make it go to appeal, I've got an Inspector up my sleeve who is crying out for promotion – very reliable chap. Remember, I want to start building on Cripplegate fairground within the year. And don't forget that justice must be seen to be done. Win the yokels in Barleybridge over to your side. Talk to Caesar Capone – his PR outfit did wonders for the PM, especially after young Luke leaked the budget speech to his merchant banker pals.'

The Country Leisure Centre plans received a mixed reaction from the members of Barleybridge Parish Council. Arthur Beckwith, bronzed from his recent Miami cruising holiday and the invigorating business discussions with Councillor Kit Jackson, moved that the members accord the plans their traditional 'No observations' verdict and pass on to the more pressing issue of whether Mrs Batty's hen-house stands in Barleybridge or Holmesmead parish. Amos Raw, Fred Tinkler and Tim Robinson are all unable to interpret

171

complicated plans, but once they were assured that no barn conversions were involved they agreed to take aboard the hen-house question followed by the 'obscene calor gas containers' reported to have erupted on the fringes of the parish. However, Sam Pullan can read plans and he was horrified by what he saw.

'Are you lot proposin' t'sit there and let these nazzarts turn t'owd village into a fairground?' he bellowed. 'By 'eck, there'll be summat said to t'Ministry of Agriculture about dairy quotas in Barleybridge if tha does!'

Confronted by such lucid and persuasive arguments the remaining councillors agreed that any decision should be deferred until a village meeting had been convened. Copies of the plans were then pinned to Mrs Fawcett's leg and paraded round the village.

Reactions within the community were no less divided. Mrs Sherman emerged as the leading supporter of the proposals. What particularly caught her eye was the offer of a site for a village community centre. In no time at all she imagined herself organising mother and toddler groups, home help agencies, best garden gnome competitions, baby-sitting circles, discussion groups on every topic under the sun (except for those featured in *The Sun*), Conservative meetings, SDP meetings – why, the scope was endless! She was even more exhilarated when she learned that Schuster and Shyster were not offering a complete community centre, just a site for one. This provided opportunities to organise building fund occasions like bring-and-buy stalls, jumble sales, raffles, tombola, fun runs, sponsor-hubby-to-do-the-washing-up competitions, baby shows and even more tedious events. Yes! At last she could assume her rightful role at the helm of village affairs. Soon the WI would be *begging* her to accept the chairmanship!

In Rev. Hobhouse she found an almost equally enthusiastic campaigner. First-time buyers meant babies – lots and lots of bawling babies. And babies meant christenings, all with good Aryan names – Amos, Joshua and the rest of the biblical village old-timers could not live for ever; one day Barley-bridge would be full of fresh-faced Harolds and Egberts. Moreover, if only one first-time buyer in twenty attended

172

the village church then the congregation would double. What a shame there were no retirement homes on the plans to boost the funeral trade! Still, it would be good to have some sensible residents who would settle for three score years and ten and not be greedy like the natives.

'Fast' Frank was a less distinguished recruit to the Schuster and Shyster banner. Following his ban on wellington boots and dominoes his local trade had evaporated, while so many of his new customers had been lost following the confiscation of their driving licences. Now he could picture droves of first-time buyers trooping down to the pub after polishing their Ford Sierras on Sunday mornings, with tourists in tee-shirts and trainers too, all jostling for his Friar Tuck hamburgers.

No less predictably, the opposition included Sam Pullan, Mr Gavestone, Albert Swales, Hector Ewbank and the other potentially homeless cricketers, Amos Raw, who had belatedly recognised the implications for Barleybridge Show, Sid Tosh, Danny Kendal and Mrs Fawcett. These stalwarts and their supporters swiftly formed themselves into an action group: Conserve Our Wonderful Countryside and Line-up Against Property Speculators (COWCLAPS).

The opposing factions assembled at the village meeting in the packed schoolroom. On Chairman Beckwith's insistence it began with a video presentation by the men in suits from Capone and Capone. In this way the villagers learned that the Pleasure Dome and Roller Coaster were specifically designed to blend into the Pitherdale countryside – and that, indeed, such recreational structures were traditional features of many northern villages. Henry I was responsible, they were told, for building a big dipper and amusement arcade at Grassington in 1107.

Mr Beckwith then introduced local celebrity Ned Withershins, bronzed from his recent Caribbean cruising holiday and present in his new-found capacity as Rural Advisor to the Schuster and Shyster Development Corporation.

'Na'then,' began Ned, who had already incorporated a little Dalestalk into his vocabulary, 'oi just want to say that Barleybridge is croying-out for a pleasure dome and rural leisure centre, 'as been for years. Oi moind moi ol' aunty

Molly Withershins down in Buckland Brewer. They were 'ard toimes down Bideford Way and there were no roller coaster in Buckland – not in Weare Gifford neither. Well, each noight the ol' gel would pray to the good Lord for a helter skelter or a pleasure dome with Olympic-size tropical swimming pool and wave machine. But when they come they come too late for ol' Molly, Gawd luv us they did! So Oi just wants to say, don't you good folk end up loik poor aunty Moll.'

Despite much shuffling and arm-raising from the COWCLAPS contingent, Chairman Beckwith then gave the floor to Rev. Hobhouse.

'Dear friends,' began the Vicar, 'is it not a miracle that testing times like this bring us all together in one great united and caring community?'

'Get on wi' it, tha sanctimonious caingy owd steg!' interrupted Hector Ewbank.

The Vicar made a hurried memo in his excommunication notebook and continued: 'Friends, I have been studying our good book from cover to cover and I can tell you all that not a word is written against country leisure centres, pleasure domes, glass-fibre cattle or roller coasters. But, dear friends, in the Book of Isaiah, is it not written, "I will sit on the mount of assembly in the far north. I will ascend above the heights of the clouds"? Here where we dwell in the far north we must ponder diligently upon these words. Could not the mount of assembly be the pleasure dome that our kind friends from London have offered to build for us? And what better than a roller coaster to send our spirits soaring above the heights of the clouds? And so we must ask ourselves whether the good prophet was thinking of Barleybridge when he wrote those words so long ago. And, do you know, in a funny sort of way I think he was.'

At this point Hector called the Vicar a northern dialect word pertaining to matter which dangles from the fleece at the posterior end of sheep; Despond and Divinity announced that the abusive behaviour of the COWCLAPS contingent was beginning to make them feel quite unclean, and Arthur Beckwith threw the meeting open to the floor.

Sooner or later it must occur to all seasoned observers of

Barleybridge debates that from time to time the discussions do tend to become becalmed in the backwaters of relevance. On this occasion the question of the Barleybridge Society of Horticulturalists' tea hut became the focus of attention. This structure, converted in 1956 (several contributors insisted that it was in 1955), from one of Fred Tinkler's father's old hen-houses at a cost to the Society of £1 11s 6d (or £1 10s 9$^{1}/_{2}$ d, if one prefers to believe Mr Reeth's heated intervention) accommodates the following essential items of equipment: one copper; one cream enamel bucket (originally white, according to Mrs Reynard); one cardboard box containing sugar cubes and bearing the price 19s 11$^{3}/_{4}$d; one formerly silver-plated teaspoon attached to a string; two gross waxed paper cups, which are religiously gathered and washed after each village show; and one of Despond Sherman's Cripplegate High School uniform stockings, whose presence here is mysterious and which does not appear on the inventory of equipment pinned to the left of the serving hatch.

The preoccupation with the BASH tea hut began when Fred Tinkler, who still regards it as something of a family heirloom, informed the meeting that if the villagers upset the new owners of the green by voting against their development plans then Schuster and Shyster might order the hut to be taken down – and then how could Mrs Carperby serve the tea at Barleybridge Show? Mr Gavestone then intervened to explain that if the development went ahead there would be no green, therefore no village show ground, therefore no show and consequently no customers for tea.

It was at this point that the assembly became transfixed by the issue of how much the late Mr Bacon was paid for converting the hen-house; the original colour of the tea bucket; whether Col. Sir Percival Hardcastle used to take one sugar lump or two; whether there *were* sugar lumps in those days; who last creosoted the shed, when, and how much it cost – and sundry related issues. This chapter in the discussions lasted for two and a half hours, during which time Mr Gavestone took Fred Tinkler over to the sand tray and built various models in an attempt to illustrate his reasoning on the secondary importance of the tea shed question. However, his efforts were not entirely successful, for when the rest of the gathering had dispensed with the topic, Fred was still muttering, 'Ah, but tha's still not towd me 'ow she can serve up t'tea wi' out t'tea 'ut.'

Thereafter the discussion drifted in the direction of whether the marquee which BASH hired in 1963 had an orange canopy; whether tea could be served through the scorer's hatch in the cricket pavilion; what BASH would pay BCC for the use of the pavilion; and whether the school uniform stocking found in the cricket pavilion matched the one found in the tea hut.

At 2.30 a.m. the vote was taken because Messrs Beckwith, Robinson and Tinkler needed a bite of food before milking time came round. Those in favour of the development numbered six. This figure included the proxy votes of Despond and Divinity who began to feel unclean during the stocking discussions, and of Mrs Carperby, who had dozed off around midnight and thought that she was voting to have the tea hut pulled down. The votes against numbered 234, and although Chairman Beckwith insisted on a recount the result thereafter was still unchanged.

The parish councillors promised to take the views of their constituents very seriously when formulating their decision. In the event the judgement forwarded to Cripplegate Area 5 Planning Committee took the form: 'The Barleybridge Parish Council has no observations to make on this matter'. Chairman Beckwith's casting vote proved decisive.

Morale amongst the COWCLAPS committee members was low when they met to review the situation. All that the parish meeting had achieved was a brief deferral of the leisure park decision until the next Cripplegate Planning Committee meeting. And the situation was even more urgent than they imagined. Unbeknown to Barleybridge, Christopher Smedley was increasingly anxious to secure the Cripplegate fairground site. Tax incentives to first-time buyers would not last for ever – or so the Chancellor had told him after his tenth brandy in the Lancers.

In the course of the COWCLAPS meeting Danny Kendal generously offered to blow up the village green. However, the other committee members were painfully aware that where Danny's explosions are concerned, results have exceeded intentions by a factor of at least five. Mrs Fawcett remarked that the accidental detonation of the entire village might possibly alienate some of COWCLAPS' support, while Sam Pullan pointed out that with the eruption of the cricket square the fruits of three generations of roller technology would be lost for ever. The possibilities of controlled flooding, the laying of a minefield, an application to have the tea hut designated as a Grade 1 listed building, claims that golden eagles were nesting in Hardcastle Hall and sundry other less-than-promising strategies were all evaluated and discarded, until the baton passed to Mr Gavestone.

Application to use the public facilities in the County Record Office were required to be logged some seven weeks in advance of an intended visit. However, Mr Gavestone, in his dogged pursuit of the Hardcastle pedigree, made advance bookings to cover the entire school holiday periods.

'Hardcastle papers again, Mr Gavestone, I suppose,' enquired the assistant archivist.

'Yes, please,' replied the headmaster, 'and also the Barleybridge Enclosure Award, if you would be so kind.'

The papers concerning the Enclosure of the common lands in Barleybridge in 1835 were not a little interesting. The Enclosure map, a legal document which portrayed the situation as it would exist after Enclosure, showed the sprawling acres of green surrounded and enmeshed in new hedgerows. The award specified that the hedges be of quickthorn, ditched on one side and protected by fencing on the other, and that the work be completed within one year of the award. Josiah Hardcastle, however, could not read maps. Indeed, he could not read at all.

Driven by intuition, Mr Gavestone then began burrowing in the papers of Sir Marmaduke Hardcastle. In amongst some yellowing pamphlets which the good knight had written on 'The Scourge of Ferreting Amongst the Labouring Classes: Deliverance Through Manly Pursuits', Mr Gavestone found a blood-stained envelope which, when opened, was found to contain the following letter:

Hardcastle Hall
Barleybridge
Cripplegate

Mr Hector Raw
Captain, Barleybridge Cricket Club
c/o Riddings Farm
Barleybridge

13 August 1903

Dear Raw

I wish you to know that Lady Alice, my relatives and I greatly enjoyed the cricketing occasion which pitted the gentlemanly qualities of leadership, discipline and style of the Barleybridge Public Schools XI against the stolid yeoman virtues displayed by the Village and Tenants XI. I feel sure that you have taken the defeat in good part, freely accepting that breeding must always triumph.

In recognition of the trusty and steadfast manner in which you and your fellow players have renounced all thoughts of the evil 'sport' of ferreting and have directed your manly instincts unswervingly towards the pursuit of cricket, the game of all true Englishmen, I do hereby grant ownership of the Barleybridge Cricket Field, also known as the Old Village Green, and of the Barleybridge Cricket Club Pavilion, also known as the Old Wart-hog House, to Barleybridge Cricket Club in perpetuity and with but two conditions. These are: *Firstly*, that the ground be made available for the annual show of the Barleybridge Society of Horticulturalists each year on the feast day of St Eric, and, *Secondly*, that no member, relative or associate of the said Cricket Club shall operate, sustain, harbour or in any manner offer sustenance to any ferret, polecat or related species of carnivore.

Your masterful and benevolent superior
Marmaduke Hardcastle

Witnesses: G.O.D. Drury, DD
Lt J.X.C. Swaffham-Bulbeck

PS. I will be inspecting your farm at 10 a.m. sharp on
Monday next. Kindly make the necessary arrangements
for the muzzling of *all* livestock, this time including the
guinea fowl. All gates to be in good order.

'Most curious,' reflected the headmaster as he furtively
pocketed the letter. 'Plainly he chose not to forward the
communication when the famous cricket match progressed
in a manner contrary to his expectations.'

Mr Gavestone next explored the ownership of Hardcastle
Park. He soon found the sale documents recording the
purchase of the 60-acre extent of hillside land from Percy
Fitzherbert, impoverished, dissolute, and the last Fitzherbert
to occupy Delacroix Hall. Sir Josiah bought the land for £35
10s 6d, a bale of worsted and six crates of port. 'Josiah
Hardcastle, his mark', was annotated beside the spidery
cross at the foot of the bill of sale.

Mr Gavestone had never investigated the Fitzherbert
lineage, but this might be a good time to do so. It soon
emerged that, with a fortune made by evicting peasants
from promising sheep-raising land, the Fitzherberts had
bought Delacroix Abbey after the Dissolution. They built
their family mansion from stones robbed from the adjacent
abbey ruins, but soon found that so much monastic piety
was seeping from their walls that it was impossible to convert
to the Protestant faith despite the recurrent persecutions of
Catholics. In 1553 an inquisition discovered some seventeen
priests concealed in nooks and crannies within Delacroix
Hall, and the Fitzherbert estates were forfeit to the Crown.
The day after the forfeiture the fifteen-year-old Edward VI
died and was succeeded by Jane, who reigned for only nine
days. She was succeeded by the Catholic Mary, but amidst
all the royal mortality it appears that nobody had ever got
round either to executing the Fitzherberts or to reconfirming
them in their estates. Convinced by now of the expedience
of maintaining a low profile, the Fitzherberts simply continued to occupy their Hall and made it a point of principle

179

to agree with whichever Protestant, Catholic or Puritan might happen by.

So who had owned the Delacroix estates – the Fitzherberts by squatters' rights or the Crown by forfeiture? More particularly, how valid was the sale of the 60 disputable acres to Josiah Hardcastle? Armed with the fruits of his researches Mr Gavestone returned to Barleybridge.

'A most singular assemblage of documents,' said Arnold Pike of Gudgeon, Gudgeon, Roach and Pike, solicitors of Cripplegate, to the members of the COWCLAPS committee now assembled in his office. 'Firstly the Enclosure Award business. Tricky one, this. You might argue that because old Josiah Hardcastle did not comply with the conditions of the award then the Enclosure was invalid. The green might become Crown property, might revert to common land, might still have been Josiah's property. Could spend a lot of time on this one.'

'Now, for the cricket field business. You say this letter has been held by the cricket club since 1903?'

'Aye, that's abaht t'size o' it,' replied Sam Pullan.

'And you are telling me that nobody connected with the cricket club keeps or has ever kept ferrets from that day forward?'

'That's reet,' answered Sam (who just the previous evening had removed twenty-seven ferrets from the village and its environs, five of them his own).

'Well, this is another tricky one. You could have a strong case. If you faced a good barrister he might argue that dogs or cats fall under the heading of what the document describes as "related species of carnivore". You're not telling me that there are no dogs or cats in Barleybridge?'

'There might have been the odd one or two,' answered Sam, nudging Trusty further under his chair.

'Then we would have to call expert zoological witnesses to argue that cats and dogs are not related to ferrets, to any significant degree. Of course the opposition would call their own zoologists – and geneticists. We would want a laboratory to do some research on the DNA of ferrets; of cats and dogs too. Bears are carnivores, perhaps – I don't suppose anyone in Barleybridge keeps a bear?' asked Mr Pike, beaming at his own joke.

'Only Mrs Appleyard's far 's I can recall,' replied Sam.

'Well, it would be a most interesting case to tackle,' mused the solicitor, rubbing his hands together.

'Now, regarding the ownership of the park. Well, this would really be an issue between the rival claimants, Schuster and Shyster and the Crown. Could run for months. No harm in writing to inform the appropriate authorities of their rights in the matter – then sit back and enjoy the fun!'

Members of the Cripplegate Area 5 Planning Committee had never looked so healthy and well-dressed as they did on the day that they convened to consider the country leisure centre application. Each member sported a ruddy tan that only rich food, white rum and a prolonged Caribbean cruise can endow. Each one had also enjoyed ample time to relax and consider the positive merits of the proposals, free from the distractions of the workaday world. And so the committee members dozed contentedly as their district's chief planning officer began the meeting by pointing out that the Barleybridge development would breach policies CG 13, CG 15, CG 16a and d, CG 18, CG 19, CG 21b, CG 23 and CG 25 of the County Structure Plan – and seven environmental health policies, too, for good measure.

'Yes, yes, yes,' interjected Chairman Jackson impatiently. 'We know all about the guidelines but we can't let initiative be strangled in red tape.'

'Quite so, quite so,' muttered sundry committee members.

'There is one more point,' added the planning officer (who had not been able to sample the mind-liberating effects of a Caribbean cruise). 'Although anybody can submit a planning application, even for land they do not own, it is my duty to advise you that the ownership of the lands in question is vigorously disputed and may, within the next year or two, be the subject of a prolonged court case involving the developers, the Crown and possibly Barleybridge Cricket Club. I therefore most strongly recommend an indefinite deferral until legal ownership can be established.'

'Pull out of Barleybridge! Pull out now!' shouted the Minister of the Environment down the telephone to Sammy Shyster when he heard of the deferral.

'Listen, Sammy, you clear that Cripplegate fairground site for me now and I'll tell you what I'll do in return. How would you like a hundred acres in Brightbourne green belt? Yes, I thought you would. Here's the deal: you buy my Towerton refuse tip for a couple of million and you can landscape that for your blessed Country Leisure Centre – but scrape some earth over all those Jollyfield radioactive waste bags before you let the press boys in. And don't worry about the green belt. Just leave that to me. See you in the Lancers with the contracts, OK?'

As the Country Leisure Park issue retreated into history, thoughts in Barleybridge turned to the special festival of thanksgiving, perhaps the last that the village will ever stage. 'Potty' Burton-Latimer returned from retirement to conduct a special service to celebrate the deliverance of the village from Shuster and Shyster and, for the first time in years, the church was packed. For once the psalms took a back seat and Potty, his walking-stick waving to the beat, led the choir and congregation in the top ten old village favourites. Season and ceremony were forgotten as the villagers sang their way through 'The Holly and the Ivy', 'For all the Saints', 'Come ye Thankful People Come', 'Ride on, Ride on, in Majesty' and a more ancient English hymn, 'Bright Morning Star'. Next the author played the organ while Mrs Fawcett descended from the loft to lead the Women's Institute in a rousing rendition of 'Jerusalem'. Finally the old vicar led the congregation down to the green and revived the ceremony of blessing the cricket square, sprinkling holy water on the mighty roller.

Then the stage was set for a commemorative cricket match between Barleybridge CC 2nd XI and the Unofficial

Anglers XI – but not until Amos Raw had delivered his opening speech. Since it diverged from its standard form, the author may be excused for quoting it in full: 'Na then, I'm, pleased you've all came. I reckon we've got t'barn situation abaht reet – but that's not t'most important thing any mower. T'owd village 'as been through some 'ard times but we done nowt to deserve all t'bother that's came us way. Back in 'Ardcastle time folks kenned where they was. Seedtime, 'arvest Rent Day an' Christmas, we wucked 'ard, we tret each other decent an' there were nowt much to pleean abaht. Cricket a Seterdays, church a Sundays, an' life just went on. But these days it seems that folks just weean't leave us alone. There's offcomers gawpin', offcomers movin' in an' wantin' to change t'owd place in ivvery way – so that I doan't ken why they came i' t'fust place. I nivver thowt as 'ow we 'ad owt much 'ceptin' usselves – but whativver we do 'ave t'offcomers want to buy it an' change it around an' sikelike. I've allus thowt that when I dee I'd like to look down an' keep in touch wi' Barleybridge, but now I'm not so suer. I'm feared o' what I might see. Any road, let's enjoy usselves while we may – and if anybody wants a load o' muck deliverin' come November I've got some good stuff that's rottin' down nicely. It's not all watter an' straw like they'll sell you at 'Olmesmead 'Ollins Farm.'

After what was by far the longest speech of his life the old farmer made his way to the tea hut, now resplendent in red, white and blue bunting and smelling strongly of fresh creosote. From the bench beside it he watched the cricket, dreamed of his old cricketing triumphs, of village shows past and those that were still to come. He dreamed he was an angel floating above the grand marquee and looking down as Bertram received the Amos Raw Trophy for Best Muck in Show. But when the players retired in the first chill of evening he did not want to awaken – he just wanted to stay there and dream and dream.

'Is owt up, Mrs Fawcett?' asked Mrs Carperby as the ladies tidied the tea hut.

'Eee, it's been a reet grand day,' replied her friend as she wiped away a tear. 'Trouble is, it's 'minded me of all t'fun we used to 'ave in t'owden times when we 'ad just usselves

183

to bother abaht. Them were bettermer times an' I just 'ad a thowt that today is t'last o' t'good owd times.'

'Nathen, Mrs Fawcett, doan't take on. Come 'ome wi' me an' we'll 'ave a nice glass o' rhubarb wine an' get out t'scrapbook.'

And so the villagers went their different ways, necks burning from the sun and the smell of fresh-cut grass still strong in their nostrils. For a while, for just a little while, Barleybridge will be at peace. Amos can dream his dreams, the farmers can deal their little deals, Mrs Fawcett can dibble with her leg and plant her wallflowers for the spring and somewhere between his yard and the Woolpack, Sam will surely catch his supper.

Meanwhile the springs still gush sparkling from the hillsides, the last of the otters ply the Pither in search of mates, while the oaks and alders hang heavily over the darkly gliding waters. And those solitary natives who stroll by the river at dusk, past banks of cow parsley, sweet cicely and balsam, may be the last to hear the song of leaf, feather and stream as it murmurs across the valley: 'All is one, all is one!'